a twin pique

A High Sierra Mystery

Terry Gooch Ross

A Twin Pique. Copyright © 2016 by Terry Gooch Ross

ISBN: 978-0-692-82328-6

Printed on acid-free paper.

Two Birds Press
2017

First Edition

High Sierra Mysteries also by Terry Gooch Ross

A Twin Falls
A Twin Pursuit

For information:

Two Birds Press
P.O. Box 7274, Mammoth Lakes, CA 93546

Acknowledgements

I am convinced you never know how many friends you have until you start to write a book. Based on the amount of support I have received for *A Twin Pique,* as well as the first two books in the series, I am one of the luckiest people in the world. When I asked for information, insight, or critical comments, I was never turned away. The greatest patience my friends demonstrated was when I particularly liked a passage I had just written and made them sit patiently while I read it to them. Never once a complaint.

If the list is too long, you might not take the time to read it. So, permit me to thank some of those I pestered the most. My extraordinary editor and facilitator, Diane Eagle; legal team of Pat and Roxanne Gooch; law enforcement team: Alysa and Jon Cole; and, my chocolate supplier, Sarah Bakewell. Then there are those to whom I sent copy after copy: Missy Stevens, Anna Gooch, Kate Page, Linda Delaney, Denise Boucher, and Pam Koslov. And, of course, my captive audience, my husband Ross and stepdaughter Erin.

Although I've never met him, a special thanks goes out to the designer of the Snow Star golf course logo, Matthew McIvor, a designer at Sinclair Printing, and of course, Joy and Bob Sinclair.

I decided to take the two local golf courses in Mammoth and combine them into a twenty-seven-hole course, I asked the golf pros at each course for their middle names. Voila "David Bernard".

And, to a special individual . . . Happy Birthday, Jeff Boucher!

a twin falls

my heart grows by half again

Mary lives there

for Ross
today is as good as the before

Chapter 1

Summers are glorious in the Eastern Sierra town of Mammoth Lakes, California. At 8,200 feet above sea level the sky is so bright and so blue it almost hurts your eyes. The air smells like pine, sage, and all things mountain. Wildflowers compete for attention throughout the landscape. Purple larkspur, blue lupine, white yarrow, red paintbrush, yellow monkey flowers, and a zillion other varieties border trails, roads, creeks, and homes.

My twin, Mary, and I were sprawled out on Adirondack chairs—legs hung over the arms like teenagers, catching late morning rays that spilled across the upstairs deck. Mary was coaxing the occasional mountain chickadee to eat sunflower seeds from her hand. They were so polite. The chickadees queued up in the trees and landed one at a time on Mary's palm. Sparrows and finches made jealous noises from the railing, but were too skittish to come closer. Steller's jays squawked their disapproval from the roof.

Through the bird noise I could hear the faint tapping of computer keys coming through the living room door. Mary's husband, Bob, a software genius by anyone's definition, was always on the computer. Fleetingly, I wondered what he was working on, but lost the thought when a red-tailed hawk swooped down and temporarily scattered the congregation.

There was so much I wanted to talk to Mary and Bob about, but their deaths in a plane crash eighteen months ago had brought a new reality. Oh, Mary and Bob regularly visit.

They leave me with an occasional cryptic message in the form of a picture, website, or some other means. They saved my life when I met their murderer face to face, and have helped me in times of danger. They've even guided strangers to my door who were in trouble and needed help. But since the crash neither Mary nor Bob have spoken a word—at least not to me.

Settling back into my chair I basked in the knowledge today's visit seemed to have no other purpose than to hang out, and that suited me just fine. I would spend time with my twin and her husband any way I could.

So, I returned to the internal debate that had been occupying my brain for the past few weeks. Was it time for Ross, the man of my heart, and me to give living together another try? Our first attempt was six years ago. What Ross and I now referred to as *Version 1.0* had been a disaster. I loved to jump out of bed and chat in the mornings; Ross liked to begin his day with a cup of coffee in the dark, slowly waking up. Ross had the financial discipline of an accountant; I hadn't balanced my checkbook in years—hell, I didn't even know if I remembered how. I liked Crest toothpaste and Woolite laundry detergent; Ross used Colgate and Tide. Needless to say, the experience proved that compromise of lifelong daily routines was something neither Ross nor I was good at.

I'd thought our current situation—separate residences with lots of sleepovers—was ideal for us. At least I did until late one evening last October when a young woman and her then-four-month-old twins appeared on my doorstep homeless and scared, eventually moving into my guest room—compliments of Mary and Bob. Michele Conners and her twins Megan and Maxine lived with me for the better part of three months. During that time they became family. Now they lived in a friend's guesthouse in Portola Valley, while Michele attended culinary school in San Francisco. I missed them terribly. My need for control and order didn't seem so important anymore. The house seemed to have lost some of its life ever since their departure in January. It felt too big and empty, and I knew only Ross could fill the void.

A chickadee landed on the arm of my chair with an inquisitive chirp, breaking my reverie. Mary must be out of seed. I glanced over. She had vanished, leaving only some disgruntled birds. The computer in the house was silent. I sighed. It must be time to go inside and get to work, and as a human resources consultant I had plenty to do.

A woman's voice rose up from below. "J? Is that you up there?" she shouted. "I hope I'm not intruding, but do you have a moment?"

The late morning sun blinded me as I glanced over the deck railing to see who was beckoning. The silhouette was unmistakable. It was Charlotte standing in my driveway, a neighbor from the end of the street.

Like most mountain houses, the main rooms—kitchen, living room, master bedroom—were upstairs so you could see out the windows when the snow came. "Sure. Come on up. The door's unlocked. You can join me for some iced tea."

I admired Charlotte. She was one of those rare people who had a strong sense of who she was and what she wanted— never looking for approval or accolades. Last year on her fortieth birthday, she retired from her position as vice president of web development for a NASDAQ-listed software company in Southern California, because it was a "young person's field," and she "didn't need any more money." Soon after, she talked her father into selling her the family's seldom-used vacation home just down the street. The day she moved in, she marched up our cul de sac and introduced herself. Before that, the closest we'd come to meeting was a brief wave as we passed on the street on the few occasions her family vacationed in Mammoth.

Memory of that first encounter still brought a smile to my lips. When I'd spotted her out my front window, striding up the street, I thought she was a kid. She stood no more than four-eleven, and had a stocky build. It wasn't until I answered the door that her gender and age became apparent. Short, red, orphan-Annie-like curls framed her freckled face, and accentuated bright, ocean-blue eyes. Within moments I could see that two of her stronger characteristics were optimism and perpetual motion. As we became better acquainted, I learned that with Charlotte ambiguous, secretive, and patient were *not* attributes I would ever use to describe her.

Charlotte's retirement lasted about six weeks. Then she decided to supplement hiking, fishing, and mountain biking with some work. She started her own web development and software consulting business, and built a loyal following in Mono and Inyo counties within a few months. Only recently had she hired a half-time assistant to help with some of the less challenging projects.

My head was deep in the pantry, as I tried to spot some cookies or shortbread to go with the iced tea, when Charlotte entered the kitchen. My muffled greeting received no response, so I abandoned my search for a sweet to see what was up. One of the happiest people I knew stood before me, shoulders slumped, eyes red, tears streaming down her face.

"What . . .?"

"My dad died this morning, J. He . . . he drowned in his swimming pool."

I put my arms around Charlotte and led her to the loveseat that anchored the back-kitchen wall. Handing her the box of Kleenex from a nearby counter, I made inane soothing noises. Finally, after telling her everything was going to be all right, I shut up and just rocked her.

Eventually she calmed enough to sip some iced tea.

"I'm sorry, J. I was just so angry I couldn't be alone."

"Angry?"

She made a face as she spit out, "Maybe if Dad's girlfriend Steph wasn't so self-involved Dad would be alive . . ." She began to cry again, grief and anger battling for dominance.

We were on our second glass of tea before she was calm enough to continue.

"Sorry. When Steph called, all she said was that Dad drowned. I had to push really hard to get the whole story." She stood and started pacing the kitchen.

"Stephanie said that when she and Dad returned from their morning jog, he decided to cool down by swimming a few laps in the pool while she went into the house and showered. It wasn't until more than *two hours later* when she was finished with her idea of breakfast—some green gook she makes in a blender—that she realized Dad hadn't come in. *She* became *annoyed* and went to find out what was taking him so long. That's when she discovered him floating face down in the pool with a gash on his head. She called 911, but didn't bother calling me until the cops finished with her and she got back to her apartment—*four hours after she found him.*"

"Your father had a gash on his head?"

"From what I could pull out of her, the paramedics and police think Dad had some kind of a medical episode as he was getting out of the pool, and hit his head on the side when he fell. Of course, they won't know until after the autopsy." Charlotte stopped pacing and took a slow, deep breath. "I booked a seat on tomorrow morning's L.A. flight. I should be at Dad's house in Cheviot Hills by early afternoon."

"Is there anything I can do for you while you're gone?"

"Say a few prayers for my Dad," she said softly. With more vigor, she added, "Perhaps you should say a few of those prayers for Steph, too—that bitch is going to need them."

Anger seemed to have a calming effect on Charlotte. Her tears were gone, her breathing even.

"I take it you're not one of Steph's biggest fans?"

"Hell no! Dad is seventy, Steph is forty. She graduated from high school the same year as my brothers."

"That's awkward. Aren't your brothers younger than you?"

"By fourteen months. You know I wouldn't even mind the age difference if she wasn't such an obvious bimbo. Mom died more than ten years ago. Dad was almost catatonic for the first few years—all he did was work, eat, and sleep. When he told me last year that he'd started seeing someone, I was thrilled . . . until I met her. . . ."

Charlotte was interrupted mid-sentence when my cell started blaring Chicago's "Does Anyone Really Know What Time It Is."

I grabbed the cell off the table and turned off the sound. "Sorry. I completely forgot. That's my alarm reminding me I have a meeting in fifteen minutes. I can't be late because I called it." Charlotte said simultaneously, "I'm sorry. I really didn't come over to rant about Steph."

We walked to the front door and hugged. Charlotte promised to call when she returned from her father's. Before I could close the door, she turned and said in a very businesslike manner, "Oh, I almost forgot. Have you met Zach, the guy I hired to help with the business?"

"No. I knew you hired someone, but that's all."

"His name is Zach—Zach Moore. His tech skills are solid, and so far, he's been reliable," she said, staring blankly, as if she had lost her train of thought.

"That's nice, Charlotte. Uh . . . but why are you telling me this?"

She shook her head as if to clear it. "Sorry. I guess this morning's events left me pretty spacey. If you see him going in and out of my house while I'm gone, it's okay. Don't call the police. He's working on a deadline for one of my clients."

I smiled at her sudden concern for safety—Mammoth is one of those places where people seldom lock their doors, much less pay attention to who is coming and going from a neighbor's house. I could tell by the way Charlotte scrunched up her face in response to my smile that she didn't think it was an idle concern. "You better describe him," I said.

"Good point," she said seriously. "He's in his late twenties, about five eleven, long blond hair. Sort of looks like a surfer."

"He should be easy to spot. I'll keep my eye out for him, and if I see someone other than Zach, I'll call the police."

"Thanks," she said gravely, and headed down the street.

Chapter 2

S even were seated around a long conference table in the Snow Star Golf Resort meeting room, the only space in the massive log clubhouse, set among twenty-seven holes of a spectacular mountain course, which was more utilitarian than opulent. Six were looking at me expectantly. I had invited them to come; now they wanted to know why.

Included were David Bernard, Snow Star's PGA head golf pro; Tony Adams, Director of the Mammoth Lakes Enterprise Enhancement Consortium, representing Town government; Helen Sheets, one of the most accomplished fundraisers in California; Bill McNulty, a good friend who founded a business law firm with offices throughout California and Nevada; Brian Jeffries, owner of Couloir, Mammoth's newest boutique hotel scheduled to open in the early fall in the Sherwin mountains; and, Linda Taylor, another good friend and principal of the elementary school. Each had been briefed on what skill or expertise I needed from him or her, but only Linda had heard the entire plan.

In the center of the table were small bottles of Pellegrino, a plate of sliced lemons, glasses filled with ice, and a basket of energy bars. After a nod of appreciation at David for the refreshments, I poured myself some Pellegrino, watching the fizzy water dance around in my glass while I collected my thoughts, and took a deep breath.

"When I phoned to invite each of you to our meeting today, I only told you I needed you, not *why*. I'm ecstatic that with no information you were all still willing to come today. I'll begin by giving you some background, next describe what I'm hoping we can achieve as a group, and finally," giving them my most engaging smile, "if you're still here, discuss what I hope each of you can contribute to the effort to achieve our goal.

"I was recently contacted by Jean McBride, Chairman of the Board of *Hope for Our Children,* a Bay Area nonprofit. It's an organization my twin, Mary, actively supported when she was alive, which I think is the reason Jean phoned *me.* The mission of her organization is to provide whatever resources and assistance are needed to enrich the lives of disadvantaged, abused, and neglected children in California. The purpose of Jean's call was twofold. She explained that the HFOC Board has decided to expand its services to small rural California counties, and they've chosen Mono County for the first site of a new multi-service program aimed at assisting poor working families."

Helen, a petite silver-haired woman in her fifties, asked, "I know *Hope for Our Children.* It's a solid organization with a good reputation. But why here? There are a lot of small rural counties much closer to the Bay Area."

"I was curious, too," I responded, pleased Helen had asked. A woman of means, Helen had dedicated her life, considerable intellect, and energy to volunteer work. "Apparently, the Board has been discussing this service expansion to rural counties for more than a year, but didn't know how they were going to raise the funds. Then their biggest donor stepped up and said if HFOC started in Mono County, she would give the organization $50,000 toward startup costs, and fully underwrite a fundraiser. Although I have never met her, it seems she has a vacation home here."

Helen lit up. "Then we could only be talking about Roberta Hart."

"Yes, how did you know?"

"Simple. Roberta has more money than God, is passionate about giving all children a fair chance, and once she has an idea, she'll do whatever it takes to make it happen. Our paths have crossed many times over the years at various fundraisers." A flush came over Helen's porcelain complexion. "In fact, her vacation home is next door to mine."

Frenetically rolling his hand in a gesture to move things along, Tony, the only politician in the room said, "And this is important to us . . . why?"

Helen visibly bristled. She straightened her spine and said, as if speaking to a child, "Given who is in the room, and what J has said, isn't it obvious she wants us to organize the fundraiser? And since David is here, I suspect it's a golf tournament."

All eyes turned to me for affirmation. I opened my mouth to respond, but was cut off by Tony. "I don't have time to put on a golf tournament for some nonprofit from the Bay Area." His five-foot-seven-inch frame, clad in red and black spandex bike garb, rose from the table. Casting about the group, his eyes fell on Bill, the only other male over fifty in the room. "Sorry, but I'm way too busy for this."

Bill surprised me when he used his lawyer-voice. "Sit down, Tony. I know J. You wouldn't have been invited if what she has in mind isn't going to be significant to the town."

Tony didn't return to his chair. Instead he half-sat, half-leaned against a credenza, a sour look on his face.

Bill gave me an almost imperceptible nod of his head, and I continued. "Helen is correct. What Roberta wants is a gala golf tournament weekend. She has a few specific requests, and if we follow them she'll underwrite the entire event, including lodging and food, so that every dollar will go directly to the HFOC's Mono County program for working poor families."

A nervous giggle escaped Helen. "I'm not sure I want to hear. The last time I worked with her on a fundraiser, she set the goal at a million dollars."

"Then I guess Roberta is consistent, because the goal she set for this gala is precisely that—a million dollars."

Tony returned to his chair.

The conversation became animated when I announced Sunday of Labor Day weekend as the tournament date. At first the discussion was characterized by skepticism. No one believed a golf tournament in Mono County with a population of a little over fourteen thousand, could raise a million dollars in a weekend—let alone a weekend that was less than five weeks away. But, as we began to list the celebrities, politicians, philanthropists, and other notables who frequented Mammoth, the mood began to shift. Tony, however, apparently clueless to the purpose of the event, focused only on marketing the town. His primary contribution was, "We could showcase Mammoth to California's rich and influential."

It was Brian who got the full group on board. "I don't know what all the fuss is about," he said. "If we tried we could raise a million dollars with just a few phone calls for the right cause. If we do this right, it will achieve both Ms. Hart's goals for the county's children, and Tony's tourism goals. I'm in."

Within moments we were off and running. We decided that in order to have a chance of meeting the goal, a foursome should cost $10,000, and the twenty-seven hole-sponsorships should bring in $20,000 apiece. If we had full participation, we'd reach seventy percent of our financial objective. Tony balked, until Brian suggested he might be a little out of touch. Tony was not pleased.

By the time we were through, everyone had committed to contribute time and resources to the fundraiser. Brian said he'd have an early, soft opening of Couloir to provide all the lodging for the out-of-town golfers, and host the awards dinner. David stated his management had already agreed to host the tournament. I announced that Andrea Revy, owner of the Rock & Bowl, was excited to host an opening affair the night before the tournament. Helen and Bill decided to work together on individual and corporate hole-sponsorships, as well as coming up with strategies to fill all the golf carts with the rich and famous. Helen would also work with Roberta Hart on a raffle idea she had that "just might get us to our goal." Tony volunteered to contact local restaurants and businesses to get contributions for goody bags and the on-course lunch. Not surprisingly, he also said that he would handle public and media relations.

Finally, as prearranged, Linda volunteered to serve as the event committee's team leader, assuming responsibility for meetings, communications, and coordination.

Overwhelmed at the scope of the project we had taken on, we all just sat for a moment in silence. That's when I noticed David's absence. Being one of the youngest in the group, his departure didn't surprise me, but I was a little disappointed. In my mind David was more than the golf pro; he was the guy everyone wanted at the party. He had boundless energy and an irreverent sense of humor. I'd been counting on his charisma to keep the group going when things got tough.

I stood, announced the date of the next meeting, and began to thank everyone. Our good-byes were interrupted when the door flew open.

David, pushing a well-stocked portable bar cart, grinned and said, "Anyone interested in a million-dollar cocktail?"

Chapter 3

Only Tony declined the offer of a libation. He left as soon as the meeting ended to cycle back to his office.

The two chardonnay drinkers, Brian and Helen, moved toward the corner of the room, talking quietly. At six-foot-two Brian towered over Helen by almost a foot. He was built like he lived in a gym, with black hair and a tropical tan. Only his boyish, round face and impetuous nature seemed out of character with the successful hotelier he was. Couloir would be his third mountain-boutique hotel in six years. It was hard to believe he was only thirty-two. In contrast, Helen gave the impression of a English country lady. Short white hair framed her porcelain face, her mannerisms were refined, her comments thoughtful and respectful. Although there was an age difference of more than twenty years, they discovered they had many affluent acquaintances in common. From the few words I could overhear, it sounded like many of them wouldn't give a second thought to sponsoring a hole for fifty thousand dollars. Their conversation gave me hope.

David was at the front of the room, giving Linda a crash course in the mechanics of putting on a golf tournament while they sipped bottles of Paranoids Pale Ale, a locally brewed favorite. They made for an odd pair—the outgoing, cheeky golf pro and the meticulous, business-like elementary school principal. A perfect match in my opinion. Linda and I became friends a little less than two years ago, when she first hired me to ferret out the culprits in what could only be called Robin Hood thefts at the elementary school—instead of stealing things *from* the school, the thieves stole *for* the school. It took us a while and help from our police chief, Ian Williams, but eventually the troublemakers were exposed.

I moved on as David gestured enthusiastically and Linda took notes on her iPad. For someone who had never played golf, she asked some surprisingly astute questions. My confidence was growing.

I headed toward Bill at the bar cart, who held up a bottle of vodka in one hand and tonic in the other in silent question. I nodded and continued my way to the back of the room. Bill's wife, Ellen, and I had been cross-country ski buddies until almost eight years ago when a truck hit a nasty patch of ice and took her life. Ellen's sudden death was hard on everyone, but none more so than Bill and Ellen's fifteen-year-old son, Wes. Since Nordic skiing was one of Ellen's passions, Bill thought the activity would help Wes work through his grief; Wes agreed as long as I showed him his mother's favorite runs. The three of us have been cross-country skiing every winter since.

"Thanks," I said, as Bill handed me the drink. "I haven't heard from Wes recently. Is he still enjoying law school?"

"He loves it and has the grades to prove it." The pride in his voice brought a smile. Then he looked at me disapprovingly.

Following his gaze, I saw the empty glass in my hand. I was so thirsty from meeting nerves and talking, I'd downed half my drink in two gulps.

Bill shook his head as if he were my father, and filled up my glass with tonic, asking, "Do you mind if we talk a little business?"

I eyed him suspiciously. Bill had hired me late last year for an assignment that was way outside my skill set and comfort level. It involved coaching a depressed, suicidal senior partner of the firm, and it was one of the toughest assignments of my career.

Bill laughed at my reaction to his question. Throwing up his hands in surrender, he said, "Don't worry, J. This time my problem really is a human resources issue."

Taking a sip of my mostly tonic, I relented. "Sure. What's the problem?"

He led me out of earshot of the others. "It's my Bishop office. I have three attorneys, a paralegal, an office manager, and an administrative staff there. Or at least I did. Four weeks ago one of the lawyers walked out, giving no notice or explanation. Two weeks ago, our paralegal indicated she would be leaving at the end of the month. She, too, gave no reason for her departure."

Bill looked aggrieved as he paused, studying his hands as if they had the answer. "In addition, I've recently started receiving complaints from two of our longstanding clients about the quality of the work coming out of the office. The final straw came a few days ago, when Lynette Germaine, the Bishop office's managing attorney, met with our biggest Inyo County client in preparation for final negotiations in an acquisition we've been facilitating. All the numbers were wrong."

"How did Lynette explain that?"

Bill shook his head, looking befuddled. "She said one of the staff must have sabotaged her."

"Do you think she's lying?"

He massaged his chin. "I really don't think so. Lynette is considered *the* expert in her field. After graduating from Stanford's dual JD/MBA program, she finished off her education with a Ph.D. in Water Resource Management from UCSB's Bren School of Environmental Science. Her credentials, experience and reputation are impeccable. When the opportunity arose several months ago, I engaged her as a consultant to lead a very sensitive water rights negotiation in Bishop. Her results were remarkable, and I thought she worked well with my Bishop staff. I immediately offered her a generous salary package, relocation expenses and a hiring bonus to become the managing attorney of the office. When she told me she would only come if I also hired her assistant, I agreed."

"So you think the staff *is* sabotaging her?" I asked in disbelief.

"I honestly don't know what to think. I tried interviewing each of the employees, including Kyle, the attorney who quit. No one will say anything . . ." Bill's voice trailed off.

He placed his club soda on a nearby table. His face showed his fatigue. "I was hoping you could meet with all of them and tell me what you think."

We stood for a moment while I contemplated his request. "Let's take it in baby steps. If the Bishop employees won't tell you what's going on, they probably won't tell me, either. How about if you send me to the Bishop office to conduct a two-day audit of personnel files and employment procedures—you know, something mundane so I can blend into the background— and I'll see what I can learn?"

Bill's customary smile returned to his face. "Thanks, J. I'll have Elise phone you to schedule your time and anything else you might need. You remember Elise, don't you?"

"Are you kidding? I don't think your Mammoth office could function if she weren't there."

Bill laughed. "None of our offices could."

"Did any of the staff have objections to Lynette being hired to manage the office?" I asked just before we said our goodbyes.

"Kyle, the attorney who recently left, asked me if anyone else had been considered for the position. I told him no one of Lynette's caliber. That seemed to satisfy him; at least he didn't express any concerns." Bill looked out the window, as if revisiting the conversation. "I think he thought he should be promoted into the position, but of course, never came out and said so." He shook his head back to the moment. "It was a real shame. His IT experience coupled with his understanding of the law made him a good attorney. I had big hopes for him." Bill took one last swig of his soda. "It's getting late. Thanks again, J." He rushed towards the door.

"Hey, Bill. Hot date?"

Bill's face was pink when he turned to give me an unconvincing lawyer's stare.

"Say hello to Deb for me."

He resumed his exit without a word.

I smiled. Bill had given all his attention and energy to Wes and his law practice after Ellen's death. Until he met Deb

Moore at the beginning of the year. Now they spent most of their free time together. Both Wes and I were thrilled.

On my way to the parking lot, my phone buzzed with a text from Ross, asking me to meet him at Burgers restaurant at seven. I felt a twinge of anticipation and excitement. While many unmarried couples have intimate discussions over a candlelit dinner and expensive bottle of wine, Ross and I usually held our serious deliberations over hamburgers and beer. Since Burgers restaurant offered the best comfort food in town, it was where we went to talk.

Perhaps he'd also been affected by Michele and her toddlers' departure in January. Could he be thinking about giving our living together another try, too? It was the only topic I could think of that would trigger a dinner invitation to Burgers.

I rushed home to change into something more appealing.

Chapter 4

My mood turned apprehensive when I walked into the restaurant. Ed Hurley, Burgers' owner, wore a concerned look on his face as he directed me to the corner table where Ross sat staring at his empty beer mug. I thanked him and took the seat opposite Ross, while Ed left to fetch more beer.

Ross's shoulders were slumped and there was a hint of perspiration on his upper lip. Either he was breaking up with me, or asking me to marry him. My stomach did flip-flops.

Ed returned with two chilled mugs and a pitcher of beer. As he left, he guided the waitress who was coming to take our orders away from our table, whispering something in her ear. After a quick, inquisitive glance, she turned and walked off to the other side of the restaurant.

I have never been one for relationship suspense. I took a big gulp of beer, almost choking because I forgot to breathe first. "Whatever it is, Ross, just tell me . . . *please*." I added with some urgency in my voice.

He drained half his glass and cleared his throat. "An old high school friend is getting divorced and wants to come live with me for a while." Ross looked at me for a reaction. "You know, a place to stay while checking out job opportunities, and finding a place to live."

The world came back into focus. The tears that had been pushing at the corners of my eyes retreated to wherever tears come from. I let out a relieved laugh, which, if truth be told, probably sounded like a snort. "That's all? Oh, Ross, of course one of your high school buddies should stay with you while he gets back on his feet. The way you looked when I sat down, I thought . . ."

I stopped mid-sentence when I noticed Ross didn't share my exuberance. His large hands were still wrapped tightly around his mug. He returned to staring into his beer.

Without breathing I asked quietly, "There's more?"

"The *old high school buddy* is Olli," he said barely above a whisper.

My stomach returned to the trapeze it had just left. Olli. Olivia Parker. Ross's high school girlfriend. She'd been the head cheerleader when he was captain of the football team. They'd been the king and queen of the senior prom. Olli—his first love.

Although I had never met her, I Googled her a few years back when Ross said he had received an email from her and I was feeling particularly insecure. Her face appeared immediately after I typed in her name, as if she had been waiting for me. I stared in horror. A young Cameron Diaz with boobs smiled back at me.

As I scrolled through the pictures I saw *Olli extreme helicopter skiing in Banff, Canada; Olli receiving a medal for taking first in her age group in the Honolulu bike century ride; Olli finishing her third marathon in as many weeks; Olli winning her golf club championship for the second year in a row.*

Now, *that* Olli was getting a divorce and moving in with Ross.

"J?" Ross was staring at me intently.

I took a few quick sips of my beer, hoping the cold liquid would shrink the giant lump in my throat. Did I want this to happen? Absolutely not. Should I tell Ross I was against it? Tell him how jealous it made me feel that he was even considering it? No. That wasn't how *we* were. We gave each other space. We supported one another. We trusted one another. It's why we were still together. It was why we still loved one another.

I took one more swallow of beer. "Of course you should give Olli a place to stay," I said with all the airiness I could muster.

Ross visibly relaxed and sat back in his chair, relief preventing him from hearing the angst in my voice. The restaurant, which had been freeze-framed throughout our discourse, let out a collective breath. Diners laughed, noises came from the kitchen, and waitresses called out orders. Ross picked up the menu and started to tell me about his day. I tried to take it all in.

I was grateful for his obliviousness as he chatted amiably through dinner. Focusing all my attention and energy on what he was saying, I pushed Olivia Parker to a small compartment in my head and shut the door. I would not think about her until I was alone, no matter how hard she pounded on the box to get out.

There was one last question to be answered this evening, and I wanted to put it off as long as I could. But as we were getting up to go back to my place, he said casually, "Olli arrives the day after tomorrow. Perhaps we could have her for dinner at your place on Sunday. You know, so you two can meet, and we can make her feel at home."

What else could I do but smile and nod?

I was sweating profusely, trying to elude Cameron Diaz in her *Charlie's Angels* garb, when the bright morning sun roused me out of a fitful sleep. The digital clock indicated it was past seven. A folded note next to the clock told me Ross had left early for his summer job mowing the fairways at Snow Star. I was alone and bummed.

My mood worsened when I read his note.

J. I won't be able to come by after work tonight. I need to clean the condo and stock the pantry before Olli arrives tomorrow. Thanks for understanding that I really didn't have a choice. Most girlfriends would have gone ballistic. Love R

p.s. Are you still up for making dinner for Olli and me Sunday?

Girlfriend? I was more than a girlfriend. *Olli and me?* When did it become Olli and me? Since I could no longer call Mary to vent my jealousy and rage, I'd do the next best thing. I'd call Kate, Mary's former assistant and dear friend. A woman I barely knew eighteen months ago. A woman who helped me find Mary and Bob's murderer, and almost lost her life in the process. A woman who was now one of my closest friends. She would help me figure out what to do.

As I picked up my cell I remembered Kate and Nathan, Kate's husband of less than six months, were vacationing in Paris. I wouldn't dream of interrupting their romantic getaway to burden Kate with my problems. "But I could email her," I said out loud, and went in search of my laptop.

It was in the living room where Bob had left it the morning before. Momentarily forgetting my pique, I opened it up to see what he'd been working on while Mary and I had sunned on the deck. Oddly, I found a tabloid page. There were four articles on the page: Domestic Violence in the LGBT Community, Dangers of Plastic Surgery, Secrets of Internet Dating, and lastly, Don't Let Jealousy Ruin Your Relationship.

Okay, Bob, I get your point.

Chapter 5

Bob's prescience put an end to the idea of emailing Kate. I grumped around the house until I realized Ross wasn't the only one who needed to clean the homestead. For the next few hours I dusted, Windexed, vacuumed, and—I admit—rearranged pictures to more prominently display those of Ross and me in various forms of recreation and intimacy.

Next I assessed the decks and the front porch. The flowerpots definitely needed freshening. Each boasted a perennial like white lilacs, or pink veronicas, but they needed some annual color to liven them up. I noted what colors and plants I needed, and began to relax. The chores gave me the illusion I was back in control of my life and my relationship.

Heartened, I opened cookbooks to plan Sunday evening's repast, thinking casual but elegant. Eventually I decided on an appetizer of grilled shrimp and bruschetta with cocktails; a tri-tip roast with chimichurri sauce and a medley of summer vegetables accompanied by a 2002 Lang & Reed cabernet franc, to be followed by berries and crème fraiche, and cappuccino with a touch of Courvoisier for dessert. I was going to make certain Olivia Parker knew I was all Ross needed or wanted.

With shopping list in hand and confidence surging, I reached for the front doorknob when my cell rang. I looked at the screen to see if I had to answer it, and saw I wanted to. It was Michele Conners.

I was able to get out "Hello, Michele, how's culinary school . . ." when she interrupted with a loud, "Why didn't you tell me the couple who sent me to your house last year was Mary and Bob?"

Almost a year and a half ago Mary had sat with me in the hospital while I recuperated from the plane crash that took Mary and Bob's lives. At first I thought she had survived, unharmed. When I was told she and Bob were dead, I thought she might be a grief-related hallucination. After realizing she wasn't a figment of my battered imagination, I told Ross, whose first reaction was to suggest I seek the services of a mental health professional. It wasn't until he had his own encounter with Mary and Bob that he finally believed me. The only other two people who knew of Mary and Bob's appearances were Kate and Nathan. And, we had all sworn to keep it our secret. Michele had encounters with Mary and Bob—the first when they sent her to my house for shelter. But she never knew they weren't flesh and blood. It had been difficult to keep their real circumstances secret while she lived with me. I thought we had succeeded.

"Uh . . ." I wasn't prepared for this conversation. Thankfully my phone pinged with another call. As I glanced at the screen to see Kate's name, Michele demanded, "Don't answer that. Don't put me off. Talk to me. Why didn't you tell me about Mary and Bob? Didn't you think I would understand? Do Kate and Nathan know?"

I exhaled, long and loud, and then asked calmly, "What do you think you'd have done if I'd told you my dead twin and brother-in-law had given you my address the night you arrived on my front porch?" I could hear Michele suck in air, gearing up for a shrill comeback. I preempted her. "Yes, Kate and

Nathan know. I'll tell you the whole story, but first, please tell me how you found out."

"Their pictures are in the Chronicle," she said stridently. Her voice declined in volume and fervor. "Next to a story about the man accused of their murders. Apparently, he goes to trial this fall."

After a minute, she murmured, "I'm sorry, J. I get why you couldn't tell me, especially when I first arrived. I guess I'd have thought you were nuts. But I never could understand why every time I was in trouble the same couple showed up and helped me. It just didn't make sense."

Trying to keep the tears out of my voice, I said, "If it's any consolation, the only people they have visited are you, me, and Ross." I told her the story.

Thirty minutes later, emotionally exhausted and a bit tearful, I climbed into the car to run my errands. The ring of the cell sent a jolt of electricity through my nerves. I almost threw it into the back seat, but recalled that Kate had phoned. I answered, "Kate, sorry I didn't call back. I just got off the phone with Michele."

I heard a chuckle. "This isn't Kate, J."

"Sorry, Ross. I'm in the car and didn't check caller ID." Trying to sound cheery, I added, "In fact I'm on the way to the market to pick up the ingredients for Sunday night's dinner."

"Great! Perfect timing," Ross said with unusual enthusiasm. "Olli was able to get away a day early. In fact, she just arrived and I was hoping we could move up our dinner to tomorrow night. Will that work for you?"

In the background a feminine voice said, "Sunday is fine, Ross. I can make dinner for us tomorrow."

"Tomorrow will work just fine." Before he could respond to the invitation, I said, "Gotta go. Lots to do. Love you, Hon. See you tomorrow evening." I terminated the call, fuming.

I made a mile and a half detour on the way to the grocery store, and drove to the Lakes Basin. I parked in front of Tamarack Lodge and walked to the bridge over the Twin Lakes to collect my thoughts. I needed to get my jealousy—*Yes, Bob, jealousy*—under control.

Twin Lakes is really an hourglass-shaped lake, with a bridge where the lake narrows like an hourglass. I've always thought of it as conjoined twins, spectacularly set off by the craggy peaks of the Eastern Sierra as a backdrop.

While I admired the aspens, pines, willows, firs, and of course, wildflowers, I began to calm. Dragonflies skimmed the surface of the water. Families of ducks paddled around in circles, occasionally nabbing fish. I closed my eyes and breathed in the scent of mountains, camping, and freedom. Gradually my sense of composure returned.

I had faced far greater challenges than an old girlfriend of Ross's, no matter how beautiful and accomplished she might be. Besides, Ross and I had always trusted one another; now was not the time to stop. I took a minute to imprint the landscape on my psyche, so it would be readily available to me for its soothing effects over the next few days.

As I turned to leave, three ducks caught my eye. The striking bottle-green head of one indicated a male, which was accompanied by two brown-speckled females. I watched with perverse fascination as the females pushed and bumped up against one another, each trying to take the lead following the male. They made quite a ruckus. While they were busy battling it out, the male suddenly lifted his neck, stretched his wings and with a great honk, flew away. It didn't appear the squabbling females noticed his departure.

Chapter 6

A sleepless night gave way to a late start the next morning. I consumed coffee in large quantities—not my usual morning beverage of choice—while adding pansies and petunias to flowerpots, sweeping decks, washing windows, setting the dinner table, and prepping the ingredients of the evening's meal. Tasks I thought would only take a few hours stretched to consume the entire day. As I placed the tri-tip in the oven to roast, I realized I had just about enough time to shower and change before Ross and Olli arrived. So, of course, the phone rang.

Bill McNulty's office. I took a deep breath, forcing myself not to rush or sound frantic. It was Elise from the McNulty Law Group, Bill's firm.

"Hello, Ms. Westmore, I hope I'm not intruding so late on a Saturday?" Without waiting for a response, she continued, "I understand you're going to be working with us again." Her formality made me forget my angst and I smiled.

"Yes, I am, Elise. And, please call me J. After all we went through together earlier this year, don't you think we can be on a first-name basis?"

She didn't respond, so I upped the ante. "If you call me J, I'll tell you how our favorite McNulty senior partner, Alex, attempted to take one-year-old twins to the San Francisco Zoo by himself."

I heard Elise make a low hum. As she made up her mind I thought about Alex Rossi. A single dad who lost his twenty-one-year-old son in a ski accident last spring. The senior partner Bill had hired me to coach as he returned from his bereavement. I wasn't successful. But a chance encounter with my houseguests, Michele and her twins Meg and Max, saved his life, and gave him a new family to care for. Now he headed Bill's San Francisco office so he could be close to Michele and the twins. I smiled at the memory.

"J? J, are you still there? Elise sounded like this wasn't the first time she asked.

"Sorry, Elise. I was having a twin flashback."

"Alex really took Meg and Max to the zoo by himself? Oh, goodness, J, that must have been a disaster," she exclaimed.

"Apparently, Alex thought that since the twins would be in their stroller, it had to be easy. I wouldn't have known about how wrong he was if it hadn't been for a friend of Michele's who happened to be at the zoo with her five-year-old, and took a picture of Alex. His clothes were peppered with milk and food stains, and he was weighed down by bags of diapers, food and toys. In the photo one twin is howling and the other is throwing everything within reach—including her sister's shoes—into the moat around one of the animal cages."

Elise asked me to forward the picture, and I knew it would quickly make the rounds of the firm's various offices.

Clearing her throat, Elise took on a slightly more formal tone. "Back to business. Am I correct that you agreed to conduct an audit of the Bishop's office personnel files and procedures?"

I waited for her to continue, but was met with silence.

"Uh, yes. That's the cover. I'm really there to . . ."

Elise cut me off, saying, "Oh, I know the real reason, and I hope you succeed in finding out what is going on down there with all the turnover. But, since I am responsible for the firm's human resources compliance, I want to make sure you actually perform an audit." Her unwavering confidence made it hard to believe Elise was an attractive redhead in her twenties instead of a decades-seasoned professional from my mother's generation.

"I guess I could conduct a real audit . . . I mean . . . uh, if you really want me to." *Damn, the last thing I want to do is spend a couple of days catching up with all the current local, state and federal requirements.*

"Yes, please, J." There was a pause while I could hear Elise typing something into her computer.

"I have spoken with Ms. Germaine, the office's managing attorney, and she would like to meet with you at noon for lunch on Monday at Jack's restaurant. Then if all goes well, you can begin working in the office on Tuesday morning. I told her you estimated two to three days to conduct the audit."

"She wants to meet with me for lunch before I begin? Isn't that unusual? I mean, I assume she'll want to speak with me when I arrive at the office, but lunch the day before? That seems a little over the top for someone coming in to conduct a clerical audit?"

"Ms. Germaine is a very unusual woman. She's gracious and responsive, but my impression is that she leaves nothing to chance."

We made our arrangements and I promised to forward her the picture of Alex and the twins. Just as I was about to hang up, Elise said, "Ms. West . . . er, I mean J."

Smiling, I said, "Yes, Elise."

"Please be on time. Ms. Germaine is a stickler for punctuality."

The call must have captured my full attention, because I hadn't heard anyone enter the house. As I headed to my bedroom to get ready for dinner, I literally bumped into one of the most stunning women I'd ever seen. She was around five foot nine, couldn't have weighed more than one hundred and twenty pounds, with honey blond hair pulled back into a haphazard ponytail. Dressed in well-worn jeans and a man's white dress shirt, her most striking features were her wide, sensuous mouth and deep olive-green eyes.

For a moment, we just stared at one another, then Ross stepped out from behind her, and we all spoke at once.

"J, this is Ollie."

"I'm so sorry, J. I was so anxious to meet you I insisted we come early."

"I got waylaid by a call from a client. I should have paid attention to the time."

Our chorus was followed by awkward silence.

As we took a collective breath, I held up my hand. "Ross, why don't you and Olli get something to drink while I shower and change." I scurried to my room, yelling every swearword I knew inside my head.

I could smell the tri-tip cooking when I entered the kitchen thirty minutes later. I let out a sigh, satisfied that at least dinner would be delicious and on time, even if I hadn't been. Ross and Olli were talking quietly on the back deck, so I arranged the shrimp in the center of a cobalt blue platter, and placed the bruschetta on the perimeter, adding a few springs of basil to soften the presentation. I was delighted to find a martini waiting for me in the freezer. *Thank you, Ross.* Finally starting to relax, I grabbed the hors d'oeuvres and my drink, and joined my guests—though I was loath to think of Ross as a guest.

At first glance Olli and Ross looked supernatural as they sat chatting, heads together. Behind them, the late afternoon sun obscured their features and framed them in an aura of yellow and gold. It both frightened and compelled me to interrupt their conversation.

I shook my head to clear it, and heard Ross say, "Just tell her, Olli. J will understand."

"Tell me what?" I asked in my best hostess voice.

Olli looked at her lap, and Ross answered, "Olli doesn't eat red meat."

It was going to be a long evening.

Chapter 7

Olli was still looking at her lap as I sucked down half my martini, and racked my brain for something I could serve instead of the tri-tip. "It really isn't a big deal, Olli. It's an easy adjustment to make," I said with all the nonchalance I could muster.

She gazed up, and I was once again struck by her incredible beauty. "Really? Are you sure you don't mind?"

I nodded my head, and secretly vowed to make it my mission to find Olli her own residence as soon as humanly possible.

An hour later dinner was ready. I had set aside the roast, cooked some quinoa, tossed in the medley of summer vegetables, mixed in some fresh greens and basil vinaigrette and added some goat cheese, turning it into a summer salad. I exchanged the cabernet franc for a bottle of Rombauer chardonnay, and called Olli and Ross in for dinner.

As I brought our plates in from the kitchen I was disconcerted to see Olli sitting in the dining chair I *always* sat in. A little unnerved, I served them mechanically. Olli seemed ecstatic with the meal, Ross looked crestfallen; he loved tri-tip.

I set my plate down in front of what I had always considered a guest chair. The slight change in order made me off-kilter. I tried to mask my discomfort by asking Olli what made her choose to move to Mammoth, as I poured the Rombauer into our glasses.

She took a bite of her salad and smiled. "Well partly because I love the outdoors. Skiing, hiking, fishing, golfing, paddle boarding, it doesn't matter to me. I just want to be outside. But mostly . . ." She took another forkful, "because Sam hates Mammoth."

"Sam?"

"Yeah, my ex. You could call Sam an intensely indoor person."

I opened my mouth to ask more about Sam when I felt Ross nudge me under the table with his foot. His way of letting me know this was not a good topic of conversation. I changed gears. "What kind of work do you do?"

Olli brightened a bit more, if that were possible, though she didn't quit eating. "I resigned my position last week as Director of Communications and Marketing for the Western Restaurant Association, a position I held for almost ten years. My staff and I handled everything from media relations to website development, to conference planning to you name it. She set her fork down and smiled. "I really loved the work, but I know there's nothing like that in Mammoth. I guess I'll have to go back to waiting tables like I did in college."

Ross interjected, "Olli, tell J about the job you got yesterday."

"You just arrived and you already have a job?"

"Just for three evenings a week. I'm going to teach Ashtanga yoga at the Snow Star Athletic Club."

"Aaasshttaa . . .?" I stammered.

"Ashtanga. It's sort of a current-day classical Indian yoga. You should sign up for the Monday class, it's for beginners."

"Thanks, but I don't think I'm the yoga type; my form of relaxation is a long run."

Through the rest of the meal, dessert, and cappuccino, we discussed Olli's various athletic accomplishments. Fortunately, I'd read about most of them on Facebook, so I wasn't overly intimidated. In fact, I had a grudging admiration for this woman, and thought, if circumstances had been different— *translated to: if she wasn't living with Ross*—we might have become good friends.

Just as I was beginning to get comfortable with the evening, Ross looked at his watch and said, "Thanks for dinner, J. This was great. I'm really happy the two of you got to know one another. But Olli and I both have early starts tomorrow, so we better call it a night."

Olli asked if I wanted help clearing the table. I declined her offer, still stunned by Ross's abrupt announcement.

We walked to the front door. Olli gave me a hug, Ross pecked me on the lips, and they were gone.

I returned to the littered dining table, pushed aside some dirty plates to make room for my wine glass and poured myself the remaining two inches of chardonnay. Ross and Olli were *calling it an early night*. Whatever the hell that meant. I took a sip, and then got up to pour the rest down the drain; I couldn't taste it.

Leaving the soiled plates and utensils where they lay, I went to my bedroom, stripped down to a T-shirt and panties, and got into bed. All I wanted was to go to sleep and escape into my dreams where I wouldn't feel so abandoned.

Completely covered in pillows and my comforter, I wondered whether I would be able to fall asleep. Then the bed shook and it felt like someone was throwing loads of laundry on me. I cautiously peered out from beneath my pillow toward the foot of the bed. There was Bob lying cross-wise on his back, hands clasped over his stomach, long-lashed lids closed. To my left, Mary reclined beside me on top of the covers, one arm draped across my body, sharing my pillow. Her eyes were closed, too.

I let out a slow breath and felt the weight of Mary's arm across my chest and Bob across my feet.

"You knew I needed you. Thank you," I whispered. Then I closed my eyes, soaking in the comfort of their presence. I no longer felt abandoned.

At first I tried to lie still, not moving a millimeter, fearful Mary and Bob would disappear if I adjusted my position even slightly. Occasionally I opened my eyes, to make sure they were still there—each time buoyed by their sleeping forms. But eventually fatigue and the wine from dinner won out, and I fell into a hard, dreamless sleep.

Chapter 8

I awoke in degrees, one sense at a time, the morning sun coming in through the bedroom window and warming my face. As memory of the night before returned, I rolled onto my left side to say good morning to Mary. But she and Bob had vanished. While not surprised by their absence, I was still disappointed. A few deep sighs later I threw back the covers, wondering if this time their visit had been a figment of my imagination—mere wishful thinking brought on by the rejection I felt after Ross and Olli left. But a quick glance of the rumpled bed bore the impression of Mary's head next to mine in the pillow. Touching it lightly with the tips of my fingers, I imagined I could still feel her presence.

My sense of peace departed abruptly as I walked through the house to get a cup of coffee. The detritus of last night's disastrous dinner covered the dining room, kitchen, and upstairs deck. Resigned to the morning ahead, I set my iPod to play Sam Smith's "Stay With Me" and began to clean up, my resentment even more acute since Ross's job had always been washing the dishes after a guest dinner.

Once the house was in order, I perched on a front deck Adirondack chair with my current copy of the California Chamber of Commerce Labor Law Digest, cursing myself for agreeing to conduct a real personnel file audit. As boredom threatened to trick me into a mid-morning nap, my cell chirped. The number was blocked, but I was in desperate need of distraction, so I answered it.

"Hello. This is J."

"I hope I'm not interrupting anything," Charlotte said. Before I could reply, she continued, "J, I need a big favor."

She sounded so unlike herself, so serious, I almost laughed, but then I remembered that she was in Los Angeles because of the death of her father. "No problem, Charlotte. What can I do for you?"

"We're having a memorial service for Dad on Tuesday, and I want to wear the bracelet he gave my Mom on their wedding day." I could hear rather than see the tears streaming down her face. "Could I ask you to go over to the house, get it out of the safe, and overnight it to me?"

"Of course. I'll get it right now so I can send it out to you first thing in the morning."

She went on as if she hadn't heard me. "I wouldn't bother you, but I've been trying to call Zach for hours and he doesn't answer his phone—or his messages."

"It's okay, Charlotte. Really. Actually, it will give me a legitimate reason for taking a work break."

"Thanks, J. This means a lot to me. I'm sure I'll be the only one who even knows its significance, but I want something my mother held dear with me when I say goodbye to Dad."

"How are you? Your brothers?"

"Frankly, it's a nightmare. Unbeknownst to any of us, Dad named me executrix, which really pissed off the twins. He also left me a confidential note expressing how he wants his estate handled, which of course, I will follow to the letter. When Corey and Cody find out what those instructions are, they'll really go ballistic. And don't get me started on Steph! I'll share all the ugly details when I get home."

"If I recall, you like a good Bordeaux. I'll pull out a La Dominique Saint Emilion and some chocolate for your return, and you can tell me all about it."

"Perfect. Something to look forward to."

She gave me the locations of the spare house key and safe, as well as the code to open the safe and a description of the bracelet. "If you have any problems getting into the house or the safe, just call. I'll keep my phone close until I hear you were successful."

More than happy to set aside the labor law materials, I headed down the block to Charlotte's.

I arrived on her front porch, perplexed to find I didn't need a key. I was fairly certain she hadn't accidentally left it unlocked, not after her request to watch the house. But thinking her assistant could be inside, I entered, leaving the door open behind me in case a quick departure was necessary.

It was an old house, probably built in the seventies, decorated to look like a Tyrolean chalet. Outside there were shutters painted bright green with stenciled designs and large flowerboxes. Inside everything was made of knotty pine, with colorful flowers painted over doorways and around windows.

I checked the downstairs, where Charlotte had converted two bedrooms into offices, and found them neither occupied nor recently used. I headed upstairs to find the safe. I called a soft hello as I ascended the staircase, but got no answer. The second floor was a mess. Empty bottles and dirty glasses littered most of the surfaces. The air smelled like stale beer, old pizza, and marijuana. I turned to leave and call Charlotte when an angry, tallish blond man walked out of the master bedroom stark naked.

"Who the fuck are you? And what the fuck are you doing here?"

Trying to look unfazed, I forced a smile. "A friend of Charlotte's, and you must be Zach, her employee." When he moved toward me, I ran downstairs into the safety of the street.

Chapter 9

The Mammoth Lakes police, led by Officer Jon Cole—someone I was encountering far too frequently in his role to protect and serve over the last year and a half—came and removed Zach and his girlfriend. When the girlfriend, a petite, punked-out brunette covered in snake and flower tattoos, saw me standing across the street, she sneered and gave me the finger. Unmoved, I gave Charlotte a blow-by-blow description of the eviction over the phone. Zach was belligerent, and insisted Charlotte had asked him to stay in the house while she was gone. That's when Officer Cole, who was escorting Zach's girlfriend, pointed at me with phone in hand, and told Zach not only was he being arrested for unlawful entry, but that Charlotte had just fired him.

Zach started screaming, "Bitch. I'll get you, you fucking bitch. Who the hell do you think you are, you bitch." In the midst of his tantrum, he inadvertently hit one of the cops in the face, and was immediately restrained. As they drove him off, Zach was still yelling over and over again, "You're dead meat." I wasn't sure whether he was referring to Charlotte or me, but I assumed we should both be careful.

I assured an apoplectic Charlotte I would get a locksmith to come to the house and change all the locks, call a cleaning service, and of course, get her mother's bracelet and send it to her the next day. I returned home thinking the Labor Law Digest didn't look so bad after all.

Late in the afternoon when I was almost numb with state and federal leaves of absence documentation regulations, I heard the familiar sound of Ross's Honda pulling into the driveway. It evoked an instant feeling of happiness—until I remembered Olli. A day of tedium, sprinkled with a few moments of fear, did not put me in a good place to be hospitable. When I heard only one car door slam I became more hopeful.

Ross walked in, arms extended, one hand holding a bouquet of daffodils. He knew I was a sucker for daffodils. I fell into him and all the angst of the past few days evaporated. He apologized for showing up early the night before then not staying long enough to clean up after dinner. I apologized for being peeved with him. He expressed surprise that I'd been upset. I expressed incredulity at his surprise. We laughed and went to the kitchen to make cocktails and watch the sun set.

Over a dinner of thinly sliced tri-tip with chimichurri sauce and a green salad, we spoke of everything but Olli. I didn't want her at the table with us, but ultimately couldn't resist the primal urge to find out what was happening with her.

I tried to choose my words carefully. "So how is Olli adjusting to life in Mammoth?"

"I guess she's doing okay," Ross responded tentatively, looking at the last few bites of roast on his plate.

"That sounds vague. Is something wrong?"

"She's . . . well, she's different. Or at least I think she is. I mean I haven't seen her in almost twenty years. But there is something off. I just can't put my finger on it." He looked up at me expectantly, as if I might have the answer.

My head went into consultant mode, and I asked Ross the types of questions I would ask an employer who told me his employee seemed just a little off. "Describe what she does that seems odd to you."

Ross sat back in his chair, stretching his long legs in front of him, eyes focused on the ceiling. "Well, she used to be very open about everything—I mean what she was doing, how she was feeling—Olli couldn't keep an opinion to herself. Now she's extremely private. She talks to me like she just met me. When I asked about her divorce, you would have thought I slapped her. She just said she was going into her room for a while."

"Perhaps she's feeling awkward, asking to stay with you after all these years."

"That's sort of what I thought at first, but there are other things. Both nights as soon as I turned the lights out in my bedroom to go to sleep, I heard her walking around the condo checking all the doors and windows."

"She's lived in the city, honey. Most people check their doors and windows before they go to bed."

"Yeah," he shook his head wearily. "But usually not every hour until it's light outside."

A long moment passed as words sank in. "Are there any other behaviors that are out of character for Olli?"

"Olli has always been comfortable wherever she is—sometimes inappropriately so. I remember when a group of us got called into the principal's office after being caught the night before drinking after football practice. There were eight of us and Olli led the way. She walked in as if she and Principal Blair were old friends, asked him how his wife and kids were doing—by name, mind you. Then she perched on the edge of Blair's desk and told him she was sure he understood we were just acting like teenagers were supposed to act. He seemed so flustered by her confident demeanor he just nodded, told us drinking was bad for us, and unceremoniously dismissed us. No detention, no lecture, nothing."

"And now . . .?"

"Now every other sentence is an apology. 'I'm sorry for intruding.' 'I'm sorry if I used too much hot water.' 'I'm sorry for being a vegetarian.' It's making me a little crazy and a lot sad."

"Do you think her personality change is a result of her marriage to Sam?"

"I think it may be, but if it is, she's not going to tell me." I could tell by the regret in his voice Ross thought he was failing his friend.

"Perhaps, J . . ." he said cautiously, "perhaps she would tell you." As he warmed to the idea, he became more animated. "She really likes you. She said so in the car last night. Maybe she'd be more comfortable talking to another woman?"

I suppressed a groan. But I was the one who had brought up the topic of Olli, so I couldn't be irritated with Ross. Giving him my best "anything to help out my partner" grin, I agreed to give it a try. I silently vowed not to bring up Olli again, and suggested we take advantage of the warm summer night and go for a walk around the neighborhood.

The rest of the night passed without thought of anyone but each other.

Chapter 10

At 11:55 Monday morning, a dozen vehicles were parked just north of Bishop on Highway 395; mine was one of them. We had been at a standstill for fifteen minutes, gawking at a sheriff and a couple of ranch hands trying to corral two rogue cows that had escaped their captivity through a downed fence. While I watched the bovines wander down the thoroughfare, I kept hearing Elise say, "Ms. Germaine is a stickler for punctuality."

Groaning, I dialed Ms. Germaine's mobile. She answered before the first ring was over. "I assume this is Ms. Westmore."

"Uh . . . yes, Ma'am." Realizing how obsequious I sounded, I quickly explained the situation, and assured her I would be at the restaurant as soon as humanly possible.

"I am sure you will," she responded. "I better order for us, I need to be back in the office by one-fifteen. What would you like?"

"Thank you for understanding. I'll have whatever you're having."

When I arrived the parking lot was full, so I had to park on a side street a block away. The trek back to the restaurant in one-hundred-degree weather did not improve my mood. The only consolation was the sign on the front of Jack's, which announced its opening in 1946—the sign of a good restaurant. I could vaguely remember years ago being served a wonderful country breakfast at Jack's by a waitress with a handkerchief pinned to her blouse by a pin with her name on it.

I wondered how long it had been since last eating at Jack's as I squeezed through a crowd of fishermen waiting for a table. I emitted a small groan when I saw how packed the restaurant was. There were so many people that the air felt warmer inside. I completed three tours around the restaurant looking for a formidable woman in business attire to no avail. I was about to head over to the McNulty Law Group office when an extremely petite brunette in a flowered silk shirtdress and summer sandals tapped me on the shoulder and said, "You walked past me three times." Then she turned and strode back to her table. I followed, trying to reconcile her appearance to her behavior. She gave a brief nod to a waitress, who immediately headed off to the kitchen.

We were just sitting down when the waitress placed a dish heaped with roast beef and mashed potatoes smothered in gravy in front of each of us. The sight of the heavy food made my stomach turn. As I thought, "Could this day get any better," Ms. Germaine said, "I had them keep our lunch warm for us. I love Jack's hot roast beef sandwich. Though, I must admit I was tempted to try the chicken fried steak instead."

Before speaking another word this pixie demolished half her sandwich. I swirled tender pieces of beef in the gravy, wishing I hadn't asked Ms. Germaine to order for me, when she looked at me with disapproval. "You don't like roast beef sandwiches?" Without waiting for a response, she continued, "No matter. We need to get down to business."

She dabbed at her mouth with a napkin. "Isn't this job a bit menial for you?"

"I beg your pardon?"

"I do my homework," she said, making it sound like a reprimand. "I never work with someone unless I've Googled them. You resolve conflicts and work on organization culture issues, you don't audit personnel files." She sat back in the booth and looked at me expectantly.

"Well, actually I *do* conduct file audits. At least for friends, I do. I've known Bill for a while. He agreed to join a steering committee for a charity gala for me, so, I agreed to conduct a file audit for him."

Ms. Germaine smiled for the first time, momentarily transforming her from a tight-assed, controlling attorney to someone approachable. She said thoughtfully, "Ah, now that makes sense. Bill is a good negotiator, and a good judge of people." She stared at me for a moment, and said tentatively, more to herself than to me, "That makes the second part of our conversation easier."

I cocked my head and gave her my best "Tell me more, I'm listening" consultant look.

"Do you think you could stretch your audit to five days, instead of two or three?"

"I could, I guess. But, why?"

"Something is not right in the office, and I haven't been able to ferret out the problem. When I looked your credentials up on the Internet I realized you might be able to help me figure it out. That's why I told Elise I needed to meet with you before you came to the office."

"To ask me to help you?"

"First, to check you out. I *really* couldn't figure out why you would do a clerical audit."

"So what are you asking me to do?"

"Get a feel for the office. Talk to the staff. See if something is amiss or you think I am imagining it. You can still conduct the audit. But I will pay you for the extra time you need and for your counsel out of my own pocket. Other than complete honesty, the only thing I ask is that this remain confidential, between you and me."

"Is there anything you want me to know going into the assignment?" *This was a critical question. Even though I had already accepted the same assignment from Bill, if she tried to shape my perceptions before I began, I couldn't trust her intentions.*

"No. I don't want to influence you. I want you to go in with fresh eyes."

"You have a deal, on one condition."

Her expression changed to suspicious. "One condition?"

"I will conduct the audit on Bill's dime. Any additional work I do for you will be strictly gratis."

Her face and torso relaxed. She smiled ever so slightly. "I won't ask why. I will just say we have an agreement."

She looked at her watch, placed a twenty and a ten-dollar bill on the table, and stood. "I'll see you tomorrow morning." With a raised eyebrow, she added, "at eight-thirty."

Chapter 11

D riving down the Sherwin grade to Bishop in the early morning—and I consider seven a.m. to be early—is always spectacular. Small mountain communities interspersed among the Eastern Sierra give way to ranches, farms, and open space. Clusters of firs and pines become oak and birch trees. In forty minutes, you descend from eighty-two hundred feet to forty-one hundred feet above sea level. And of course, as the elevation drops, the temperature rises.

Originally populated by Native Americans, the Bishop area's beauty and resources appeal to almost everyone: hikers, artists, rock climbers, fishermen, campers, hunters, cyclists, runners, basically anyone who likes to work or play outdoors. And its popularity is never more evident than in the middle of summer. Main Street's sidewalks boast a full contingent of western life, and this day was no exception.

I picked up an espresso at the Looney Bean and drove the few blocks to the law office that was located in a mixed neighborhood of residences and small business. I had to smile in admiration. Instead of a small office building, the McNulty Law Office occupied a vintage Craftsman home in its purest form: a large front porch, gabled roof with corbels, sash windows, blue-gray with white trim, and lots of wood and glass. It was perfect.

I downed my coffee and exited the car thirty minutes before I was expected. I was *not* going to be late today. To my dismay the front door was locked. I checked the address again, and knocked loudly. No answer. I took a seat on a porch swing and waited. At eight-forty, a harried looking Ms. Germaine bounded out of an Audi A3. She did not look happy. When she saw me on the porch she looked even less happy, if that was possible.

"Why aren't you in the office?"

Before I could respond, she grabbed the front door knob and tried to turn. "Oh."

While she searched her purse for her keys, she mumbled, "First I get forced out of the house because of a broken pipe in the middle of the night. Then my cell phone won't hold a charge. And, now the only person who shows up for work is a consultant . . ."

Ms. Germaine seemed to have a habit of asking a question, not waiting for an answer, then talking to herself.

When she managed to unlock the door, I held it open while she bustled in, still mumbling. As I entered I took in the room—or perhaps I should say the downstairs. I finally understood what the term "open concept" referred to. Hardwood floors, mission-style wood furniture with touches of soft leather, beveled glass mirrors, simple accents of color achieved mostly with art pieces and flowers. The effect was simple and elegant. The line of sight ended at the rear of the house through large wood-framed windows to a beautifully tended rose garden, set off by velvet green lawn and sturdy wooden benches. I felt a stab of envy as I mentally catalogued all the varieties of roses—*Mammoth's short growing season means the only roses I see at home come from the store.*

I was so absorbed in the décor I hadn't been paying attention to Ms. Germaine. "Ms. Westmore. Ms. Westmore. We seem to have a situation here."

I shook my head as if to clear it, trying to focus on my employer. "A problem?"

She sat at a reception desk with the landline still in hand. "My assistant and office manager Mags, Margaret Barry to you, has a . . . um . . ." Her voice faltered. Then she spat out, ". . . a family emergency, and was unable to return to Bishop yesterday. She also informed me that Shari Miller will be in court today, our receptionist Brittany won't be in until noon because she has a doctor's appointment, and Christine, our paralegal, has a job interview and does not know when she will arrive."

"A job interview?"

"She gave notice and is leaving at the end of the month."

Was that a note of regret in her tone? I smiled and shrugged my shoulders. "So I guess it's just you and me."

"I'm afraid not," she answered without humor. "I have a meeting with the Los Angeles Department of Water and Power in fifteen minutes." A hint of a smile crossed her lips. "How are you at answering phones?"

By noon I was a basket case. I had messages haphazardly scribbled on a legal pad, having given up on message slips. *Didn't the staff have cell phones?* I hadn't left the reception desk since nine. The phone wouldn't quit ringing. I'd been regretting my espresso for the last hour, since I didn't even have time to use the bathroom. Hell! I didn't even know where the bathroom was.

I was about to mutiny when a young woman with raven hair ran into the office, yelling, "I'm pregnant!" Her face fell when she looked around to find a stranger sitting at the reception desk.

"May I help you?" I asked politely.

She dropped into a chair across from the desk. "Who are you? You don't work here, do you?"

"It's a long story. The short version is that I'm here to conduct an HR audit, and was conscripted to answer phones since no one else was here to do it. My name is J, J Westmore. And you?"

"I'm Brittany Liano, the receptionist." After a long moment, she looked up at the ceiling and said smugly, "And . . . I just found out I'm pregnant and am finally getting out of this hellhole."

Chapter 12

"Well, I hope you're not quitting today, Brittany, because I'm in way over my head."

She blanched. "Did I say that out loud? I didn't mean to. Please . . . pleeeze don't tell anyone what I just said. They'll fire me. And first I have to convince Don, that's my husband, that I should be a stay-at-home."

"Don't worry, your secret is safe with me. Oh, and congratulations. That's exciting news."

Her beaming smile made her look fifteen. She stood. "Well, J. You did say your name was J, didn't you? Why don't I take over the desk now?"

I thanked her with more gratitude than I'd shown anyone in a long time, and asked where the bathroom was.

As I made a hasty retreat, I pointed to the legal pad I'd been using for messages. "When I get back I'll go over the messages with you."

She glanced at the tablet, shaking her head.

It took about forty minutes, with phone interruptions, to interpret the phone messages. As we neared the end of my almost incomprehensible notes, I believed I had someone who would tell what was going on in the office. Since we were alone I took my chance. "If you don't mind me asking, I'm curious. What makes this place a hellhole? Has it always been like that?"

Brittany shook her head earnestly. "Oh, no. When I started a little more than two years ago . . ."

The door burst open and Ms. Germaine strode through. "Ah, Brittany, you're back. I hope your doctor's appointment went well?" Without waiting for an answer, she turned to me. "Ms. Westmore, I assume you've had lunch. I've set you up in our small conference room." She headed off at a brisk pace. "Come with me," she trailed.

Brittany and I made eye contact, and we both shrugged our shoulders.

By five o'clock I was exhausted, hungry, bored, and, okay I admit it, a little pissed. As I was getting ready to head home, Ms. Germaine poked her head into the small conference room I was using. "I must apologize for forcing you to act as our receptionist today."

I began to respond, but she continued without looking at me. "It was the perfect storm. It just all went wrong. And Mags wasn't here." She slumped into one of the conference room chairs. I could feel more than see her defenses fade. "I took this job for us because I thought it would get her away from her fucking brother . . ."

She stopped midsentence and just sat there, looking at me with such sadness I almost wanted to cry. "Sorry, you're not a therapist, and I shouldn't have said that." She stood and straightened her shoulders. "I do appreciate your willingness to be so flexible and *confidential*. Thank you."

I acknowledged her compliment and instruction with a nod and a smile. As I picked up my purse to leave, she added, "And, you were the only one on time."

My first order of business was food. At the north end of town, I stopped at Mahogany Smoked Meats and picked up a half black forest ham sandwich on sourdough with pepperoncinis. Other than my morning espresso, it was the first sustenance I'd had all day, and I'd devoured it by the time I got back to my car.

Before pulling out of the parking lot I turned my mobile back on and checked for messages. There were three. The first was from Ross, letting me know some of the employees at Snow Star were going to play a late round of golf and go out for a few brews. The second was from Bill McNulty asking how my first day went. The last must have come in while I was getting my sandwich. It was Helen Sheets, asking me to return the call as soon as possible.

I texted both Ross and Bill, wishing Ross a nice evening, and telling Bill I would call him later in the week and give him a full update. Then I punched in Helen's number. She answered on the first ring.

"Oh, J, I'm so glad you got back to me so quickly." She sounded excited, but somewhat formal.

"No problem. What's up?"

"Do you have time to stop by? I have a couple of people I'd like to introduce you to."

I was tired, and felt grimy from sitting around an office all day, but Helen never imposed or wasted anyone's time.

"Helen, I'm on my way back up the hill from Bishop. I need to stop by the house and freshen up. I could be there in say, an hour or so."

"Lovely. That will work just fine. We can have a glass of wine and some light hors d'oeuvres."

"Who am I meeting?"

"Oh, that's a surprise." I could hear a smile, and perhaps a little excitement in her voice.

"All right. I'll be there as quickly as I can . . . and Helen? Please don't make the hors d'oeuvres too light."

I was still famished.

Chapter 13

Denis, Helen's husband, had clearly been waiting for me, and he ushered me into the mudroom before I could even knock on the door. His enthusiasm was contagious. "Helen will be so happy you're here. Come on in. While you meet the ladies, I'll get you a glass of wine?"

"Do you have anything stronger? It's been a very long day."

Denis nodded. "Helen said you might ask."

"Do you know what this is all about?"

He grinned like he'd just won the lottery, but said nothing.

Helen and Denis's home had an unusual entry. After a small foyer Denis led me through a glass door down a long hallway bordered by full-length windows on either side. Very little light was needed, as the night sky illuminated the outside gardens. The impression was magical but fleeting, as we walked through a French door and down a step into a sunken living room. The room's three occupants rose: Helen, her cheeks rosy from wine, excitement or both; a large sixtyish woman with close-cropped gray hair and an air of authority; and, a stunning, tall, elegant, dark-eyed, dark-haired beauty who could have been anywhere between twenty and forty. Helen hugged me, and then introduced me to Roberta Hart and Susanna Montoya.

As I took my seat Denis handed me a chilled vodka martini. I almost got up and kissed him on the lips before deciding it wasn't socially inappropriate.

"It's a pleasure to finally meet you in person," I said to Roberta. "Your support of *Hope for Our Children* and now of the Mono County youth is awe-inspiring."

"Thank you," she said graciously, looking down at the floor—which I later learned was out of character for Roberta. "I am a blessed woman, and was raised to share my blessings with those who are most vulnerable." She raised her eyes to mine. "But first I want to offer you my condolences and tell you what an honor it was to work with your twin Mary. Now there was someone special."

I was caught off guard. Of course, Roberta had known Mary, how could I be so dense? It was just hearing Mary's name spoken by someone I didn't really know, and so unexpectedly. It brought on a kind of emotional paralysis.

My feelings must have shown on my face because Helen instinctively began to move toward me. Embarrassed, I held up my hands, trying to signal I was all right; I just needed a minute. Roberta started to apologize. "Who's Mary?" Susanna asked. I opened my mouth to respond and nothing came out.

Out of the corner of my eye I saw Mary sit down on the arm of the chair Helen occupied, shaking her head and rolling her eyes at me, as she always did when she thought I was being overly dramatic. I couldn't help but smile. *Okay, Mary. I'll lighten up,* I whined in my head.

"Roberta, I'm so sorry for my reaction to your sincere words." Turning to Susanna, I said, "Mary was my twin. She passed away last year. I still get a little choked up when I speak about her." I took a long, thoughtful sip of my martini. "Tell me, Susanna, since I assume this evening's subject is our *Hope for Our Children* Mono County fundraiser, how did Helen manage to talk you into helping."

I could tell Helen was relieved we were back on topic. She jumped up from the chair that Mary was no longer sharing. "Susanna is our first $100,000 donor, who outside this room wishes to remain anonymous . . ."

"Wow," I started to say, when Helen shook her head to let me know she wasn't finished.

". . . And, she's going to loan us one of her consulting firm's professionals to assist in any way we need him."

"That's fabulous, Susanna."

Susanna's smile made me want to go to the dentist to have my teeth whitened. It was dazzling. She nodded toward Roberta. "I have a small marketing consulting firm, and have done some work for Berta in the past. When I heard about how ambitious your goals were, I wanted to be a part of it. I must admit, loaning you one of my staff is selfish. He has strict orders to record all your strategies so we can replicate the effort next year in Santa Barbara."

"Without sounding too anxious, we don't have much time, when do you think he can start?"

"Whenever you want him."

"I don't want us to prematurely take him away from any projects he may working on."

"Actually, John hasn't started working on anything yet."

Susanna had our attention.

"Perhaps I should explain. He started an executive search firm twenty years ago, which became quite successful. He sold it in January, quickly grew bored with leisure, and he starts work for me on Monday."

Helen jumped in. "Search firm? I thought you were a marketing consultant?"

"I am. And it took a while to convince John that he'd been in the marketing business for twenty years—it was just people instead of products or services he was selling. Now he's excited about the transition."

My excitement was ebbing, and I was skeptical. "I don't think someone who owned his own firm is going to be happy doing our legwork."

"On the contrary, your 'legwork' is his classroom. My firm puts on a lot of corporate and charity events. You'll find John is a nuts and bolts guy. He can answer phones, take and distribute meeting notes, use Outlook to schedule appointments, and comfortably work with anyone from city clerks to chief executive officers. Versatility. It's what made him so successful."

We spent the rest of the evening discussing Roberta and Helen's auction strategy. It was an idea in its infancy, but if I understood it correctly they wanted to auction off celebrities. Ideas included a round of golf at Pebble Beach with this year's FedEx Cup winner, a dinner party with the outgoing President after he left the White House, an evening with a Pulitzer Prize winning novelist, a picnic with an Academy Award winner. Susanna seemed as blown away as I was at Berta—Roberta's preferred name—and Helen's confidence they could pull it off.

By ten o'clock I was ready to go home and go to bed. Berta and Susanna were surprised when I told them I had to be at work in Bishop by eight thirty the next morning. We exchanged business cards—a practice that was sadly going the way of public telephones and fax machines. Susanna also gave me one of John's cards, and told me he was awaiting our instructions.

A warm summer breeze caressed my face as the Sheets's front door closed behind me. It had been a long day with a very good ending. Relaxed by the cocktail, hors d'oeuvres, and refined company, I finally spent a moment taking in my surroundings. I loved how Helen and Denis's landscape flowed into, rather than competed with, the natural mountain setting. I also appreciated the two cars parked in front of their house, which I must have missed in my hasty arrival. Our two sponsors had nice rides. I admired the silver Mercedes Benz S600 and the midnight blue Audi A8L as I got into my aging Subaru to head home.

I stopped in my office on my way upstairs and placed the business cards I'd been given on my desk: Roberta McCarthy Hart, Susanna Angelina Montoya, John James Collins. Two very generous ladies and a mystery man.

Chapter 14

I was filled with relief the next morning when I found the front door unlocked and the office bustling. I wouldn't have to answer the phones again. As I approached Brittany to ask her if we could lunch together, a woman intercepted me. She was fortyish, about the same age as Ms. Germaine, average build, average height, not blond but not brunette, not pretty but attractive. And although she wouldn't stand out in a crowd, there was something oddly compelling about her.

"You must be Ms. Westmore. I'm Margaret Barry. I heard you had a challenging morning yesterday. I'm afraid that was partly my fault."

"It was nothing. I just hope I didn't screw up any of the messages." She looked at me as if what I had to say were important. Her smile made me smile. "Please, call me J. All my friends do."

"Gladly, J, and you may call me Margaret. Why don't you come with me? We're having a client meeting in the small conference room today, so I moved you to the top floor into our vacant attorney office. It's much more suitable for conducting an audit since there's more privacy and it will keep you out of the fray."

Clearly Margaret didn't know I was supposed to be in the fray.

I followed her upstairs and to the back of the house. "There are some perks to being up here," she said, pointing to a small kitchen that had a cappuccino machine and a Keurig coffeemaker. "Everything you need is in the cupboard above the machines and in the refrigerator. There're also fruit and snack bars over there," she said, pointing to another counter, "and a variety of cold drinks in the fridge. Please help yourself."

"This is great. Thank you." I couldn't help but inwardly groan. This was all upstairs yesterday when I was starving to death?

"It's helpful when staff have to work through lunch or into the evening."

She opened a door with a plaque that read 'Kyle Wilson.' Glancing at the nameplate, she said absentmindedly, "That should have been removed by now."

I looked around the spacious corner room. The desk was set off to the side, with a small round table and four chairs under beveled windows. As with the rest of the house, it had beautiful cream-colored crown moldings, and rich oak furniture with leather accents. The HR files I'd been working on were in orderly piles on the small table.

As I set my bag on a chair and pulled out my electronic tablet, Margaret said, "Oops, I forgot something," and left the room.

She returned almost immediately with a tall vase of yellow roses and white gerbera daisies. She placed them on the credenza behind the desk. "These are from our garden. I've taken it over. I think of gardening as a form of meditation.

And, I'm a firm believer that flowers make a workplace less stressful."

"I think this is one of the nicest workplaces I've ever been in." I flinched, remembering a third of the staff had quit and Brittany referred to it as a hellhole. I regained my concentration. "I think I'll make a coffee and get to work. Thanks, Margaret."

"I only wish I had been here to do this for you yesterday," she said, her voice trailing off. She cleared her head with a shake. "I'm next door if you need me."

I went to the kitchen and made myself an espresso—for someone who rarely drank coffee I was in peril of forming a new bad habit. I returned to the office, and began reviewing files. There was a tap on the door and Margaret poked her head in.

She pointed to a small cardboard box on the floor next to the credenza. "When Kyle, the former occupant of this office, left, he failed to take his personal items. If he comes by and I'm not here, all his belongings are in there. Please don't let him take anything else." With a smile, she added, "Thanks, J," and left.

A little after eleven o'clock I went downstairs to see if Brittany wanted to go to lunch with me. She turned me down because she'd signed up for a prenatal exercise class at the hospital during her lunch hour. I decided to drive over to Mahogany Smoked Meats for a sandwich I could eat at my desk. As I pulled out into the street, a beat-up Camry took my parking spot, and a rather angry looking man got out. Under different circumstances I would have called the office to warn them, but I believed Ms. Germaine was more than capable of handling any situation that arose.

I returned, lunch in hand, to find the Camry still parked in front of the office. I expected to hear some shouting or at least loud discussion as I entered the office, but all was quiet. I headed back to my office, making a stop in the kitchen for an Honest Tea.

I opened my office door and discovered the angry Camry driver was tearing apart the office. He was huge, at least six feet two, and he was pissed. He paused and looked me up and down. "You must be the newest stooge. I'll be out of here in a minute. I'm looking for my thumb drive; I thought I left it in the top desk drawer. Have you seen it?"

"Are you Kyle?" I hadn't moved from the doorway.

"Yeah. That's right. I haven't seen you around the area. They must have imported you." His tone was snide.

The office was a mess. All the files I'd been working on were in a heap on the floor. I wanted to yell at him to take his box and get out, but that would be a missed opportunity.

I nodded toward the box next to the credenza. "I was told if you stopped by to pick up your things, they're all in that box."

He leapt at the box and emptied its contents on the already cluttered floor. A couple of framed pictures and a diploma, a Slinky, a couple of law books, a sleeve of golf balls, and an unopened split of champagne tumbled out. No thumb drive. As he pawed through the contents he kept mumbling to himself, "It's got to be here. It's. . . ."

"It's what? I don't understand," hoping he would take the bait.

"Oh you will, girlie. You'll understand soon enough."

Someone from behind gently move me to the side. "Hi, Kyle. I see you're looking for something."

Kyle's body stiffened and his anger was palpable. He looked up, focused on Margaret, and the tension left his body. "Oh, Mags, I thought you were the bitch."

Margaret gave him a sad smile. "What are you looking for?"

"My Goddamn thumb drive. It was in my drawer. Have you seen it?"

"I'm sorry, no. And I'm the one who cleaned your office and put your belongings in the box." She nodded in the direction of the overturned box on the floor. "If there had been one, I would have found it and placed it with your other possessions."

"Then SHE got here first," he said as he replaced items in the box. He stood up and looked at me. "Sorry about the mess." He touched Margaret on the shoulder. "Sorry, Mags." And left.

Chapter 15

Margaret and I cleaned up the office in awkward silence. I wanted to ask what she thought might be on Kyle's thumb drive. "Why was Kyle so angry?" I asked instead.

Wearily, Margaret stood. There was a tear in her eye. "Kyle claims someone gave him false information, which he used in court," she said so softly I had to strain to make out her words. "The end result was that he looked less competent than a first-year law student."

"So he was fired?"

"No," she said, shaking her head wearily. "He was so humiliated he quit."

"Someone gave him bad information?"

"He claims Lynette. But I'm positive it isn't true. Lynette . . . Ms. Germaine, has no reason to sabotage her own office, her own negotiations."

"Then what do you think happened?"

Margaret's head snapped back as if she were coming out of a stupor. She straightened and became a little guarded. "I don't know. I'm an assistant—a secretary—not an attorney." As if noticing her words and tone of voice, she said gently, "It's all quite depressing. And it seems like your first two days in the office have been a nightmare. I'm so sorry."

We returned to working in silence. When we finished, Margaret gave me one last wistful smile and left.

I sat at the table and ate my lunch, but didn't really taste it. I wanted to know what was going on in this office. None of it made sense. And it felt so sad. A few hours later I packed up and departed. As I passed Margaret's closed door I thought I heard a muffled sob.

Ross phoned as I was driving up Highway 395. "Hi, J. Where are you?" He sounded amped up, like he was the one who had three espressos today.

"About halfway home from Bishop . . . Why?"

"Go straight home. I'll meet you there."

"Sure, Ross. Is something wrong?"

He laughed. It sounded like a nervous laugh. "Nothing's wrong. I have . . . er . . . there's a surprise waiting for you at the house."

"There's nothing wrong, though?"

"No, J. I promise this is a good surprise."

"Can you tell me what it is? It's been a long day and I'm not sure I can handle a surprise."

"This is a really good surprise. Just come home."

Before I could probe anymore Ross disconnected.

Everything appeared normal when I pulled up to the house. Ross's Honda Pilot sat in the driveway. I could smell a faint whiff of cigar smoke, which most likely meant he was on the back deck having a martini. But I was a still little uneasy. Guiltily, I hoped the surprise didn't involve Olli. I was not in the mood.

When I entered the house, I could hear Ross talking to someone female, and my heart fell. I threw my workbag into the office and trudged up the stairs to the evening ahead.

I heard Ross yell, "J, is that you?"

I took a deep breath. "It's me." I hoped I sounded enthusiastic.

As I reached the top of the stairs I felt rather than saw someone grab me and yell, "Surprise!"

"Kate," I exclaimed. "You're supposed to be on your honeymoon?"

"We got back this morning, or at least I think it was this morning."

"This morning? Then what in the hell are you doing here? You must be totally exhausted."

Nathan responded from the living room. "She couldn't wait to tell you about her surprise for you, so we had all our luggage sent home, and caught the United flight to Mammoth." For a moment, he looked at Kate with such love I thought I should leave the room. "I hope you have a couple of extra toothbrushes. We brought nothing."

"What surprise? YOU are the surprise."

Kate just smiled like she was going to burst. Nathan said, "Let's join Ross on the back deck, and Kate can tell you both what she has planned." He took a sip from his wine glass. "He told me to tell you your drink is in the freezer."

And so it was.

When we all settled on the back deck, Kate said more solemnly than I would have expected, "As you know, Steve James is set to go on trial the end of this year."

The mention of the man who murdered my twin and brother-in-law smothered all the joy I had been feeling. "Yes," I whispered. "I keep hoping he'll just plead guilty and we can be done with it. But . . . but I know he's not going to."

Ross laid his hand on my shoulder. Oddly, Kate's excitement had not diminished, and Steve had almost succeeded at killing her too. *The night Steve broke into Mary's house to kill me, he unexpectedly ran into Kate who was spending the night in my guestroom. Kate was lucky to escape with a concussion and badly fractured leg.*

She took both my hands in hers and leaned toward me. "So to get through a shitty time, we need something to look forward to," she giggled.

I could feel anticipation returning. "What are we going to look forward to? Oh my God, are you pregnant?"

Kate Laughed, "No, I'm not pregnant, or at least I don't think so."

Nathan's eyes widened.

"The surprise is . . ." Turning to Nathan, she said, "Drum roll, please."

He mimed a drum roll and Kate clasped her hands in delight.

"Even with a worst-case scenario, the trial will be over by the beginning of December. So, Nathan and I are taking you and Ross to Paris for three weeks, beginning December 16! We're going to stay at L'Hôtel, in a two-bedroom suite that overlooks La rue des Beaux Arts," she squealed. *I'd never heard Kate squeal before.* "We've already booked the suite, so you can't say no. We're going to eat too much. We're going to shop too much. We're going to go to art museums and galleries. We're going to drink Bordeaux and champagne. And we're going to celebrate Christmas and the New Year and never having to think about Steve James again."

Kate was so happy she stood up, dragging me with her because she was still holding onto my hands. "What do you think?"

"I think you've gone bonkers, and I love it!"

By nine o'clock—six in the morning Paris time—Kate and Nathan had crashed, and Ross and I were talking quietly on the back deck. My excitement had ebbed. The December holiday season was a peak time for ski patrollers, which meant it would be difficult, if not impossible, for Ross to get the last two weeks of the year off to go to Paris.

"I'll call Bobby in the morning and make my case. In my fifteen years on patrol, I've never asked for time off in December. Besides, with this much advance warning, maybe we can work something out. But, J, don't get your hopes up. You may have to go without me." He didn't sound optimistic.

"Perhaps if you tell him the reason for the trip . . . "

Ross understood what I was offering. Both of us were loath to share personal details with people, especially anything related to Mary and Bob's murders. But I was feeling desperate.

"J, I'll do everything in my power to try and make it happen."

I was glad it was dark so Ross couldn't see the tears welling up in my eyes.

But he knew me well, and took me into his arms, whispering into my hair, "I promise."

Chapter 16

E arly the next morning I sat on the back deck drinking tea and playing scrabble on my mobile in a lame attempt to put off the inevitable. Finally disgusted by my cowardice, I punched in her number.

Ms. Germaine answered her phone on the first ring. "Good morning, J."

While Ross had dressed, I rehearsed a number of reasons why I would not be going into Bishop for work today. When he'd heard enough, Ross reminded me I was a grown woman, and should just tell the truth. So now I replied to Ms. Germaine's salutation with a tentative, "Good morning. I'm calling to let you know some friends dropped in unexpectedly last evening, and I will not be in the office today."

"Some friends *dropped by* so you decided not to come to work? And you call yourself a human resources consultant?" she barked sarcastically.

Squelching the urge to lash back, I said calmly but deliberately, "Yes, they flew in from their honeymoon in Paris last night to surprise me. They're leaving late this afternoon. I will be in the office tomorrow."

I felt a gentle touch on my shoulder and looked up to see Kate in my green and blue plaid pajamas smiling at me. Despite the seriousness of the call, I couldn't help but notice the pajamas were way too short for her.

"I realize it's unprofessional, but due to the circumstances I was hoping you'd understand."

I heard Ms. Germaine's long sigh. "I'm sorry for snapping, J, of course I understand. Another day or two isn't going to make a difference. It's just that . . . Well, I guess it really doesn't matter . . ." Her voice trailed off.

"What's wrong? Did something more happen?"

"No. Nothing more has happened. It's just that . . . I guess I've never had a problem I couldn't figure out for myself. I'm not used to asking for help."

In an effort to lighten the mood I said, "If everyone quit asking for help, I'd be out of a job."

Clearly it was the wrong response. I could almost hear her straighten up and reassume her professional persona. Her voice came through crisp and businesslike. "I'll expect you at eight-thirty Friday morning. Is there anything else?"

"Actually, there is. If you want me to observe staff, I need to be moved back downstairs where the action is."

"Hmmm. I suppose you do, now that Kyle has picked up his personal belongings."

I gave Kate a puzzled look as though she could hear both sides of the conversation. "I beg your pardon?"

"Oh, didn't I tell you? I asked Mags to move you to Kyle's office. I was hoping when he came by to pick up his things, you could talk to him. You know, inquire as to why he left. He wouldn't tell Mags or me anything, just that he was leaving.

His manner made it clear that he did not like the way I managed him, but he didn't offer any specific explanation."

As I chastised myself for not guessing my presence in Kyle's former office was deliberate, Ms. Germaine moved into her "self-talking" mode, a habit that could be both annoying and informative. "Sometimes I think Kyle quit because I accidentally handed him the wrong client file before one of his union negotiations, but that couldn't be it. I mean all he had to do was peruse the file and he would have known. Besides, quitting because of a mistake is juvenile, and I never thought he was that puerile."

Her voice changed, and I knew Ms. Germaine was talking to me again. "But Margaret told me he picked up his box without a word to anyone." After a beat, she added, "I'll have your files moved back downstairs to the small conference room. See you Friday morning. Don't be late."

I took a moment to process what I'd just heard. It seemed Margaret was protecting Ms. Germaine from the worst of Kyle's anger. I wondered whether that was a good idea or not. When I looked up, Kate was watching me with some concern.

"J, if you need to go to this job, don't worry about us."

"Are you kidding me? I'm taking advantage of every minute you're here. After we lounge around the house for a while we can clean up and go to the Village for a long lunch. It's a beautiful day. We can sit outside and people watch. Besides, we spent all last night talking about *our* December trip to Paris, I want to hear about your honeymoon." At her blush, I quickly added, ". . . the public part."

A little after noon, Kate, Nathan and I walked the four blocks downhill to the Village—which includes a hotel, condos, several restaurants, stores, and gondola access to Mammoth Mountain's thirty-five hundred acres of (winter) skiable, (summer) mountain bike-able terrain. Our destination was the Smokeyard, a wonderful barbecue steakhouse owned by two South African brothers, Alon and Guy Ravid.

The Village bustled with mountain bikers, hikers, tourists, and locals—some shopping or people watching, but most looking for a place to lunch. So, we were excited to get the last table outside on the Smokeyard patio.

We ordered our drinks—chardonnay for Kate and me, Real McCoy Amber Ale for Nathan—then I begged them to tell me about Paris.

Kate grinned. "Did I mention that we were robbed, or at least Nathan was, on the Metro?"

"Robbed?" This wasn't what I'd been expecting to hear. "And you're just mentioning it now?"

"Well," said Nathan sheepishly, "it was a little embarrassing."

He did not continue. After a full minute of silence, and a little smirking on Kate's part, I asked, "Will someone please tell me about it?"

Nathan nodded at Kate. "We decided for our last day we would go to Bois de Boulogne Parc in the 16th arrondissement, and picnic on the shore of Lac Inférieur." Kate frowned when I started to giggle. "Why are you laughing?"

"Sorry. You just sound so . . . so French. Please, go ahead with your story." I tried to look serious.

Kate arched an eyebrow at me and continued. "The hotel prepared us a lunch basket, and we boarded the Metro. There was only one seat available, which was next to the door, so I took it and Nathan stood next to me. A minute or so before the train took off, two young teenage girls rushed into the car. They walked right up to Nathan, and . . ." She paused when a slight groan escaped Nathan. Now it was her turn to giggle.

". . . One of the girls pulled up her shirt to expose rather nice breasts. While Nathan was gawking, the other grabbed his wallet right out of his front jeans pocket. And then as the train doors started to close, they rushed out."

"Oh, Nathan. I'm sorry." Picturing the scene, it was hard not to laugh. "How much did they get away with?"

Before Nathan could respond, Kate said, "Actually, *they* didn't get away. Only the girl with the wallet managed to detrain."

"Because the door closed too quickly?"

"Because my husband managed to grab the teenager with the boobs before she could flee."

Startled, I turned to Nathan. "You actually caught her? Your reactions were that fast?"

"Well I am an attorney, after all."

Kate and I rolled our eyes at one another. Our drinks arrived in time to toast Nathan's lightning-quick reflexes.

"So what did you do with the teenager once you . . ."

Kate cut me off. She was looking at something over my shoulder. "Didn't you tell me earlier Ross's old high school sweetheart was a stunning honey blond with olive green eyes, around five feet nine?" she asked.

My spirits fell. "Yes. Why?"

"Because a woman fitting that description, accompanied by a man in bicycle clothing, is headed this way."

Chapter 17

Tony Adams, Director of the Mammoth Lakes Enterprise Enhancement Consortium, a.k.a. man in bike clothing, stopped directly in front of me, saying without preamble, "J, I'm glad you're here." He pointed to Olli. "I want to hire your friend Olivia here to help out with the public and media relations for the Mammoth Lakes Labor Day Golf Gala, and I need a local reference. Will you vouch for her?"

I unclenched my teeth and took a deep breath. "Hello, Tony. Permit me to introduce you to my guests." He had the grace to look slightly mortified as I made the introductions.

"Of course, I'll provide you with a reference for Olli . . ."

Tony spoke over me. "In writing?"

My patience was getting thin. I really did not like this man. And what was up with his always walking around in bike clothes?

"I'll email it to you once my guests depart this afternoon," I said stiffly.

"Good," he said tersely as he turned to leave.

"Tony," I said. When he didn't turn around, I said a bit more forcefully, "Tony."

I guess my voice came out louder than I intended, because not only did Tony turn to look at me, so did half the diners on the patio. "It's not the 'Mammoth Lakes Labor Day Golf Gala,' it's the 'Hope for Our Children Labor Day Golf Gala,' being held in Mammoth Lakes."

"Sure. Though what we call it doesn't matter that much."

"It does to the sponsors of the event," I said evenly. "Remember *all* press releases and other marketing materials need to be approved by Linda or myself *before* they go out."

Tony gave a slight nod, and left.

We watched him depart.

Olli was the first to break the silence. "I'm sorry for the interruption. Tony was interviewing me over a cup of coffee at Starbucks," she said, pointing at the café across the brick walkway. "When he spotted you, he said if you would vouch for me I had the job. Then before I knew it, he rushed over here."

"It's not your fault, Olli. Unfortunately, Tony is short on manners." Looking around the table, I said, "And I guess, so am I. Would you like to join us?" I hoped my invitation didn't sound as hollow to her as it did to me.

Olli shook her head. "Thank you, no. I don't want to further disrupt your lunch." With an embarrassed smile to Kate and Nathan, she added, "Nice to meet you. Enjoy your time with J," and headed off.

Before I could share my relief at Olli's departure, I felt a sharp pain on my shin. Kate silently signaled with her eyes and head for me to go after Olli and bring her back. Sighing, I went to retrieve Olli.

Thirty minutes later we were devouring our lunches and talking about Paris, except this time there were animated side conversations in French between Olli and Kate. As the two went on with one of their longer dialogues, my feelings started to get hurt. It was bad enough Ross's old girlfriend was living with him, but now that same old girlfriend was charming one of my closest friends. And that close friend was ignoring me when we only had a few short hours left to spend together. I turned to Nathan, irritation all over my face. He just shrugged, and took another swig of his ale.

Kate saved me from giving voice to my annoyance. "J, Olli was at L'Hôtel last year," she said. Turning back to Olli, she asked, "Où vous . . . sorry, I meant to ask in English. Were you with anyone or by yourself?"

Olli seemed to shrink in on herself. She whispered into her lunch remains, "Sam."

After a moment of what seemed to be introspection, she said somberly, "I stayed much longer than I should have. It's been a real pleasure, but I must go now." She took her wallet out of her purse, and Nathan said, "Please put that back. You're our guest."

Olli looked uncomfortable, until Nathan added, "I particularly liked the story about your disastrous trip to La Rochelle."

Olli's face softened to a smile.

Once Olli was out of earshot, I turned to Nathan. "You speak French, too? "

"Sûrement. Je suis un avocat, après tout. "

"What did he just say?" I demanded of Kate.

"He just reminded you once again that as an attorney he knows everything," Kate said, trying to stifle a giggle.

On our walk back up the hill to the house we discussed Olli. Kate was convinced she'd been through some kind of trauma. "Every time I asked her something personal, she changed the subject. I understand she's getting a divorce, but it felt like something more."

I shared with them Ross's observations and concerns from Olli's staying with him—her hyper vigilance about locked windows and doors, always shutting down when anything of a personal nature came up.

"I think Kate's supposition may be right," Nathan said. "It sounds like she's been abused, either emotionally or physically. And now it makes much more sense that she would want to stay with her old boyfriend for a while instead of getting a place of her own."

I felt like a jerk as I said, "Yeah, so do I. But did it have to be Ross? And does she have to be so beautiful *and* accomplished?"

Both Nathan and Kate laughed at my whining. "You have nothing to worry about, J, and you know it," Kate said.

"Besides," Nathan added as he looked up the final hill to the house, "we may not live long enough to worry about Ross or Olli. Why didn't you warn me about how difficult walking uphill is at eighty-two hundred feet above sea level when I suggested a second round of drinks?"

I had an ache in my heart as Kate and Nathan boarded the plane. They'd become so dear to me I wished we lived closer. When they disappeared from sight, I reluctantly headed toward the parking lot. After a few steps I heard a commotion coming from the door of the plane. I turned to see Kate signaling for me to come closer, despite the irritated look she was getting from a flight attendant.

"I almost forgot to tell you," she shouted over the sound of the engine.

"What?"

"M ...... and ......"

"What?"

The attendant now had Kate by the arm, trying to guide her back into the plane.

I saw her take a deep breath and yell, "Mary and Bob had chocolates and Bordeaux waiting for us at the hotel when we arrived in Paris."

Kate must have known I heard by the tears spilling down my face, because she meekly followed the steward back into the plane.

As I started my car I realized I hadn't found out what happened to the teenage girl Nathan caught in the Paris Metro.

Chapter 18

My cell rang the next morning as I pulled up in front of the McNulty Bishop Law Office. It was Charlotte, and since I was twenty minutes early, I answered it.

"Oh hi, J. I rather expected to get your voicemail at this hour of the morning."

I guess it was no secret I liked to sleep in. "Well then, Charlotte, you'll be surprised to learn I just arrived in Bishop for a job."

"That *is* impressive. I won't keep you. I wanted to let you know I'll be home tomorrow." Was that relief I heard in her voice?

"Sounds like you'll be happy to be back in Mammoth."

"Oh, J, you have no idea. The short version is that my brothers and my Dad's girlfriend aren't speaking to me and have threatened litigation—for different reasons, of course. The twins want money and they want it now. Steph insists that Dad promised her most of the artwork in the house if anything ever happened to him. It's a mess."

"I'm sorry, Charlotte," I said gently. "What time does your plane land? I'll pick you up."

"Not necessary, but thanks. My car is at the airport. I'll call when I get back. I've been looking forward to the

Dominique Saint Emilion with a side of chocolate you promised."

"It's ready when you are. Travel safely, my friend."

As I exited the car Brittany pulled up behind me. Although it was way too early to look pregnant, she did not look well. "Are you all right, Brittany?"

"The doctor says it's just a touch of morning sickness. If this is a *touch* I can't imagine what full-blown morning sickness could be." She was sallow and unsteady on her feet. She had a point.

"Maybe you should have stayed at home?"

"Wouldn't work. Ms. Germaine is going to be in meetings at the Energy Council all day; Mags is in court supporting Shari Miller, our other attorney, and Christine has a job interview. It's just you and me." She gave me a sickly smile. "And I didn't think you wanted to answer phones again."

By the way she laughed I knew she saw how relieved I was at not having to play receptionist again.

"Now that you bring up Shari, is she ever in the office for more than a few minutes? I've seen her rushing in and out, but that's the extent of it."

"Not often," Brittany said as she unlocked the front door. "She doesn't like the 'office vibe.' But really, who does? If I could leave, the only person I would miss is Mags."

We entered the office and went to our respective stations. I was pleased to discover the boxes of personnel files on the table of the small conference room. I'd been expecting to haul them all down from Kyle's old office myself. My first order of business was a cappuccino, so I dropped my purse and notebook on a chair, and went to see if Brittany wanted one, too. I was amazed to find that in the few minutes we had been apart, Brittany had managed to cover every open space on her desk with crackers, pretzels, ginger ale, and lollipops.

"What are these?" I asked, holding up a sucker.

"Preggie Pops," she answered proudly. "They help ease nausea."

What would they think of next?

"Can I get you anything from the kitchen? I'm going to make myself a cappuccino."

Brittany turned a little green when I said cappuccino. She shook her head a vehement *no*, and the phone rang.

By mid-morning I was on my way to check if the Office's required federal and state employment postings were current, when Brittany called my name. She stood next to her desk, doubled up. She managed to say, "Please cover my desk," and ran in the direction of the ladies' room. Of course, the phone started ringing.

There was finally a lull about twenty minutes later. Brittany hadn't returned. I went to the door of the ladies' room and knocked. "Are you all right? Is there anything or anyone you need?"

I heard a muffled, "Okay. Just need a few more minutes."

Four or possibly five phone calls later, a young, very large, harried-looking man ran into the office and demanded, "Where's Brittany?"

"You are . . .?" I wasn't sure if I should just tell anyone where Brittany was.

"Don. Her . . . her husband. She just called . . . It wasn't like this the first time." He looked like he was going to be sick, cry, or both.

I pointed to the ladies' room, pondering his statement "the first time." I thought this was Brittany's first baby. "Let me know if you need help or if I should call anyone. Last time I checked up on her, she said she was getting a little better."

Don hadn't waited to hear what I had to say.

Moments later he emerged carrying Brittany in his arms. "I'm taking her to the doctor's office. We're not leaving until he gives Brit something to make her feel better."

I went to the reception desk to get her purse. While I was filling it with the various foodstuffs that littered the space, I saw a document on her computer screen. "Is there something you want me to do with this document, or should I just turn off the computer?"

Don glared at me, anxious to leave. "What does it say on the top of the page?" Brittany asked.

"Let's see . . . Madison Manufacturing."

She let out a little yelp. I had her attention. "Oh, J, I'm so glad you saw that. I just hope it's not too late." She wriggled to get out of her husband's arms and stand on her own, but Don was having none of it. Giving up the struggle, she said, "Just hit enter, save, and close. In that order!"

While I held the front door open for them, Brittany kept saying, "Enter, save, close." And then the phone rang.

Shortly after one o'clock I decided to mutiny. I didn't know how Brittany did it. People called and asked the dumbest questions, and when you didn't have an answer, they got angry. It was time to call Elise, the administrative glue that kept all of the McNulty law offices functioning, and ask her to send someone to replace me as receptionist. But of course, as I went to dial her number the phone rang.

"McNulty Law Group, Bishop office. How may I help you?"

A hostile voice ordered, "Put Mags on, and do it NOW."

"I'm sorry, Ms. Barry is out of the office. May I take a message?"

"Where is she? And why doesn't she answer her fucking cell phone? And while I'm at it, who the hell is this? It certainly isn't Brittany." As he continued ranting, Ms. Germaine flew into the office and without a glance at reception, ran up the stairs towards her office. ". . . If you don't tell me where my sister is I'll have your job."

I was beyond pissed. I practically yelled, "I'll tell your sister you called." Before I could disconnect, he bellowed, "NO. You tell her she lied. She said she'd be back by now and help me. Well she isn't, so I am going out and help myself. And whatever happens, it's her fault." The line went dead.

This was Margaret's brother? What a jerk.

The phone rang again, but I placed the ringer on mute and headed up stairs to talk to Ms. Germaine.

Her door was partially open, so I knocked on the frame as I walked in.

Ms. Germaine was sitting in one of the client chairs, sobbing.

Chapter 19

C oncern replaced irritation. The last person on earth I would expect to be crying uncontrollably was Ms. Germaine. She was so *in control*, precise, unemotional. Since she hadn't yet noticed me, I went to the kitchen first and got a cold bottle of water, placed it next to her, and sat down in the companion client chair, and waited.

Slowly she regained some degree of composure. She reached for the water and took a few sips, then turned toward me. She looked startled and said to herself, "Of course you couldn't be Mags; she's in court today. . . ."

It was another few minutes before she addressed me. "I'm sorry you had to witness that. I seldom break down, and never in the office." Her voice was stiff, verging on formal.

"What's wrong?" I asked, ignoring her attempt at distancing. "Perhaps I can help."

A brief flash of resentment crossed her face. "Nothing I can't handle. Thank you for your concern." She started to stand.

Placing a hand on the arm of her chair, I said, "Please don't dismiss me. *You* asked me to help when I began this assignment. Now let me. What do you have to lose? Let's start with what made you so upset today."

I watched an internal debate play out on her face before she finally fell back into her chair. "All right. What does it matter anymore," she replied softly. "Today I may have lost this office's most important client, because of rookie mistakes in the contract documents I brought with me."

"Who prepared the documents?"

A half sob escaped her lips. "I did."

"I find that difficult to believe."

"So did I. I went over everything last night, and was pleased with the work I'd done. Then this morning as I was presenting our analysis, conclusions, supporting documentation and recommended plan of action, I saw that all my work could have been that of a first-year law student." Ms. Germaine sat very still for a few moments. "I think I'm losing my mind," she whispered.

We sat in awkward silence.

"Could someone have changed your work between last evening and this morning?"

"When I first saw the mistakes, I thought so. But who? Shari has been working at her client's office for the last week, getting ready for a trial. Kyle no longer has access to the building. Christine has virtually quit, we're just still paying her for a few weeks—and she's a paralegal, not an attorney. There's no one else left."

"Who would have had access to the documents between last night and this morning?"

Ms. Germaine unconsciously rolled a pen back and forth on her desk. "They're stored electronically, so anyone in the office. I came in early this morning and printed a hard copy in case I needed it, but most of my clients don't like to work with paper until all the changes have been made to whatever documents we're working on." She studied her hands. "Why would someone change them? If we lose clients because of incompetency, Bill will just close the office, and everyone will lose their job."

I was at a loss.

"No, the simplest answer is usually the right one. I must be going through some kind of breakdown."

"You are *not* losing your mind. There *is* a logical explanation, and together we can figure it out," I said with a bit more confidence than I felt. "Let's talk it through."

"We can try," she said almost timidly. Then as if a switch in her brain turned on, she sat up straight and said, "Why don't I hear any phones?"

I told her about Brittany's morning sickness, her husband picking her up, and how I put the ringer on mute.

With a mirthless smile, she asked, "So you're on phone duty again?" Without waiting for an answer, she got up from her desk. "I'll go downstairs and put on the 'we're all in a staff meeting' recording, and then we can talk without losing any more clients."

While Ms. Germaine went downstairs to change the phone message, I went into the kitchen and gathered some energy bars, a couple of apples and bottles of Honest Tea. I didn't know about Ms. Germaine, but once again, I was starving. By the time she returned, I was jotting down some questions on a scrap of paper.

"Where do I start?" she asked, unwrapping a Clif bar. She looked tense, but almost eager to see where the conversation would take us.

My strategy was simple. I didn't know what questions to ask, but I wanted her to start talking, hoping that something she said would trigger a clue one of us would recognize. "Tell me why you took this job. My understanding from Bill is that you have an exceptional reputation in your field. So, why Bishop?"

A smile crossed Ms. Germaine's face. "As you know, my expertise is where water resource management meets the law. Bishop, well basically, all of Inyo and Mono counties, have been engaged in water wars since the early 1900s. A few years ago Bill lured me into a consulting agreement with a particularly messy water contract negotiation. I loved every minute of it. And it seems Los Angeles has pretty much guaranteed we will never have a shortage of similar problems. When my assignment ended, and Bill asked if I wanted a full-time position, I was delighted."

"So it was just the nature of the work?"

She sat back in her chair and closed her eyes. "No, it was a combination of factors. On the professional side the McNulty Law Group has a solid reputation, practicing not just law, but problem solving in a variety of technical areas. I also liked the staff here. They were hard working and earnest."

This was interesting, but I didn't want her to quit talking, so I asked, "You said from a professional side?"

Her face tensed up, and I spied a flash of anger in her eyes. "Yes, she said quietly and deliberately. "Personally I was concerned about Mags. I wanted her out of the reach of her narcissistic user of a brother. He has an unhealthy control over her, demanding that he should be her first priority. He has always monopolized most of her free time, and constantly interrupts her at work. Bishop seemed the perfect place, because I was fairly certain he would never consider moving here. Too much nature, not enough night life."

"So Margaret was always part of the equation? How did the two of you first meet?"

Ms. Germaine leaned back again into her chair, a faraway look in her eyes. "I moved next door to Mags in Pasadena when we were six, and we've been best friends ever since. We went to elementary, high school, college, and law school together. We consistently finished one and two in our class. And I was always second."

"Law school? But Margaret's not an attorney. She's your assistant." I was stunned.

She didn't seem to hear me; she was still reminiscing. She shook her head. "I tried so hard to beat her, but no matter how studiously I worked, she was always smarter."

"So why is Margaret not practicing law?"

Tears came to her eyes, but none fell. "Margaret's parents were killed in a head-on collision on their way to our Law School graduation ceremony at Stanford. Her fourteen-year-old brother was the only one to survive. Mags blamed herself for the accident; she claimed that if she hadn't insisted they come they'd still be alive. Actually, I'm the one who should feel guilty." Her voice cracked. "A few days before graduation, Mrs. Barry called and said she thought it was too far to drive. She never liked long car rides, and hated planes. I got on the phone and convinced her to come." Ms. Germaine's tears were flowing freely now. She shook her head as to if to force the memory back into its box. She looked at me with such sorrow I thought I would cry, too. "The day of their funeral Mags said she would never practice law. And, she never has."

"Is the accident the reason Margaret's brother is so . . . um . . . needy?"

"No," Ms. Germaine said vehemently. "Eric was the only child I ever met who was born a self-centered little shit and only got worse as he aged."

Chapter 20

"I'm so sorry," I whispered. I didn't know what else to say.

Ms. Germaine shook her head regretfully. "It's water under the bridge."

I recalled the phone call I'd received earlier. "Does Margaret have just one brother?"

Ms. Germaine became alert. "Yes. Why?"

I told her about my phone encounter with Margaret's brother, and his final words.

"Oh dear. This means Mags will rush back to Pasadena to save him." She looked thoughtful. "Why don't you give me the message, and I'll give it to Mags. Perhaps I can talk her out of going."

"I better go downstairs and get it right now, or I'll probably forget." I was grateful for the few minutes it would take me to get the message. It would give me some time to formulate more questions. I particularly wanted to know what changed with the staff from the time of her consulting assignment to now.

When I returned Ms. Germaine was on her mobile, and she sounded serious. Taking the phone message from me, she excused herself to her caller, covered the speaker, and said we would have to continue later. My face must have betrayed both disappointment and frustration. "I promise we will finish this conversation, J. Just not now."

I grabbed an Honest Tea and a protein bar, and reluctantly walked back to reception.

At five-thirty I still had not seen or heard from her, so I collected my things, and left a note on top of the day's messages, asking her to call me so we could schedule some time to resume our discussion.

I checked my cell as I got into the car. There were five new texts, but I gave my attention to Ross's message. He was in Bishop golfing with friends, and wanted me to meet them for a drink at the course. I texted back and asked if I was too late to join them. He immediately responded with "perfect timing . . . we just finished our round." *No,* I thought as I drove to the Bishop Country Club, *your timing is perfect, Ross.*

It was a late Friday afternoon in the summer so the parking lot was packed. As I strode toward the clubhouse I wished I had my golf clubs in the car. The golf course is rural and open, giving one the feeling of old California and space. This Round Valley golf course boasts views of the Sierra Nevada mountains on one side, and the White mountains on the other. It is bordered by Highway 395—the main thoroughfare—on one side, and working farms on the other three. The effect is breathtaking. With a few hours of daylight left, the long shadows made the giant oaks, birch and willow trees look like something from a fairytale.

Lost in the course's magic I failed to notice the large man coming toward me until we were almost touching. It took a moment to recognize Kyle, the disgruntled, unemployed attorney I'd met a few days earlier. He still looked angry.

"You're Ms. Westmore, aren't you?"

"Yes," I said tentatively. Holding my small purse between us as if it were body armor, I said more assertively, "And you're Kyle. What can I do for you?"

He took a step closer. I took a step back.

Kyle held up his hands in surrender. "Sorry, I didn't mean to scare you."

I was still unsure of his intentions. "What can I do for you?"

His arrogance fell away. "I want to apologize for being such a jerk the other day."

"You do?" The words were out of my mouth before I could stop them. "That's very nice," I stammered. "Why the change of heart?"

He looked down at his feet, which I now saw were clad in golf shoes. He wasn't *stalking* me. "Mags phoned Wednesday night and read me the riot act. She said you were a consultant who had nothing to do with the firm, besides conducting a one-time procedural audit. She also said she was ashamed of me, and that I had no excuse for acting like a child." He looked at me so contritely I no longer saw an attorney in his mid-thirties, but a boy in his mid-teens. "She was right. I was an ass. I hope you'll accept my apology."

I dropped my hands to my sides, no longer needing protection. "Of course, I do." As I held out my hand to shake, I said, "You must think a great deal of Margaret."

"She's one of the most gracious, kind, and intelligent ladies I've ever met. She's always treated the staff like family. She goes to lunch with us, has us over to her house. Hell, she's been mothering Brittany since the first day she came to work. You know, just a great soul. The hardest part of not working at McNulty is not working with her."

He cocked his head slightly as if someone were whispering in his ear. "Though I think Mags would be a lot happier if she could go back to Pasadena," he said.

This would probably be my only chance to ask, "If it's not too personal, what happened?"

I watched his body tense and the color rise in his cheeks. He said slowly, as if trying to maintain control, "The b . . . er . . . . I was set up to fail." He must have noticed the puzzled look on my face, because he added, "I had a client who was having labor union issues. After working with his management team, I prepared a proposed plan of action for negotiations, citing relevant state and federal regulations and laws. During our first meeting with Labor, I found that everything was based on bad information. The client was livid. He fired us the next day."

I didn't want Kyle ranting again, but I needed to know. "And this is the situation that caused you to leave McNulty?"

"No." His voice was so quiet I almost couldn't hear him. "I tried calling Mr. McNulty but he was in the middle of a court case. When I couldn't reach him, I sent an email and told him what I believed, no *knew*, had happened."

"And what did Bill . . . er . . . Mr. McNulty say?"

"He never responded."

I was about to ask another question, when I saw Ross approaching us. "Is everything all right?" he asked. "I was expecting you twenty minutes ago." Noticing the other man, he said, "Hey Kyle, I didn't know you and J knew one another."

Kyle looked surprised, then laughed. "She's your lady, Ross? I wish I'd known that a few days ago."

"Why don't you join us for a drink and explain what you mean?"

Kyle shook his head. "I need to head home. *My* lady and I are going out. I just saw Ms. West. . . um . . . J, and wanted a word with her." He shrugged, said goodbye, and started toward his Camry. After a few steps, he turned and added, "If you're still working over at the office next week, keep your eyes open."

I raised my eyebrows at him.

He just shook his head derisively, making a sound between a laugh and a grunt, and headed to his car.

His words sounded ominous. Ross and I just looked at one another, and then strolled to the clubhouse. As we walked I asked, "Do you golf with Kyle?"

Ross laughed and shook his head. "Never. The guy takes himself way too seriously."

A drink with Ross and his buddies was just what I needed. Instead of focusing on the crises that had defined my day, I listened to Jeff brag about the eagle he had on the second hole, and to John badgering Jeff to tell me about his score on the other seventeen holes. It was perfect.

Since we were forty miles from home, it was a one-drink maximum. After saying good night to everyone, Ross walked me to my car. "Shall I follow you to your place?" he asked, moving his eyebrows up and down.

"I was just going to ask if you would." I giggled, throwing my purse onto the passenger seat. As I watched it land, I realized my laptop was not on the seat where it should be. "Uh oh. I'm going to have to stop by the law office. I was so busy with reception, I forgot my computer."

"Still want me to follow you?"

"No, it'll only take me a few minutes—less if Ms. Germaine has locked the office and gone home for the day." This time my eyebrows were raised in anticipation. "That would give you time to stop by the Village and pick up a couple of salads from the Side Door."

"No problem," Ross said. "See you at home."

Five minutes later I pulled up behind Ms. Germaine who was exiting her car with purpose. She looked at me curiously. "J, what brings you back to the office? You're not expecting to resume our discussion now, are you?"

"No, I forgot my laptop." Looking up at the office, I asked, "How about you? Did you forget something too?"

"No. Less than an hour after I got home I realized I was too restless to stay, so I thought I would come back to work. Besides, I think I may have an idea of how to get back into Mike Madison's good graces, and I want to start working on it now." She strode deliberately to the front door, a woman on a mission.

"Is that the client you, uh . . . met with today?" I asked gingerly.

She assumed her normal stiff-backed posture. "If you mean, is that the client I lost today. It is."

"Were you able to give Margaret her brother's phone message?" I asked, changing the subject.

Her shoulders slumped. "Yes. And as I predicted, she's on her way back to Pasadena to rescue him from whatever mess he got himself into this time."

"I'm sorry," I half whispered, as Ms. Germaine unlocked the front door of the office.

Her response was a slow shake of her head. "It's been a long day for both of us, J. And don't think I'm not aware of all you did for me. Thank you." With the hint of a smile, she added, "We'll finish today's conversation Monday morning. Now get your laptop and go home and start your weekend." She headed to the stairs.

I stopped her halfway up. "May I ask you something?"

She looked at me wearily. "Certainly, J."

"I know it's none of my business, but I was curious . . .?"

"What is it?" I heard impatience in her voice.

Now I felt guilty about bothering her with such a trivial question, but one look at Ms. Germaine, I knew I better get on with it. "Was Brittany ever pregnant before?"

Her face tightened. "That's an odd question." Before I could tell her about Don's remark when he came to get Brittany, she continued. "Yes. She had a miscarriage about six months ago. She was about four months pregnant at the time." I didn't think it was possible, but Ms. Germaine's face tightened even more. "Why? Did she tell you it was my fault? That's what she told everyone else in the office." Without waiting for a response, she turned and finished her climb to the second floor.

I was flabbergasted by her statement, but too exhausted to pursue it. Perhaps Bill McNulty knew what this was all about. I did a quick inventory of my belongings as I packed them up. The only thing missing was the silver Cross pen my mother had given my father on their twenty-fifth wedding anniversary. After inheriting it, I had carefully packed the pen away in a bedroom drawer so it wouldn't be lost or damaged. Only a few weeks ago I rediscovered it, and the pleasure of using the pen far surpassed the wisdom of preserving it for posterity.

I flipped off the small conference room light switch, and went to reception. My precious pen was perched on top of the computer keyboard. As I picked up the cherished heirloom I couldn't take my eyes off the computer.

Milliseconds later I was walking into Ms. Germaine's office. "I assume Mike Madison works for Madison Manufacturing?"

Startled and mildly irritated, she responded, "Yes. Of course, he does. He owns Madison Manufacturing. But . . ."

I cut her off. "Did you ask Brittany to make corrections to any of the Madison Manufacturing documents this morning?"

"Brittany has nothing to do with any of our client documents. She's a receptionist, for God's sake."

"I don't know much about computers, but when changes are made to a client document, is the time of the change tracked in the program?"

"I think so. But what is this all about? What are you implying?"

"Can you check? Now?"

"Check what?" she shouted. Ms. Germaine's irritation was no longer mild.

"What time the last change was made to the Madison Manufacturing documents?"

She rapidly tapped at her computer. The widening of her eyes signaled she found what she was looking for. Her voice was hoarse. "The last change was made at 10:41:17 this morning. Are you saying Brittany changed my documents?"

I fell into the client chair across from her. "No. I think technically speaking, I changed your documents."

Chapter 21

After a quick text to Ross so he wouldn't worry, I told Ms. Germaine about the document that had been on the computer when Brittany's husband carried her off to the doctor. And her instructions to, "Hit enter, save, and close."

We were dumbfounded. Neither of us could believe sweet, innocent Brittany could be the source of the changed documents. In the midst of mentally listing all the reasons it couldn't be Brittany, a small groan escaped Ms. Germaine and she picked up the phone.

"Who are you calling?"

"Brittany. I want to know why she's been sabotaging us."

I leapt out of my chair, grabbed the phone and disconnected the cord. "No. You're not calling and accusing Brittany based on one small piece of information. You're an attorney. Think about it. Calling any employee at home on a Friday night, much less a pregnant one with severe morning sickness who has already had one miscarriage, and accusing her of sabotage will only result in disaster. Besides we really don't have any proof. Remember, technically, I made the changes."

"You're right," Ms. Germaine said, slumping back into her chair. "I'll wait until Monday morning to ask her about the changes."

"We need more information, and we need proof before you confront anyone."

"How do you think we are going to get that information if we don't confront anyone?" She was getting angry again.

"First, I suggest you list all the documents you suspect have been changed over the last several weeks. And for each on record, who prepared the documents, the day and time of the client presentation when the errors were discovered, and then look at the computer record to see if changes were made right before or during the presentation. That way we can get a handle on the extent of the problem."

I marveled at how quickly professional resolve replaced Ms. Germaine's fury. She stood. "I'll do it this weekend."

"Good. Then, on Monday morning let me speak with Brittany unofficially about the Madison documents. It's been my experience that you learn more by chatting than accusing."

"All right. I don't like it, but I can see your logic. However, if Brittany is not forthcoming with you, I may take a more forceful approach."

Knowing this was the best I could expect from Ms. Germaine, I agreed, asked her to email me the results of her research when she was finished, and said good night.

I was so blown away by the possibility Brittany could be single-handedly destroying the McNulty's Bishop Office reputation, it wasn't until I was halfway up the Sherwin Grade to Mammoth I realized I'd forgotten my computer again.

Ross awakened me the next morning with a mug of coffee and a kiss. He was on his way to work at Snow Star with a promise to return by six. It was Saturday and I was on my own. Most Saturdays followed the same routine: Begin with a run up to the Lakes Basin, clean the house, do the laundry, and restock the pantry. Today I was particularly eager for the challenge since it didn't involve answering phones for a law office.

I ran a soul-cleansing ten-mile loop from my house to Lake Horseshoe and back. It was a run that always made me vow I would never live anywhere but Mammoth Lakes. If the elevation gain of a thousand feet didn't take my breath away, the scenery would. The running vista included Crystal Crag, a giant rock monolith marking the Eastern Sierra Mammoth Crest; four lakes: Twin, Mary, Mamie, and Horseshoe; and, a cascading waterfall—and that was just on the way up to Lake Horseshoe. If these landmarks weren't enough to distract me from my daily worries, running by an occasional family of deer, or mother bear and her cubs would. By the time I was finished, my heart was full and I was ready for whatever the day brought. Or so I thought.

By three o'clock the laundry was done, the house sparkled, and I was leaving the grocery store with a full cart. Out of the corner of my eye, I saw a familiar figure with red curly hair pass me in the parking lot. "Charlotte? When did you get back?"

"About thirty minutes ago," she said. "I thought I'd pick up something for dinner on my way home from the airport, and save myself an extra trip. I'm beat."

She looked more than beat; she looked like she hadn't slept in a week. "Save yourself some work and have dinner with Ross and me. We're going to barbecue some fish."

"Thanks, J, but I'll pass. I'm looking forward to an evening of mindless TV and early to bed." She grinned. "But tomorrow night I'm free."

"Tomorrow night it is." We parted, Charlotte to buy her dinner, and I to load the car.

Twenty minutes later I was leaning against the back of my Subaru in the Vons parking lot frustrated, terminating a call to the local garage, when Charlotte spotted me. This time she was the one with the full shopping cart. "Problem?" she asked.

"My car won't start, and it's not the battery," I whined.

"Did you call the auto club?"

"No, better. I called my friend, Chuck Addy at Norco. He's sending a tow truck."

"Why don't you leave your keys in the car, and I'll give you a lift home."

"That would be perfect. I'd really like to get the fish and milk products into the refrigerator before they spoil."

Minutes later we'd loaded Charlotte's Toyota Rav 4 with all our provisions and headed home. While she drove, I called Chuck to tell him where the key was, and asked him to call as soon as he knew what was wrong with my car. "I really need my car by seven Monday morning, Chuck. I have a critical meeting with a client early. I know you're closed on Sunday, but I'd much rather pay your mechanic overtime and a bonus than rent a car. Is that possible?"

Charlotte turned onto our street as Chuck assured me his mechanic would jump at the chance to make some extra money. She automatically reached up and pushed the remote to open her garage. Chuck was still talking, so I tapped her on the arm and motioned for her to continue to my house at the top of the cul de sac. She mouthed "sorry," and drove up the street.

We hadn't made it fifty yards when a deafening explosion shook the car, causing Charlotte to veer off into a neighbor's front yard. The concussion left us dazed and confused. What brought us both out of our stupor was someone faraway yelling "J! J! Are you okay? J! Answer me."

I looked at Charlotte who pointed to the phone still tightly clasped in my hand. As I began to answer a frantic Chuck, we both looked around to find the source of the blast. We saw it at the same time. "I think we're okay," I responded shakily. "But you better send the fire department and police to my street."

"I guess you'll be having dinner with us after all," I said. Then Charlotte and I fell into the silent stupor of those who had just had a close brush with their own mortality.

Chapter 22

C haos replaced civility. People from blocks away came running to see what had happened. Some stood in front of Charlotte's house, which was now missing its garage and most of its kitchen. Others rushed to the car. Fortunately, my next-door neighbor, Bill, reached us first and held them at bay. When he opened the driver's door Charlotte and I became aware of the screeching car and house alarms; we remained in the car, unmoving and in shock. Bill helped us out of the car one at a time, checked for visible injuries, and walked us the few hundred yards to my house. Once we were seated on the front porch bench and out of harm's way, he returned to move Charlotte's car out of the yard it was parked in.

By the time Bill pulled Charlotte's car into my driveway, police had cordoned off the entrance to the cul de sac and firemen were unraveling their hoses. As he stepped onto the porch I pointed toward the commotion, but couldn't remember what I wanted to say.

Bill nodded. "I'll go down and tell them Charlotte's here with you." He left before I could murmur thanks, more for understanding what I wanted to say than for performing the act itself.

The next hours were madness. An anxious Ross came running in the house while paramedics were examining Charlotte and me. Police and firefighters entered and exited, asking nonstop questions. Neighbors stopped by to see if we needed anything and to find out what happened. At Charlotte's behest Ross found a firefighter he knew to take him into her house to check out the damage and gather some of her belongings. Perishable groceries were discarded after spending too much time in the car trunk, and the rest were put away. And after much protesting, Charlotte moved into my downstairs guest bedroom.

Through all of it we were clueless about what had actually happened. We didn't know if the blast was an accident, such as a propane tank explosion, or a deliberate act. We did, however, exact a promise from Officer Jon Cole that someone would come by in the evening to give us a preliminary assessment.

The knock came a few hours later just as the last of the concerned had left, and Ross was making us martinis. Both Charlotte and I jumped at the unexpected noise, nerves still on edge. Before Ross could go downstairs to answer it, we heard the door open and Police Chief Ian Williams bellow as he walked up the stairs to the living room. "I should have known when I heard about the bomb, you would be involved, Westmore."

We all froze, Ross in mid-pour. Bomb?

Ian looked taken aback by our expressions. "No one told you? It was a couple sticks of dynamite that were triggered when the garage door was fully open, or at least that's what it looks like. The explosives investigator should confirm it in the next few days." Ian smiled when he spotted Ross, and added, "Perfect timing. I'd love one of your perfect martinis. I've had a tough day."

Charlotte and I rolled our eyes as Ross poured Ian's cocktail.

I formally introduced Ian to Charlotte, and we sipped our drinks while trying to process this new information. "So, whom did you piss off so badly they wanted to kill you?" Ian asked Charlotte.

Charlotte burst into tears.

"Nice going, Ian," I said.

I rose to go to Charlotte, but she held up her hand to stop me.

"It's been a week and a half since my father died of what I consider suspicious circumstances." She sniffled. "In that time my only employee trashed my home; I've had to get a restraining order so my father's girlfriend doesn't steal all his valuables; my brothers hate me because I won't deviate from Dad's written estate instructions; and someone tried to blow me up." She stood up to her full four-feet-eleven inches and looked at Ian. "And, you want to know if I've pissed anyone off?" She blew her nose loudly and asked Ross to make her another martini.

Interest piqued, Ian said, "Let's start with your father. Why . . ."

I cut him off with a glare and a promise we would talk to him tomorrow.

The rest of the evening was fuzzy. What little substantive conversation we had focused on the process of the police and bomb investigations. Dinner consisted of cheese, crackers, tapenade, and berries. Eventually, Charlotte fell asleep on the couch and began to snore softly. This prompted our police chief to head for home, only after reminding me of my agreement that Charlotte and I would be available to meet with his detectives Sunday afternoon. As soon as he left, Ross and I guided a semi-conscious Charlotte downstairs, laid her on the guest bed, removed her shoes, and covered her with a quilt. We were all asleep by ten.

As on most summer mornings, it was the sunlight and bird chatter that woke me. I knew Ross would already be at work, but I was hoping he'd left me some coffee—regardless of how overcooked it would be. However, I wasn't prepared for what I found in the kitchen. A high-end espresso machine, a French press coffee maker, a coffee grinder, and several bags of exotic looking coffees covered one of the counters. Charlotte was stretched out on the kitchen loveseat smiling. "Really, J, a Mr. Coffee? How do you kick-start your mornings? Not with that tea-shit I found in your pantry, I hope. Fortunately, I always have replacement equipment for making a good cup of coffee, *and* it was stored on the side of the house still intact."

"You must have gotten up at the crack of dawn to haul this here," I said sweeping my arm over the array of coffee-making products.

She rose from her perch, shaking her head. "J, it's almost noon. Now, what's your pleasure?"

"I'd love a cappuccino," I said, putting some scones and fresh berries on a plate.

Charlotte placed my coffee with its foam of cream in front of the loveseat and returned to the nest she had created with pillows and an afghan. The cappuccino was beautiful. *For a tea drinker, I really was developing a serious coffee addiction.*

I went to sit beside her, anxious to hear about her trip to LA. And, naturally, my cell rang from the bedroom.

The call was short—over by the time I returned to the kitchen.

"You have a really strange look on your face, J. What's wrong?"

Mentally sorting through the implications, and only coming up with one I couldn't share—*Mary and Bob*, I answered. "That was Chuck at Norco. His mechanic did a full inspection of my car and found absolutely nothing wrong with it. Because Chuck couldn't start it yesterday, either, he made the mechanic check a second time."

Charlotte looked astonished. I tried to appear dumfounded while silently thanking Mary and Bob for their intervention.

"Well, J, your car breaking down when it did saved my life. I'll be damned if I'm going to question it."

Relieved by her reaction, I took a long sip of coffee. "If you're up to it, let's start with your brothers."

At the mention of her brothers, she stood up and began pacing. "I'm not even sure where to begin."

"I hate to be trite, but how about at the beginning. I don't really know anything about them except they're twins."

Charlotte paused, nodded in agreement, and resumed pacing. "Corey and Cody are forty. Corey is a philanthropist and Cody is a philanderer. And for both of them, Dad was their bank." Then she sat back down on the couch, nodding to herself as if in appreciation of her succinctness.

"I think I could use a bit more information. Let's start with Corey. He's a philanthropist? That sounds pretty noble. Is this a full-time vocation, or does he have other interests?"

"By training he's a plastic surgeon, specializing in facial reconstruction."

"Wow," I said, unsuccessfully hiding my surprise. From the way Charlotte talked about them, I thought her brothers were uneducated and unemployed. "Living in Southern California, he must make a pretty good living."

Once again Charlotte left the comfort of the loveseat and strode back and forth across the kitchen. "Actually, you would think so." She said with more than a note of disdain. "But Corey thinks making money is for the lower classes. He donates all his time to Doctors Without Borders, and similar organizations. I don't believe he's ever made a dime."

"How about Cody? Does he work?"

Charlotte's laugh was laced with derision. "No, though Cody, too, is well-educated. He has a Ph.D. in earth, environmental and planetary studies. He likes . . . or should I say, loves women. I think he chose his field of study to distinguish himself as a desirable pundit on climate and environmental issues, making him popular at dinners and parties."

"Do the twins have trust funds or some other means of support?"

"Up until last Monday their sole means of support was Dad."

"You mean to supplement their income, provide them with the lifestyle they wanted?"

Charlotte looked frustrated. "No, J. Not certain I could be much clearer. Dad housed them and provided all their income."

"Wow," I said, trying to comprehend how two highly educated forty-year-olds could still be dependent on their father. "Are you sure they're *your* brothers?"

A small giggle escaped Charlotte. "As a matter of fact, I did ask Dad about that once or twice over the years. But he always insisted we had the same lineage."

I chose a blueberry scone. "So, what were the estate instructions your father left that made your brothers so upset?"

"He forgave all the outstanding loans he'd given them, of which there were many. We're talking thousands and thousands of dollars."

"That sounds pretty generous. What do they have to complain about?"

"Dad also gave them one month from the date of his death to move off his estate and support themselves. If they want any inheritance whatsoever, they must be financially solvent in two years when his estate will be disbursed."

"I guess I see why they might be a little upset. What happens to the money if neither of them achieves financial independence?"

"The estate's assets will be divided equally between the Leukemia & Lymphoma Society and me."

Letting curiosity get the best of me, "Just how much was your father worth?"

"At last accounting . . ." Charlotte paused to calculate. "Four hundred, seventy-one million dollars and some change."

"Holy shit. Was your Dad born rich? Was he a hedge fund manager?"

"No. He manufactured ball bearings for shopping carts." She paused for effect. "Lots and lots of shopping carts."

Chapter 23

"Okay, so I get why Cody and Corey are a little put out. . ."

"That's a bit of an understatement," Charlotte said under her breath.

"But why are your brothers so angry with you? It was your father's decision, not yours."

Charlotte dropped back to the couch. "This is where it gets a little complicated."

"A *little* complicated?"

"Dad and Mom created the family trust agreement fourteen years ago, a few years before we knew Mom was sick. They were quite open about all of its provisions."

"So, you, Corey, and Cody knew about this two-year financial independence clause?"

"We did."

"If this isn't news to them I go back to my original question. Why are they angry with you?"

"Because Mother insisted on a second clause stating that if all the survivors agreed, the financial-independence condition could be voided." Charlotte's voice softened, and love for her mother poured out of her eyes. "Mom worried that there could be a circumstance they couldn't anticipate, and she didn't want any of us to be punished for their lack of forethought."

"And . . ." I was getting more confused by the minute.

"And the instruction, I suppose a better term is the plea, Dad left for me was to not void the independence clause."

We sat, staring at the table littered with dirty coffee mugs and half-eaten scones. My cell whistled an incoming text. Neither of us moved. Then Charlotte said what I was thinking.

"A pretty good motive for murder, don't you think?"

As if by some unspoken agreement or atmospheric change, we both rose and started clearing away the dirty dishes. Before Charlotte could start washing them, I led her away to the Adirondack chairs Mary and I had occupied on the deck a little more than a week before.

"Tell me about Stephanie, then we'll cleanse our palates and psyches with a glass of the La Dominique Saint Emilion I promised you."

Charlotte's eyes brightened at the mention of a good Bordeaux. "Don't forget, J, chocolate is part of the deal!"

I showed her a gift box of 32 assorted squares of Valrhona chocolate. "A gift from my dear friend Sarah in Hanalei."

Charlotte's instant smile indicated she recognized the brand and the quality. "Perhaps you should open up the wine to breathe, this shouldn't take long."

I took the bottle out of its place in my pantry, and opened it while she started her recitation.

"As it turns out, it was my fault Dad met Stephanie. To celebrate my decision to move to Mammoth I took Dad to Mélisse restaurant in Santa Monica. It's one of our favorite restaurants in the area, since they serve both vintage French dishes for me and haute French cuisine for Dad. Anyway, I guess it was the first time we had dressed up together in a while, because I noticed how shabby his clothes had gotten. That's when I suggested he buy some new clothes. Dad complained Mom had purchased all his clothes. J, I was mortified. I should have remembered. He started to suggest I could shop for him, but I think he saw the horrified look on my face and stopped mid-sentence. Clearly," she said, pointing down at her ensemble of army green T-shirt and cargo pants, "Dad realized fashion was not my forte. That's when I got the idea to arrange for him to meet with a personal shopper at Saks . . ." Her voice trailed off.

"Well?"

"The personal shopper turned out to be Stephanie," she said dejectedly.

"And she lived with your father?"

"Yup. Moved in less than a month after he met her. There has to be something immoral about continuing to make a large commission off someone you live with, but she did. I couldn't believe how many brand-new suits, pants, jackets, and shirts I found in Dad's wardrobe that had never been worn."

"She kept working after hooking up with your Dad?"

Charlotte frowned at me when I said, "hooking up," but answered, "Yeah. She went from full time to part time. But kept working. I'd bet money Dad was her biggest client."

"Anything else about her?"

Charlotte pondered this question while eyeing the bottle of wine on the table. Without a word, I fetched two Bordeaux glasses and the chocolate. I placed the Valrhona on the table and poured the wine. Charlotte continued.

"Let's see. Stephanie grew up on the Westside of town, quit school after two years at Santa Monica College because she was bored, and has been in the fashion industry ever since. She's a vegan, works out at least two hours a day, and likes to sunbathe topless."

"You've sunbathed with her?" I asked, handing her a wine.

"No. But remember, my brothers live at the house, too. They've sunbathed with her."

"And they told you about it?"

"No, Mrs. Simpson did. And, I should add, she did not approve."

I raised my eyebrows in question.

"Mom hired Mrs. Simpson to be her assistant, then she started managing the household when my Mother became ill. She never left. I don't know what Dad would have done without her. It was because of her I could move to Mammoth and know someone was watching out for Dad."

"Your brothers wouldn't have?"

Charlotte's look screamed, "Did you really just ask me that?"

"Does Mrs. Simpson . . . uh, did she live in the house?"

"She lives on the property, and will until the house is sold. When Mother was alive she lived in the house, after Mom died she moved into the largest of the three guest cottages on the grounds. The twins have the other two."

"I don't mean to pry, but was your Dad in love with Stephanie?"

Charlotte shook her head slowly, as if the motion helped her find the right words. "Mom was Dad's soul mate; Steph was his playmate. I think what Steph did for Dad was pay attention, though I could be wrong. But a few weeks before Dad died, Mrs. Simpson said she overheard him talking to his attorney about a pre-nuptial agreement, so he must have been serious."

"Do you think your Dad was really going to ask Stephanie to marry him?"

"I can't believe he would have taken such a significant step without talking to me first. We were always close, but after Mom died . . ." Tears welled up in Charlotte's eyes. "We got closer. I can't believe he had any secrets from me—to my knowledge he never had before."

We each reached for a piece of chocolate, sipped our wine, and stared at the firs and pines that surrounded the deck. Sometimes the sense of loss sneaks up on you and takes your breath away. When I glanced at Charlotte, I could tell she was in its grips too. A friend of mine used to tell me "death sings no duets." He was wrong.

I delayed taking a second confection. "Did your Dad leave anything for Stephanie?"

"Not in the trust, of course. But he left a number of bequests with his attorney, including one for Stephanie."

"And . . .?"

"He left her fifty thousand dollars." Charlotte continued to stare over the deck railing into the distance for a long moment. "And, Steph doesn't think it's enough."

My cell phone whistled an incoming text, reminding me I had received one earlier I never looked at. I picked up my phone and saw a message from our police chief, reading: "Where the hell are you and Charlotte? Been waiting an hour. Not the way I want to spend my Sunday."

"Oops," I said as I showed Charlotte the text.

We each took a big swig of wine and headed for the police station.

Chapter 24

My head was swimming the next morning as I drove to Bishop. I was frantically trying to change gears from the bomb and other Charlotte events of the weekend to an inquiry about sabotage with Brittany. The stretch was mind-boggling, and called for a treat. I pulled into the Starbucks drive-through and ordered a double-shot cappuccino, completely ignoring my latest promise to eliminate excessive stimulants from my life.

Two sips of liquid energy gave me the focus I wanted: Find out why Brittany was changing the Madison Manufacturing documents. The problem was how one casually encourages a young, pregnant, fragile woman to divulge her reasons for altering client papers. I was still processing this dilemma when I pulled up in front of the office—right behind an emotional, teary Brittany getting out of her car.

"What's wrong?" I handed Brittany a packet of Kleenex from my purse.

"Don told me this morning I have to keep working here until I'm ready to deliver. He says we can't afford the baby if I quit."

I placed my arm around her. "I'm sorry." She grabbed onto me as if I were her mother. When she quieted, I asked, "Is it so bad?"

"No one likes each other anymore. We used to have fun when we worked. Everyone pitched in and helped each other. Now it's all anger and suspicion, everyone avoids coming into the office when they can get away with it. It's so negative around here. People demand rather than request. Other than Mags, they all treat me like I'm a frigging idiot." Her voice was getting louder and her face was turning red.

"Brittany, I don't think you're an idiot. I think you're quite smart," I said gently. "Now take some deep breaths, for you and the baby."

Tears rushed to her eyes. "You're right. Don says I take things too seriously. I don't want to lose another baby because of this office." She began to cry again.

Well, there goes asking about the Madison documents.

She began to calm. "What do you think changed?" I asked as we headed into the office.

She opened her mouth to respond. Nothing came out. Her face transformed from despair to anger. I turned to see what caused such a negative reaction. Ms. Germaine was pulling up in front of the office. Before I could say another word, Brittany was through the front door.

I knew Ms. Germaine would want to confront Brittany. I also knew it was the wrong approach. Mentally regrouping as Ms. Germaine parked her car, I decided to accompany her to the privacy of her office, where we could come up with a reasonable strategy. As we strode toward the entrance, she talked about all things inconsequential. I supposed this was in case someone could overhear our conversation. While she prattled about working all weekend, Margaret going to

Southern California to see her brother, and so on, I thought about Brittany's anger, Kyle's ominous words, Shari's job search, Madison Manufacturing, and the clients Bill told me had left McNulty because of continued errors; how everyone in the office had worked well together until Ms. Germaine had accepted leadership of the team. Someone held the clue to what was going on.

When we reached her office, I closed the door. "Before we fire Brittany, I want to tell Margaret what we're doing. I think it's only fair. She's really her supervisor."

Ms. Germaine didn't look surprised. "I take it your conversation with Brittany didn't go well this morning?"

"You could say that." I was about to say more when Margaret poked her head in to let Ms. Germaine know she had arrived.

"Can you join us for a moment, Mags?"

"Just let me get a coffee and I'll be right there. Would either of you like anything?" We both declined.

By the time we were seated at the small table in Ms. Germaine's office, I'd found my words. "Ladies, I came to this office under somewhat false pretenses. Bill hired me to investigate the high rate of turnover you've been experiencing."

Ms. Germaine's eyes widened. "That's why you said pro bono."

I gave her a slight nod and proceeded. "It appears that Brittany may have been altering documents after they were prepared by staff." I addressed Margaret, who seemed to have frozen in place. "I do have the proof, at least in one case. As her supervisor, you need to terminate her for cause. I'm sorry, but we have no other alternative."

Margaret's lips trembled. "But she's pregnant."

"I'm sorry, Margaret, but there is no doubt she has been altering documents. She should be terminated—today."

Ms. Germaine made a slight sound. A quick glance silenced her. Margaret didn't notice. She shook her head. "I don't . . . I don't think I can do it."

"If we do it together, will that make it easier?" Without waiting for a response, I stood. "I'll go downstairs and ask Brittany to join us."

Ms. Germaine sat watching, but made no response.

"I need air," Margaret said, rushing from the room. I walked downstairs and asked Brittany to place the phones on hold and come with me.

By the time I returned with Brittany, Mags was back in Ms. Germaine's office. The two women were sitting woodenly at the small conference table. Brittany gazed around the room, glancing everywhere but at its occupants. Ms. Germaine had assumed a posture of almost indifferent authority. Margaret just looked panicked.

There was a long, awkward silence as Margaret tried to compose herself. Finally, she looked at me and said, "I can't."

I took a long, calming breath; this was not going to be easy. I hated these moments when I had to switch persona from helpful-but-not-threatening consultant to the hired-voice of authority. This role required an unemotional, firm, and objective voice.

I looked at Brittany. "I was not hired to conduct a personnel file audit. I was asked to find out why there is such high turnover in this office." I paused, giving my words and change of demeanor a chance to sink in.

Surprisingly, Brittany, who had been looking at me intensely, visibly relaxed.

I realized my omission. "Client turnover, not staff turnover," I said.

Brittany seemed to stiffen.

"There is no other way to say this but . . ."

Margaret abruptly stood up. Ms. Germaine tried to take her arm and guide her back to her seat. She shook herself free. "It's not Brittany; it's me!" she exclaimed, falling back into her chair and covering her face with her hands.

I took Brittany's arm, and escorted her back downstairs, leaving the two old friends to their angst. Brittany was more bewildered than traumatized, for which I was grateful. Her main concern was for Mags. "What is Mags talking about? What's her and not me?"

"It's really not my place to say. I think when Mags is ready, she'll explain," I said gently.

Before she could ask any more questions, I told her that she should take the rest of the week off. She looked at me as if I were a child, and said she would take the rest of the day off, but clearly Ms. Germaine and Mags would need her in the morning. She was much more committed than she let on.

Chapter 25

After a long thirty minutes, I headed to Ms. Germaine's office, passing a red-eyed Mags in the hall. Ms. Germaine looked beaten. "What did Margaret say?" I asked.

"Nothing."

She flinched when I said, "You've been in here alone for almost half an hour and she said nothing?" My directness both surprised and mortified me. Something didn't feel right, and I was taking my inability to figure it out on Ms. Germaine. "Sorry," I mumbled.

"Don't worry, I'm frustrated, too. I pushed Mags, harder than I wanted to. The only time she spoke was right before she left. She asked for some time to compose herself."

After a moment, I prompted, "And?"

Ms. Germaine straightened up in her chair, and for the first time since I entered the room, looked directly at me. "And . . ." she said, her professional demeanor returning. "We are meeting here at four o'clock, and I would like you to be here. I'll call Bill to ask if he can also attend." She picked up her phone. I had been dismissed.

"One last question, Lynette." She looked up curiously at the sound of her given name. "Do you think Mags is telling the truth?"

Lynette put her phone back into its cradle, and looked thoughtful. "I don't know. Something's off. What I do know is disloyalty is in absolute contrast with Mags's character."

As I was closing her door, she asked, "J, will Brittany be all right?"

"Confused but fine. I told her to take the rest if the week off . . ."

Lynette made a small moan, and looked alarmed.

". . . but she said you and Mags needed her, and she would return tomorrow morning."

Lynette smiled approvingly.

I spent the next hour trying to finish up the damn HR audit, but I couldn't concentrate. I was actually so happy for the distraction when my cell chirped that I didn't look at the caller ID.

"Hi, J. This is Brittany. Would you mind meeting me at the hospital?"

Adrenaline shot through my body. "What's wrong?" I almost shouted. "Are you hurt? Is it the baby?"

"No, no, both the baby and I are fine. Sorry, I should have explained. I need to speak with you, and my pre-natal exercise class begins at noon. Besides, we can talk in the hospital lobby without being overheard."

After a few long breaths, I told her I was on my way.

I saw her sitting on a couch in the corner of the lobby farthest from the entrance. She was not alone. Mags sat next to her, and they were so deep in conversation neither noticed me until I sat down.

Without preamble, Mags said earnestly, almost joyfully, "Brittany didn't do it! I mean, she made the changes, but she was only doing it because someone told her to."

"I'm confused," I said slowly. "You said you . . ."

Brittany interrupted. "Don't you understand? The only reason Mags said she gave me the instructions, was because she thought I was trying to get fired."

They looked at me like it all made total sense.

"Walk me through it, so I understand how changes were made."

"When Mags is out of the office and wants me to do something, she texts me instructions and I do it," Brittany began. "Lately that includes making changes to documents she's reviewed, and wants entered into the system. Like last week when I got a text from her asking me to make some changes to the Madison documents so they would be ready for Ms. Germaine's negotiation. Or at least, so I thought."

Mags broke in. "And I do send instructions from my mobile to Brittany all the time. But I never send document changes. I don't need to. With the Cloud I can make changes to master documents from my tablet, wherever I am."

"But I didn't know that some of the instructions weren't coming from Mags because the texts always came from her cell number."

I was beginning to understand, but wasn't quite there yet. "So, when you get text instructions to change a document, was a picture of the document attached to the text so you could see what to change?"

"No," Brittany said thoughtfully. "The text would just instruct something like on document 3, make the following changes to line 24."

"Do you still have any of these texts on your phone?" I asked, excited.

Brittany shook her head. "No, each time I was told to delete the text once the change had been made because the information was confidential." She looked at Mags. "I always thought that was a little over the top, even for you, Mags. I mean who would know what $150,000 on line 24 in document 3 means?"

They exchanged a look more like mother and daughter than supervisor and employee. Mags looked at her watch. "You better get to your class. You don't want to be late."

As Brittany left, I asked, "So who has regular access to your cell phone?"

"That's the question," Mags said, slouching in her chair. "To my knowledge, no one does."

"Well that should make our four o'clock meeting interesting."

Chapter 26

"Speaking of our meeting, we need to prepare for it, Mags . . . if I may call you that?"

She looked a bit sheepish. "Now that we know each other, of course you may. I know it might sound a bit formal, but I've always thought nicknames should be used by friends, not acquaintances." She glanced uncomfortably at her watch. "I'm afraid I won't be able to help you prepare for this afternoon. I have to finish up some family business."

"Your brother?" I asked tentatively.

"Yes," she said with more verve than I expected. "Lynette told me how rude he was to you on the phone the other day. I apologize."

I began to object but she raised her hand to still me. "Believe it or not, this morning's drama shocked me out of a very long malaise. I always believed family should be my closest friends. Today I was reminded that's not always true. What is true is that good friends can be your family." She stood up resolutely. "While I'm still clear on the concept, I need to close a few joint accounts I've opened over the years and let my little brother know he's responsible for his own life."

I smiled as I watched her go, unable to stop myself from thinking about the friends I now called family.

All the way back to the office I kept asking myself: Can you send a text from someone else's phone without their knowledge? When I reached my computer, and did a Google search, I was astonished by all the options. A tech-savvy person might be able to pull it off.

Kyle was the obvious choice because he was an attorney and a disgruntled ex-employee, who up until a month or so ago had access to all the firm's client files. But I needed to study his personnel file. When I first went to work for Bill he told me that every attorney was hired because he was a lawyer and had significant experience in one other field. And, as I accessed the electronic file, there it was. Before law school Kyle had been a software engineer for a video gaming company. And that's when I remembered Ross's response to my query if he and Kyle golfed together. *"Never. The guy takes himself much too seriously."*

I went to share my news with Lynette, but her door was closed, her strident voice in full negotiation mode. I could imagine her pacing across her office with her headset on, driving home point after point to one of her clients. I went to the kitchen for a bottle of water and an energy bar and returned to my workstation.

First order of business was to text Bill. *Whatever you've heard, I don't believe Brittany or Mags are your culprits. Can't prove it, but I think Kyle is your man. He has the IT skills to commandeer someone's cell number. Lynette is talking to a client so she doesn't know yet. Will explain all at the four o'clock.*

The next order of business was return to the damn HR paper audit.

A few minutes before four I walked upstairs with Mags for the meeting. She looked like a different woman than the one

I'd been working with over the last week or so. Ten years had vanished from her face in the matter of a few hours.

"You look like you were able to handle your family matters successfully."

Mags smiled. "Yes, and it feels wonderful." Her smile turned into a frown, and she asked in a more serious tone, "Did you tell Lynette about our conversation?"

"I tried, but she was on the phone with a client most of the afternoon. But I did text Bill."

Her brow knitted. "Oh dear. She won't like being the last to know." And minutes later, Mags's words proved correct.

The beginning of the meeting was quite solemn. Lynette paid no heed to my insistence for a brief word before she commenced. She was a woman on a mission, trying to remain professional at great personal cost.

She began by acknowledging Bill, and summarizing the situation, as she understood it. "This morning Margaret admitted to altering client documents, changing accurate data with inaccurate data. She did so by sending instructions to our receptionist via text, thus involving an innocent employee . . ."

Pacing while she spoke, she uncharacteristically looked at everything but the people in the room. Had she glanced up she would have seen our faces: Mags affectionately smiling, Bill amused and entertained, and me, resigned and uncomfortable.

". . . I have known Margaret almost my entire life, and I have never known her to be disloyal or dishonest. In fact . . ."

I couldn't take it any longer. "Lynette," I beseeched. "I'm sorry to interrupt, but I think you need to sit down and listen." She was startled into silence. She looked at each of us, trying to match our demeanor to the occasion. "Bill," I continued, "why don't you take over."

His grin widened. "Why don't *you* tell Lynette about your meeting today with Margaret and Brittany, J. I'll chime in as needed." I couldn't believe it; Bill was enjoying the spectacle.

So, I did. First, I explained Brittany's call, my surprise to see Mags with Brittany, the texts Brittany received from Mags, Mags's denial that she would ever ask Brittany to change a document, my initial belief in both women's declarations, the review of Kyle's personnel file, my attempt to tell Lynette, and the text to Bill. After the first few words, Lynette fell into her desk chair looking bewildered.

I ended with, "I can't prove it, but I think Kyle is your culprit."

"Well, I can," said Bill. Without another word, he turned on the recording playback app on his iPhone.

"Kyle, this is Bill McNulty. Do you have a minute?"

"Sure. What can I do for you?"

"You know me, son; I like to cut to the chase. I think I underestimated you, so first I want to apologize."

"Underestimated?" Kyle sounded cautious but pleased. "How so?"

"Well, I know it was tough working under Lynette Germaine . . ."

"You can say that again."

"And everything I knew about you seemed to indicate you were not going to let her get the better of you. But I have to admit, your strategy was absolutely brilliant." If Bill hadn't made the recording, I would have sworn he was oozing admiration for Kyle.

Kyle's voice became stiff. "I don't know what you're talking about, sir."

"Well I hope I'm not wrong, son. The McNulty Law Firm needs innovative problem solvers running its offices."

Neither man spoke for more than a minute—a long time on a phone call.

"If you could be more specific, sir."

"No *man* could let someone like Lynette Germaine force him out of *his* office with no consequences."

"No, sir!" Kyle almost shouted.

"The problem was how does one discredit a bitch . . . like her?" Bill shrugged an apology to Lynette, who was so engrossed in the recording I don't think she noticed. "I mean, she's pretty formidable—lots of degrees and a national reputation."

Another long silence.

"Ah, it would be hard, Bill." I could hear a tinge of smugness in Kyle's tone.

"Almost impossible."

"But not totally impossible, sir. One just has to know how to use the tools at hand. You know, be creative."

"Well you certainly were creative, son. As I said, I'm impressed. Is my apology accepted?"

"Yes, sir. It is."

"Please, Kyle, enough with this sir-shit. Call me Bill. After all, we're colleagues."

"You're right, Bill." Kyle's voice was riddled with arrogance.

"I don't mean to pry, but as one colleague to another, where could a guy find the kind of app we're talking about?

Without hesitation Kyle said, "There's a whole world out there beyond spoofing, Bill. For the average person, it's a little too technical to grasp, but not for us geeks."

"Spoofing? Not sure I ever heard the term."

"That's what I mean, Bill. Let me explain. Spoofing is basically tricking a computer system or user. It's often used to scam old or stupid folks, or load spyware. Pretty mundane stuff, but it's morphed into all sorts of accessing features. I think you know what I mean."

"I do, Kyle. And thank you. This has been a most beneficial conversation."

"You're welcome, Bill. Perhaps we can grab a beer sometime."

"Indeed."

Bill hit the stop button on his phone.

Chapter 27

The forty-five-minute drive back up the grade to Mammoth took forever. I was so exhausted I almost stopped at a scenic overlook to take a nap. It wasn't until I pulled into the driveway that I thought to look at my cell phone. When I turned it back on, it chirped, whistled, and rang its annoyance at being ignored—five calls, eight emails, and four texts. I was nowhere near ready for any more intrigue, and didn't even look to see who had called for fear I'd have to phone them back. The emails were advertisements and news updates. Two of the texts were from Charlotte, who I would see in moments since she was living with me; the other two were from Helen Sheets. I read Helen's message telling me the consultant lent by Susanna Montoya had arrived in town, and would like to meet me. No sooner had I tapped in, "Tomorrow, noon, Whitebark restaurant," when there was a knock on my car window. I was so startled I dropped my phone between the driver's seat and the console.

Not bothering to see who had almost scared me to death, I rooted in and out of car crevices trying to retrieve my phone. When I finally had it in hand, I looked up to see Ross, sheepish look on his face, holding an ice-cold martini. I opened the door to apologize for my rudeness and ask why the cocktail special delivery.

"Bill phoned and said you might need this."

"Boy, was he right." Ross traded me the drink for my computer bag, and I took a large sip.

Ross, Charlotte and I kept our chatter to trivialities as we made dinner. Ross barbecued swordfish that had been marinated in olive oil, balsamic vinegar, garlic, sage, rosemary, thyme, and parsley; Charlotte made a salad of summer squash and red quinoa; and, after opening some Rombauer chardonnay, I dipped strawberries into a rich chocolate mixture for dessert.

"I saw that you sent me a couple of texts today," I said to Charlotte as we finished up our meal. "Sorry I haven't read them yet. Was it something important?"

"Don't worry. Ross told me about your day while he was making your martini. From an IT professional's perspective, it sounds like you had an interesting day."

"Actually, if it hadn't been surrounded by so much drama, it would have been intriguing. But what were the texts about?"

Charlotte was unusually subdued. Her head lowered, she spoke into her wineglass. "Well, here is some more drama. It appears that Dad's autopsy was inconclusive but suspicious."

"That doesn't sound good," Ross said. "What does it mean?"

"They can't match up the blow to the back of Dad's head with anything at or near the pool. Now they're investigating his death as a homicide."

It felt like the air had just been sucked out of the room. A quick glance at Ross said he felt the same. "Charlotte, I'm so sorry." I paused briefly, remembering how I felt when I began to suspect the accidental plane crash that took Mary and Bob's lives was murder. "This must come as a huge shock. Is there anything I can do for you?"

"Glad you offered," she said, shaking her head and looking toward the heavens. "Because the first thing you can do is tell the investigators where I was around the time my dad was being murdered."

"Of course, I will. But isn't that a bit ridiculous? Stephanie called you to tell you what happened, didn't she?"

"Yeah," Charlotte said, the irony thick in her tone, "on my cell, which means I could have been anywhere when I answered it. I'm a suspect until they can confirm my alibi or phone records."

Not long after, we all went to bed. It had been a long day for both Charlotte and me. Ross hadn't known what he was getting into when he came to my house to make dinner. My last conscious thought returned to my ongoing internal debate about changing *my* house to *our* house?

The next day my phone, as reliable as a dog at mealtime, whistled a text as I was leaving to meet Helen and John Collins at the Whitebark restaurant in the Westin Hotel. It was from Helen. "Broke a tooth this morning eating granola. Can you believe it? Sorry but you will have to meet Mr. Collins on your own, am on my way to the dentist. Will call later."

Damn. What I was going to talk to John about for an entire meal? Helen was the accomplished communicator in social situations. I always sounded like I was conducting an interview—a downside of my profession. At least I'd made a reservation, which meant I could be a few minutes late and give him a chance to be seated. I was not in the mood to walk up to strange men in a hotel, asking if they were John.

He stood when the hostess showed me to our table. I was a little dumbfounded. John could have been Susanna's brother, though where she was dark, he was light—blond hair, light blue-gray eyes, fair complexion. But the rest was the same: fortyish, tall, stunning, and elegant. When he smiled, he evoked the same desire I had experienced when I met Susanna—to go to the dentist and have my teeth whitened.

He took both my hands in his, half shaking, half holding them. "You must be Janet, who likes to be called J. We already have something in common; I am John James who likes to be called JJ. But you may call me John, so it doesn't get too confusing." He gave me another dazzling smile and we sat down.

I was at a loss for words, but it didn't seem to matter. He continued, "I hope you're not offended, but I took the liberty of ordering us each a glass of wine to mark the occasion of our meeting." Looking up, he said, "Ah, here it is. My research indicates you like an oaky, buttery chardonnay. I do hope you approve of my selection."

I held up the glass of wine, as if I'd never seen one in my life. "Your research?"

He smiled again. "I think a much better toast would be 'to a successful fundraiser for the children of Mono County'."

The last time I'd seen someone this smooth was in a James Bond film. It both terrified and fascinated me.

While John was charming and somewhat entertaining, I wanted to get back on a business footing. "You had an executive search firm in Santa Barbara?"

A fashionably self-deprecating chuckle escaped him, as if he recognized my attempt to change the tenor of our conversation. "Actually, my executive search firm was based in Boston, but you wouldn't have known it from my travel schedule. I can't complain. For twenty years, I loved the work and the travel."

"Why did you sell your firm?"

There was that chuckle again. "When I started in the business it was about people. We were always scouting. We specialized in finding talent, getting to know their strengths and weaknesses, matching companies with candidates. It also meant we had to learn about our client companies' visions and values, and make sure the candidates we recommended shared the same commitments. The impact of the Internet and social media has changed most of that. Bottom line, it was no longer fun."

"It's scary. I understand and agree with everything you said." Now I was annoyed with myself for thinking this guy was fluff.

"I forgot. Susanna told me you were a human resources consultant." His 007 voice was back.

"So how did you meet Susanna?"

"Ahhhhh," he said so smoothly I thought I missed something. "She didn't tell you we were long-lost cousins? We met less than a month ago at my father's funeral in

Cambridge." No chuckle this time, just the lift of an eyebrow with a "who could have known" look.

For a moment, I thought I might be on a daytime soap opera, but that passed. The rest of the lunch was more entertaining than informative. It quickly became apparent that John would be a great asset to this project—especially with the women.

"Unfortunately, Susanna won't be able to participate in any of the preparations. This is her busy season, getting ready for winter and spring promotions. But she wants me to keep her informed. I'll provide her with regular, written updates."

John picked up the check. I would have objected, but I knew he could afford it and he didn't know if I could. "I officially start tomorrow, so I'm available if you need anything," he said as we walked out to our cars.

"Thank you. It was lovely to meet you. And please thank Susanna for me."

"Ah, glad you brought up Susanna. I don't know if you remember, but I was to remind you, she wants to remain totally anonymous. Only Berta, Helen, you, and I should know she exists."

Chapter 28

Instead of going home to Charlotte, I decided to go to Mimi's Cookie Bar for a coffee and salted caramel chocolate chip cookie, and return phone calls without interruption. I loved Charlotte, but she took up more space than Michele and her twins ever did while staying with me—and that included their baby paraphernalia.

I listened to all my messages and started to make a list. *Since my freshman year of college, I've been a diehard list maker, despite the ribbing I've taken over the years from other students and friends. Ross always rolls his eyes when I begin list making. I can't operate without one; he avoids them whenever he can.*

Elise – HR audit

Bill McNulty – Kyle update

Linda Taylor – golf tournament update meeting

Ian Williams – Charlotte's whereabouts July 7 a.m.

Charlotte – drama update

I phoned Elise, who congratulated me on solving the problems with the Bishop office, and who wanted to know if I could deliver the completed HR audit by Monday morning. I promised to bring it by on Friday. *Now I knew what I was going to be doing for the next two days.* I asked to be transferred to Bill, and was told he was in court. After confirming he'd be in the office on Friday afternoon, I asked Elise to let him know I would talk to him then.

Two down, I dialed Linda. She answered immediately. "Hi, J. Are you free on Saturday?"

"Sure. Ian finally popped the question and you're getting married this Saturday?" I joked.

There was an unusually long silence. In a whisper, Linda said, "Actually, he did. Last night. That's between you and me." She switched to her *principal* voice. "If you're available, we want to schedule a meeting of the Labor Day Gala committee. I want to introduce John, and bring everyone up to date."

I was dying to ask if Linda had accepted, but her rushed tone indicated this was the wrong time. "Tell me when and where and I'll be there, though I would appreciate an afternoon meeting. I've been getting up early to go to work in Bishop for the last several days and I'm ready to resume my late mornings."

Linda chuckled. "I'll bet you are. How about five o'clock at the golf course? David said he would serve refreshments again."

"Perfect. How are things going?"

"Beyond expectation. We have pledges for fourteen of the twenty-seven hole-sponsorships, and eighteen foursomes, plus the mysterious $100,000 donation. J, we're halfway to our financial goal and most of the marketing information hasn't gone out yet."

"How?" I was flabbergasted.

"Brian knows everyone in sports and entertainment. I think he's housed most of the contributors at one of his boutique hotels at one time or another. And it seems Berta knows just about every major corporate CEO in the country. I've never witnessed anything like this. Money just rolls in. And the names of the people signing up! It reads like a 'Who's Who'."

"Congratulations. Now I'm really looking forward to this meeting." I couldn't hold out any longer, so lowering my voice to a whisper, I asked. "Linda, did you say yes?"

She giggled and disconnected.

I decided that was an affirmative, so I went back to the list. I would see Charlotte at home, so Ian would be my last call. He, too, answered immediately.

"Hi, Chief. What's up?"

"On the morning of Thursday, July 7, did you meet with Charlotte Caron at your home in Mammoth Lakes, California?"

"Wow, Ian, you're awfully formal."

"This is a formal investigation, J. Would you like me to repeat the question?"

"No, you don't have to repeat the question." I tried not to smile, and used my most serious tone. "On Thursday, July 7, Charlotte Caron visited me at my Mammoth Lakes residence to tell me that her father had died."

He ignored my lack of seriousness. "At approximately what time did she arrive at your home?"

"Uh . . . around eleven. I remember because I had a meeting at the golf course at twelve-thirty the same day."

"Thank you, J. Would you please stop by sometime today and sign a statement affirming these facts?"

Before I could agree, Ian hung up. *This* was the romantic who had just proposed to Linda.

At home I found Charlotte at the kitchen table with her head almost completely buried inside a large box of jumbled photographs. "Are you telling me one of the most tech-savvy, organized people I know stores her photos in a cardboard box?" I quipped, as I took out my smart phone. "I think I want a picture . . ."

The sight of her tear-stained face shut me up. After a moment, I whispered, "That's not your box of pictures, is it?"

. She shook her head.

"Your father's?"

She shook her head. "My mother's."

"You phoned earlier. You said you had something to tell me?"

The tears vanished. She almost toppled the box in her rush to stand up. She could shift moods faster than anyone I knew. The grief and angst she had been experiencing boiled to the top.

"First," she said stridently, "my attorney called to tell me Steph claims she and Dad were engaged."

Charlotte started pacing. I moved out of her way before she ran me over.

"I tell him I don't believe her, but what if they were? He says she thinks she's entitled to more compensation than the maid. I ask, what maid? Mrs. Simpson, he says. I say Mrs. Simpson isn't a maid. She was an assistant and nurse to my mother, she ran the household during her illness and thereafter. She and I took care of all Dad's affairs after Mother died. Mrs. Simpson is part of the family, not a goddamn *maid*. He says I should calm down and perhaps we should consider a settlement so this doesn't get out of hand, and besides there's plenty of money. If he thinks so, I say, perhaps I should find a new attorney. And before he can respond, I hit "end," so I don't have to listen to the prick anymore."

By the time she finished I'd poured her a glass of cabernet and handed it to her, all the while thinking perhaps she should cut back on caffeine.

"That sounds dreadful," I said.

She took the glass in her right hand, and held up her left to stop me. After taking a big swallow, she said, "Ah, but I'm not finished." She drained the glass, handed it back to me and resumed her pacing.

"Then I get a call from . . ." Now she held up both hands. "None other than the bitch herself. She wants to know why Mrs. Simpson is getting more money than she is. I ask where she got this information, and she says it's none of my business. I say, well it's none of *her* business. She asks, do I know Mrs. Simpson is sleeping with one of my brothers, possibly both? I tell her that's none of my business either. She says she's going to sue. I say, bring it on, bitch. She hangs up."

Finally, Charlotte collapsed into her chair, staring morosely into the box of photographs. I poured her a second glass of wine, and after only a moment's hesitation, poured myself one, too.

Chapter 29

"Out of curiosity, how much did your father leave Mrs. Simpson?" I ventured, slightly afraid of another outburst.

But calm had been restored. "A million, after taxes."

My eyes involuntarily widened. "I guess that means she can retire comfortably. Maybe get a place in one of the new retirement communities that are becoming all the rage."

Charlotte looked at me like I had three heads. "What are you talking about? Mrs. Simpson isn't old. She's younger than I am."

"But I thought . . . uh, I mean . . . well, hasn't she worked for your family for about fifteen years? How old was she when she arrived?"

Charlotte paid no attention to me as she rifled through her box of pictures. She found what she was looking for and thrust the photo at me. "This is Mrs. Simpson. It was taken the year she came to work for my parents—you're right, about fifteen years ago."

I smiled at the photo of a tall, gangly, early twenty-something in pants too short for her, looking awkwardly into the camera. "I take it her name isn't really Mrs. Simpson?" I said, as I eyed the girl with a blue beehive hairdo.

Charlotte chortled. "No, her name is Marge. Marge Bouvier. But since the day we all were introduced; she's been Mrs. Simpson. She started as an assistant to my mother, and over time just kept taking on more and more responsibilities."

"Does she still have blue hair?"

"No, she went back to brown years ago." She smiled wistfully. "I wish she still did. Her blue hair was awesome."

"You can't believe how relieved I am that she's so young."

"Why?"

"If Steph was telling the truth, I thought your brother or brothers were sleeping with a senior citizen."

Charlotte took the picture from me and stared at it. "Truth be told; I wish Dad had fallen for Mrs. Simpson. Maybe he'd still be alive."

"Do you think one of your brothers is having an affair with her?"

"Cody would never have an affair with someone he didn't perceive as rich, powerful or famous. Though that doesn't mean he wouldn't try to get into her pants if he thought he could. But we're talking about Mrs. Simpson, so that's ridiculous. On the other hand, I've always thought Corey had a boyhood crush on her. When she'd come into a room, he'd follow her around with his eyes. If she dropped something, he'd run to pick it up. But I don't think Mrs. Simpson has ever paid attention to either of the twins, except as members of the family. She's just way too mature."

I was thinking it must be hard to have such little regard for one's brothers when Charlotte stood. "J, can you recommend a good attorney?"

"Now, that is something I can do."

It took two days to complete the full documentation of the HR audit. For a law firm, I wasn't surprised; in my experience attorneys were some of the worst when it came to keeping personnel records. For Bill McNulty's law firm, I *was* surprised. They needed to get rid of all the paper and keep their records electronically—all their records.

As I drove over to deliver the audit and talk to Bill, I promised myself this was my last audit; I hated them.

Walking into the main office of the McNulty Law Group never got old. Think of what an exclusive men's club set in a five-star ski resort should look like, and you'll understand the experience. The first time I entered the building it was winter. The large windows looked out on snowy mountain vistas, poinsettias were everywhere, and all the fireplaces were roaring. The illusion was of walking into a Christmas card. Today the windows boasted the same panoramic Sierra views, this time accented by fields of wildflowers. The flowers and scents continued throughout the entry and lobby, making it difficult to tell when outside became inside—similar to the illusion created in the Bishop office. Breathtaking.

And just as suddenly as the first time I met her, Elise appeared out of nowhere. Instead of cashmere and wool, her petite frame and red hair were set off by a cream-colored pencil skirt and an emerald silk blouse. "Ms. . . ." I gave her a stern look. "J, so nice to see you again." I handed her the audit and she directed me to the client lobby, a mini version of the larger room. "Bill will be so happy you arrived now. Lynette is meeting with him, and he thought perhaps . . ."

She opened the door, and I was taken aback when both Lynette and Bill stood up. "We were hoping our timing would work." Bill turned to Elise and said, "The refreshments?"

Elise smiled. "Of course, right back."

"The last couple of days I finally got staff—current, former, and intending to exit—to really talk to us." Bill beamed.

Lynette cleared her throat—deliberately.

Bill threw up his hands, "Okay, Mags got everyone to talk." He smiled.

"Anyway, here's where we are." He turned his smile on Lynette, and she actually smiled back.

"We will continue to try and establish precisely what software Kyle used to hijack Mags's cell number, but since we are not going to prosecute, we decided to change all the office and personal cell numbers in the meantime. We bought everyone new phones and tablets with much tighter security software, and told them it was part of an upgrade package."

"Isn't Kyle going to continue to try and insert himself?"

Bill's smile was wry. "I played him the tape, and strongly implied it could be shared."

"How about all the animosity toward Lynette?" I asked, giving her an embarrassed shrug.

"Mags spoke with all the employees from the last several months and learned Kyle had been telling staff Lynette was looking for any chance to fire them; and, he was using a gentler, but similar strategy with our clients. We spoke with all of them."

The door opened. The tray Elise was carrying held a bottle of Veuve Clicquot and three champagne flutes. Not a word was said while Bill uncorked and poured the champagne.

"Most importantly, the staff is returning, and," he smiled at Lynette who had tears in her eyes. "Mags has enrolled in a class to prepare for the Bar examination."

No more words were necessary. We clinked glasses in a silent toast.

Chapter 30

R oss and I golfed eighteen holes on Saturday, timing our round so we would finish shortly before the Gala Committee meeting. When he spotted a few of his friends in the bar, Ross turned down my offer to attend the meeting with me.

David handed me a cookie shaped like a dollar sign as I entered the conference room. Clearly, word had gotten out about all the contributions coming in. The room buzzed with energy. Helen, Bill, Brian, Linda, Berta, and John spoke in excited tones as they munched on their cookies, waiting for the meeting to begin.

As Linda tapped the table, Olli rushed in. "I'm sorry for being late. I only just got a call from Tony twenty minutes ago, telling me to represent him at this meeting."

"Your timing is perfect," Linda said. "We're just starting. Is Tony all right?"

Olli sank into the only empty chair, smiling at David, who gave her a cookie. She took a bite, and said, "Oh, he's okay. He's in Alpine County getting ready to do the Death Ride." She looked around the table at some astonished, and some blank faces. "You know, it's that gnarly bike ride that takes the riders over five Sierra passes. It's about a-hundred-and-thirty-mile ride with fifteen thousand feet of climbing?" Half the faces at the table were still lost.

Brian jumped in. "I did that last year. It's one bad-ass ride."

"Hey, so did I," Olli said. "What are the odds?" She gave Brian a big smile. *Hmmm. Perhaps Olli will find Brian interesting.*

David chimed in, "If the race starts at dawn, then I'll bet twenty Tony doesn't make it past ten tomorrow morning."

There were a few snickers around the table. Brian and Olli said, "I'll give him till lunch" at the same time, and smiled at one another again.

"I think we better get started," Linda said. "First, if anyone has not yet met Berta Hart, it's her generosity that brought us all together to raise a million dollars." Berta gave a finger-wiggle to light applause. "Since we have a few other new people since our last meeting, let's go around the table and introduce ourselves. Please include what roles you are performing for the fundraiser."

And we did.

"Okay," Linda continued, "let's start with the numbers. As of yesterday, we've raised $560,000, which includes eighteen foursomes, fourteen-hole sponsorships, and an anonymous donation of $100,000. We're more than halfway to our target goal of a million dollars, and it's all been accomplished by word of mouth. Our marketing media efforts were launched yesterday. If we sell out all 27 foursomes and hole-sponsorships, we'll be at $780,000. Since Berta has said she will pay all the expenses so that all funds raised go directly to the new program, we'll need to raise $220,000 through our raffle."

"Wow," said Olli. "Who made the big donation?"

I noticed John start, but Linda smiled. "Someone very bighearted who doesn't want anyone to know."

Berta said, "You make me sound very generous, but I must acknowledge that Brian is housing many of our guests for free, as well as paying for the awards dinner. The Mountain is giving us the use of beautiful Snow Star, and David's staff. And the Rock & Bowl has agreed to extremely favorable terms for the kick-off festivities."

David passed around a confection that looked like little gold ingots, but were chocolate-caramel candies. "Helen, please update us on the raffle strategy."

Helen stood. You could tell by the spots of pink on her cheeks she was a little nervous, excited, or both. When I saw her bouncing up and down, I chose excited.

"Oh, where to begin . . . Berta and I decided that instead of having a silent auction with a lot of stuff—you know, paintings, places to stay in exotic locations, that sort of thing, we wanted to do something that would appeal to people who think nothing of dropping ten thousand dollars on a golf foursome." She beamed at Berta, who flicked her wrist a couple of times signaling for Helen to get on with it. Berta liked brevity, Helen liked suspense.

Helen nodded. "So, we will auction off time with famous people!" She almost yelled she was so keyed up. "And we already have some tentative acceptances. I will tell you what these people do or have accomplished, but no names. They won't be revealed until the awards dinner."

She looked at Berta. "Drum roll, please." And immediately looked down at her iPad when she saw Berta's face. "Our tentative acceptances include: a round of golf for two with a former FedEx Cup winner." David gasped. "Lunch with a former Speaker of the House, dinner prepared at your home by a four-star chef, and . . ." she looked around beaming, "dinner with a former President of the United States. We want to add two more. We're trying to get one of last year's Grammy winners to sing at a party, and a member of English royalty, a very high-up member, to host a brunch."

We sat in stunned silence. Then everybody started talking at once. Once the excitement was spent, Linda said to Helen, "I think I should have saved your report for last. It begs for a toast."

David jumped up and said, "I'm game."

Linda shook her head. "Just a few other items first. Brian, you wanted to talk to the group?"

Brian nodded and remained seated. "The hotel will be ready for the Gala guests, unfortunately the full kitchen will not."

"Oh no," someone said.

"By Labor Day weekend we will be able to provide all the food services our guests will want or need, but the kitchen will not yet be adequately equipped to handle the number of people expected to attend the Awards dinner. So, I spoke with David a few days ago, and he has arranged for us to have it here at the Clubhouse. My staff will, of course, bring the food, prepare and serve the meal. But we will do so in Snow Star's fully equipped kitchen."

There was some discussion about logistics, décor, and access. In the end it was decided the Clubhouse did have easier access and would make a great venue.

Linda stood. "David, do you still want to address the group?"

David stood, looked around, sat back down, and said, "Yes."

"We're going to have a lot of people coming to this Gala weekend, and in my experience with tournament weekends, some get lost in the commotion. Sure, we'll all be here to help, but we'll also be preparing for the next event, solving logistical problems, that sort of thing. I suggest we ask a few locals who can serve as Mammoth Hosts. You know, answer questions, help people find things they forgot, provide them with some local background, chaperone them, if needed. What do you think?"

Bill had been relatively quiet throughout the meeting. "I think it's a great idea. Many of these people will have been to Mammoth before, but some will have not. And for a small town, we're complicated."

Helen chimed in. "And not everyone who comes is going to be golfing. It would be nice for them to have some options while their companions play."

Linda nodded. "Great idea. Do you have anyone in mind?"

"Jeff Boucher. He's lived here for more than thirty years, he had a heli-ski business in the Sherwins back in the day, was a Ski Patrol legend on the Mountain, and started a property management company with his wife Denise, so he knows how to talk to everyone. And most of all he really likes people." With a big smile, he added, "I mean *really* likes people."

As soon as I heard his name I knew what a great idea this was and that Jeff would be perfect for the job. Jeff and Denise were dear friends, and David was right—Jeff was ideal for the job. Looking around the table, I saw nods—everyone who knew him thought so, too.

"Great," Linda said. "Can you set up a meeting for the three of us?"

David gave her the thumbs up, and left to get the bar cart.

People stood, stretched, and chatted amiably. Only Olli remained in her chair, phone-to-ear, the color draining from her face as she listened.

David yelled "happy hour" as he barreled back into the room with his drink cart. The sudden noise drew my attention to the door. Just as I was turning I thought I saw Mary in the corner of the room, watching Olli. When I looked back she was gone, leaving me to wonder whether she had actually been there at all.

Chapter 31

"**I**s something wrong?" Helen asked as she and Berta approached.

"Huh?" I was still staring at the empty corner. I shook my head. "Sorry. I guess the excitement has my head reeling . . . Wow, a former President? How did you pull that off?"

Both ladies beamed. Berta was sharing the details of their conquests when David handed us each a drink and a small plate of mini tacos with guacamole. "Ross should be in momentarily," he whispered to me.

The next time I looked up from my conversation Ross had indeed entered the room. He was part of a tight little group of men—Brian, John, and Ross—hanging on Olli's every word. Perceptive as ever, Helen said, "Don't worry, J. She seems to have that effect on every man she meets. You should have seen Denis when Olli dropped some papers by the house."

It was almost seven o'clock when the gathering broke up. I was pleased. As usual, more work had been accomplished after the meeting than during it. I picked up my bag and looked around for Ross. My heart sank a little. He was standing where I last saw him. The only difference was that David had made it a party of five.

Ross held out his hand as I approached. "We were just talking about going out for some dinner. How does that sound?"

The first response that came to mind was "absolutely not," but even I knew that would be a mistake. Trying to squelch my jealousy, I said, "It's going to be pretty difficult to find someplace to eat on Saturday night at the height of the summer tourist season."

Both David and Ross nodded in agreement, looking disappointed. I was quietly elated.

Brian grinned. "I have an idea. Come up to Couloir. There's no real staff yet, but I have food and wine. We'll just have to prepare it ourselves." He looked boyish and slightly embarrassed. "Please do," he implored. "Only the architect, the construction crew, and a few staff have seen it. You'd be my first guests."

While I wasn't anxious to watch four men fawning over Olli, I was excited to see Couloir. Brian made a few calls before we formed a mini parade of four cars driving toward the base of the Sherwins, on the east side of town.

The small parking lot was surrounded by pine and fir trees at the base of the mountains. Exiting our personal rides, we climbed into a huge off-road vehicle and began the journey up the road. "No vehicles will come up this road except the hotel's off-road fleet," Brian explained. "In another two weeks there'll be a garage and valet station just the other side of those trees."

"A garage?" John made a face. "Doesn't sound like that will make a very good first impression for your guests."

"I think you'll be surprised. All the hotel's buildings, including the garage, are mirrored—the outside walls reflecting the landscape. The roofs are all tiered and planted with flora native to the Sierra."

"Wow," said Olli, her eyes wide.

"How about light pollution?" Ross asked. "I know a lot of folks in town were concerned Couloir would ruin our night sky."

"We took those objections quite seriously. As with my other hotels, we followed the guidelines set forth by the International Dark-Sky Association for all the lighting. And because of the uniqueness of the Sherwins, instead of one or two large buildings, we clustered small dwellings, placing all the ground lights between the buildings and the mountains, not toward the meadow or town. Even our fire pits outside each room-pod are set into the natural rock formations, with low fires and low to the ground."

Brian reached another cluster of trees. Momentarily stopping, he said, "Ladies and Gentlemen . . ." and drove through the trees, sweeping his arm toward the mountain. "Voila!"

A collection of small and medium-sized mirrored dwellings shimmered in the setting sun. It was hard to distinguish the natural scenery from the buildings' reflections. Trees, wildflowers, and alpine bushes lined streams that meandered between the structures. A few of the more cube-like dwellings at the end of the property seemed to be suspended from trees. The blurred boundary between nature and man-made took my breath away.

Brian beamed as he led us through the entrance, which, true to his word, was between the structures and the mountain. He must have sensed how impressed we were since no one had uttered a sound except for David whose "this is freaking unbelievable" spoke volumes.

Rocks, plants, and water had been used to ensure the lobby was an extension of the outside. As we crossed the threshold our eyes were drawn to the windows. We could see west for miles—the meadow, the town of Mammoth Lakes, the Sierra Crest, and Mammoth Mountain.

The interior décor was modern, tasteful, and sparse. Wood, glass, and more rock, accented by muted earth tones, gave the impression we'd just entered a five-star campground.

All five of us gawked as we followed Brian through the lobby to a rock wall. When he pushed an invisible panel, the wall disappeared, revealing the lobby bar. There was even a welcome surprise. Waiting patiently on one of the wood and glass tables a silver tray held a bottle of Perrier Jouet Belle Époque Brut and five crystal champagne flutes.

When Brian popped the cork, we all started talking at once.

Our first round of praise ended as we finished the champagne. David eyed the bar. "Is the bar open?"

Brian laughed. "As I said, the materials are here, but we have to do our own preparations. Since you asked, David, why don't you take everyone's drink orders and make the drinks. You should find everything you need behind the bar. The rest of us will be making dinner in the kitchen."

Once David had our libation preferences, Brian herded Olli, John, Ross, and me through a double door, into a dark, windowless room. When he turned on the lights, we let out a collective gasp. In stark contrast to the room we just left, the kitchen was bright, sterile, and utilitarian. It was approximately a thousand square feet of white and stainless steel, configured into six peninsula-like work areas, accessible on three sides. Stainless shelves were adjacent to each work area, housing kitchen tools, platters, and dishes. Large walk-in refrigerators anchored each side of the room; grills and ovens resided in the center of the space. In addition to the overhead lights, industrial-pendant lights illuminated all the food prep areas.

Stacked neatly on one of the workstations was a note with six neatly tied bundles. Brian picked up the note, and muttered to himself. It sounded like, "Good thinking, Missy. I wish I'd thought of it."

He turned and handed each of us a package. As we untied the bundles, Brian said, "Thanks to our chef Missy, you each are an official member of the culinary team for the evening. Here is your uniform, which, of course, you may keep."

Olli was the first to get her package untied. She squealed, "This is so rad." She looked around; color shot to her cheeks. "Or doesn't anyone say that anymore?" She held up a chef's hat and apron, each had a small "couloir" embroidered on it.

Clad in our new kitchen duds, we were each given a piece of paper explaining our individual assignments, and where we would find the foodstuffs and tools. It turned out Missy must have hurried up to the kitchen after Brian phoned her and performed most of the food preparations, because our jobs were easy.

Midway through our tasks, David entered, clad in the same apron and hat, carrying a tray of drinks. "Isn't this freaking unbelievable?"

In response, we all started talking at once, and didn't stop until we had prepared and devoured grilled salmon, asparagus, and an heirloom tomato salad in tarragon vinaigrette. By the time we moved outside to a low fire pit with our cappuccinos and Courvoisier, Couloir's first guests finally ran out of questions and praise for Brian, and turned our attention to one another.

John studied Olli. "What's your status, Olli? Married? Divorced? Attached?"

Next to me, Ross stiffened when John mentioned divorce, but after a moment Olli responded playfully, "And why might you be asking me these personal questions?"

"Touché," he said, arching an eyebrow. "Just wondering whether you are available."

Brian and David leaned forward in their lounge chairs, their interest evident. Ross suddenly stood. "Thanks for the tour and a great dinner, but I think it's time for J and me to go home. Pointing at Olli's admirers, he added, "Unless you feel you need protection from these three, Olli?"

I was surprised by Ross's sudden desire to leave. Perhaps he was uncomfortable with the conversation's direction.

"Are you sure?" Brian asked. "I was thinking we could take a stroll around the grounds. It's almost a full moon."

David shook his head. "I'll pass, too. I need to be at the golf course by five tomorrow morning."

At the same time, Olli jumped to her feet, saying, "I'm not ready to call it a night. A walk sounds perfect."

Brian smiled at Olli. "Great."

John, whose eyes were also focused on Olli, said, "Count me in."

Brian handed Ross the keys to the off-road transport and asked him to leave them in the vehicle. We said our goodbyes, and headed off in opposite directions. When I turned to offer one last "thank you," I stopped before I made a sound. John, Olli, and Brian were walking up hill behind the property, Mary and Bob following a few yards behind.

Chapter 32

"Not just once, Ross. Twice today I saw, or at least I think I saw, Mary and Bob. Both times they were with Olli. They never even glanced my way. Something's wrong." The presence of a houseguest made finishing our conversation while we sat in my driveway prudent.

"I guess so, but what do you think it is?" He sounded frustrated. "You know, after the last few weeks of Olli's strange behavior, I thought she was finally returning to her old self tonight. You saw her. She was having fun. She was being the Olli I knew—sexy and free."

I could feel stirrings of jealousy rise in my chest.

"But you're probably right, J. I don't believe Mary and Bob would follow Olli around if she weren't seriously in peril." He furrowed his brow the way he always did before he told me something I didn't want to hear.

I knew what he was going to say next, and hated myself for praying that he didn't.

"J?" he inquired softly. "I need to . . ."

I interrupted, trying not to let him sense the tumult of emotion in my words. "You need to go home and keep watch on Olli . . ."

"I'm sorry, but I think I do." He leaned awkwardly over the front seat console to take my hand. "Just until we know she's safe."

"I know." My response was barely above a whisper. "I guess rescuing damsels in distress is part of your charm." I kissed his cheek and hurriedly walked into the house. Ross was doing the right thing, but I didn't have to be happy about it.

Thankfully, the house was quiet and dark when I entered. I tiptoed up the stairs, hoping to make it to my bedroom before Charlotte knew I was home. All I wanted was to be alone for a while and sulk. But as I reached the top of the stairs, the front door opened below.

"Boy, I thought you and Ross would never finish your conversation," Charlotte said. She continued breezily as she walked up the stairs, turning on lights as she did. "I went down to the house to get some of my client files. I was walking back up the street when you guys passed me. Didn't you see me? Well anyway, I thought Ross would just park and you would go inside, but you stayed in the car. Then I thought you might be having a fight or getting it on, so I didn't want to just come barging past you. I mean, that could be awkward, so I waited. It's a good thing it isn't winter; I would have frozen to death by the time the two of you finished. I think all that waiting earned me a glass of wine. What do you think?" She headed toward the kitchen. "You go into the living room. I'll pour. I found a new Cab I think you'll like. Then we can catch up." She stopped to scrutinize me. "Nice duds. When did you go to work for Couloir?"

I hastily took off my apron and hat, then resigned to my fate, went to my favorite wingback chair and sat.

Charlotte never waited for a response, just kept talking. She raised her voice so I could hear her as she got the wine. "How was your day? Didn't you golf? You wouldn't have believed my day. It started okay. Thought I'd do a little work, but then Corey called and said he needed to postpone moving out of Dad's house because he was going to Africa. Oh, and by the way, would I send him a check for twenty thousand to cover his expenses and pay a few bills? I said no, so he cried. And, J, I don't mean a few tears, he was blubbering. After a while all I could do was hang up. Then wouldn't you know it, Cody calls and yells at me for upsetting his twin, who he, and I quote: 'no longer wants to be responsible for.' Oh, and by the way, would I sign the fucking papers so he and Corey could get their fair share of the family money? I said no, so he raged. I think you know what comes next." She paused a beat to hand me a glass of wine. "I hung up."

I found myself smiling as she prattled on. No one could talk like Charlotte.

She paced the length of the living room. "You know when someone you love dies, families should come together—tell stories, share memories, comfort one another. Who am I left with? Corey, Cody, and Stephanie. Where's the justice in that? I have no one to talk to about Dad and Mom." She actually looked chagrined for the moment it took to sip her wine. "Sorry, J, I know I have you. But the truth is you didn't know either of them. I mean I guess you could listen, but it's not the same thing…"

"Charlotte," I interrupted.

". . . I can't say 'do you remember when', or 'wasn't that the funniest . . .'"

"Charlotte," I said more forcefully.

"I guess what I'm saying is that I have to cry with . . ."

"Charlotte," I yelled. She stopped her pacing mid-stride.

"Is something wrong, J?"

I took a calming breath, and said quietly but distinctly, "Mrs. Simpson."

Charlotte looked confused. "Is something wrong with Mrs. Simpson?"

I took another longer calming breath. "Why don't you invite Mrs. Simpson to Mammoth? She knew and cared for both of your parents."

Charlotte sat down. "Of course, Mrs. Simpson. I could get her a hotel room and . . ."

"Or she could stay here. The couch in my office pulls out into a bed. From what you've said about the twins and Stephanie, Mrs. Simpson might appreciate the respite."

"You would do that?"

"Absolutely."

Charlotte leaped from her chair, grabbed her glass and the bottle of wine, and ran downstairs to call Mrs. Simpson. Her parting words, "Good to hear you had such a great day."

I shook my head and retreated to my bedroom.

Charlotte's car was gone when I got up, but there was a note next to the cappuccino machine saying Mrs. Simpson would arrive around six that evening. That meant I had some work to do. I spent the morning converting my office into a bedroom, giving the house a quick clean, and putting vases of fresh flowers in every room. In the midst of sweeping the upstairs decks, Ross called.

I told him about Mrs. Simpson's impending arrival. "Good timing," he said. "That gives me a legitimate reason to hang out at my place for the next few days and keep watch over Olli."

My stomach tightened. "How is she?" I asked, trying to keep all emotion out of my voice. "Did she enjoy herself last night?"

"I haven't really spoken to her today. By the time I got up she was already out for her morning run. When she got back, she just waved and went to her room. But I did get a call from Brian who wanted to know if Olli is dating anyone. I told him I don't think so. Apparently, he asked her out and she turned him down with no reason." Ross let out a little laugh. "From the tone of his voice I don't think Brian is used to being rejected. But I was a little surprised. I thought the two of them hit it off last night."

"Maybe she's just not ready to date yet," I offered.

"You're probably right, J. Well, got a bunch of errands to run. Will you call tonight before I go to bed?"

"Sure." I said, and disconnected. Looking at the half-swept deck, I decided Mrs. Simpson wouldn't care about a few dead leaves. What I really needed was to go for a run and clear my head.

Thirty minutes later I was running down a road referred to locally as the scenic loop, but is actually a six-mile escape road that leads from town to the main highway. Built in the event of a natural disaster, it's a perfect road to run on when introspection without distraction is required: minimum traffic, no buildings, mild elevation changes, lots of trees, a little bit of wildlife. I set my watch to remind me to turn around, so I would be home in plenty of time to meet Mrs. Simpson, and took off.

During the first mile, I established a steady pace and regulated my breathing. Once I found my rhythm, I did what I normally do whenever I'm in a dilemma, I sought guidance from Mary. Only this time I had to seek answers from our past.

The summer before we started high school Mary and I made two promises to one another: we wouldn't join the same school activities or clubs, and we would never date the same boy. Those agreements were easy to keep—we liked to do different things with our time—Mary liked academics, I liked sports, and we were never attracted to the same guy.

The summer before we started college, we reaffirmed our prior commitments, and added two more, understanding college romances could lead to something significant. The first was neither of us would seriously date someone who felt threatened by our twin-relationship. The second: we would only be with someone whom we wanted, not someone we needed—a distinction we spent hours talking about. These pledges were more challenging. One of us would go out with someone three or four times, think this is it, then introduce them to her twin. For the most part, the boy in question would try to go along with the "other twin's" frequent presence, but eventually got fed up. The most common phrases Mary and I heard from these guys were, "Aren't I enough for you?" or "Doesn't she have her own life?" And when it came to wanting to be with someone rather than needing to be with someone, halfway through college we began to understand we might not be mature enough to make the distinction. So, we remained committed to the promise, but not entirely sure what it meant.

My watch beeped the end of the first mile—ten-minutes-seventeen-seconds. Good pace. My breathing was even. I went back inside my head, trying to decipher why these particular memories had come to mind.

Slowly it dawned. *After all these years, I finally understood the difference between wanting and needing. My relationship with Ross had always been one of want. Or it had been, up until Mary died.*

This sudden revelation caused my breath to quicken. I automatically slowed my pace.

So much had happened since Mary and Bob's murders, I'd never considered how their deaths impacted my relationship with Ross. Of course, it had. Without thinking about it, Ross now filled almost all the voids Mary had left. I needed him.

I decided to sprint the next mile, while I let this epiphany sink in.

Eight and a half minutes later I slowed down to my regular pace.

I told myself there was nothing wrong with wanting and needing Ross . . . I just had to understand it, and how it affected him, me, and our relationship. I sighed. *This was getting way too complicated. I needed to deal with the most immediate issue. Which was . . .*

I collided with something soft and big, and fell down into a small drainage ditch—wind temporarily knocked out of me. A doe stood over me, and she was pissed. I'd just run into her—literally—while she grazed on the side of the road. Once she made her irritation known, she turned and loped off. When my heart quit pounding, I stood, brushed off the dirt and pine needles, took several deep breaths, and vowed to pay more attention to my environs as I continued the run.

Where was I . . . Oh, yeah, the most immediate issue. That was easy. Why had I made it so easy for Olli to move in with Ross? I posed the question to Mary back in time—telepathically. If Mary had been faced with an old flame of Bob's wanting to temporarily move in with him, she would have gone ballistic. Mary always led with her emotions when it came to matters of the heart. I came out on the other side of the spectrum; logic was my go-to strategy. It was the approach I had used all my life. Olli must have asked to stay with Ross for a reason; I believed Ross was committed to our relationship; Ross and I had always made our own decisions; therefore, if Ross wanted to let Olli stay with him, it was his decision. In the end, if Ross fell for Olli, it was his choice. It would hurt, but I always had Mary.

I stopped in my tracks. Then said out loud, "But, Mary's not here anymore. Not really. And Ross is my best-alive friend now." I sat down on a nearby rock. All the emotion I had so efficiently boxed up inside poured through my eyes. By the time my watch beeped its reminder to turnaround and run home, my shirt was damp with tears.

I rose for my return run. I knew I wouldn't abruptly demand Olli leave, or inundate Ross with my insecurities. I needed to stay the course to the end. I understood what I had to lose, but I believed in the strength of the relationship Ross and I had built. And I hoped I wasn't making the biggest mistake of my life.

I heard someone coming up behind me. The rhythm of the footfalls made me expect two runners. As they pulled alongside, I saw it was Mary and Bob. I took their presence as a good omen, and fell into pace—a little of the tightness leaving my chest.

Chapter 33

At five-thirty both the house and the hostess were presentable. A chicken was roasting in the oven, and I looked forward to meeting Mrs. Simpson. As I put the finishing touches on a cheese and fruit tray, Charlotte paced and talked at a speed that defied nature. Obviously, my fearless neighbor was nervous about the visit. Since she abhorred subtlety, I asked, "Are you uptight about Mrs. Simpson's stay?"

She collapsed on the kitchen loveseat. "A little, I guess."

"Why?" The surprise in my voice bled through. I didn't think anyone could intimidate Charlotte. "You've known her for years. Hell, she's younger than you are."

Charlotte sat perfectly still. Had I not been worried, I'd have appreciated the brief calm. "I'm in awe of her. I think she's one of the best people I know. Mrs. Simpson was the glue that held our family together through Mother's illness and death," she said reverently. "She made decisions when we were all paralyzed. She kept us moving forward . . ."

The doorbell rang. "She's here!" Charlotte sprang to her feet and ran downstairs.

"Come on up after she's settled," I yelled at the back of her head.

Several minutes later I heard, "J, this is Mrs. Simpson."

For some reason, I thought she'd look like her picture minus the blue hair—a tall, gangly, thin, awkward girl, wearing pants that were too short. I was wrong, of course. All her pieces had come together elegantly. Her slender figure was clad in a pair of white leggings and a long pumpkin-colored tee. Her thick brown hair was long and straight, tucked behind her ears. She had a heart-shaped face with high cheekbones, and the deep brown eyes of an old soul. She appeared both fragile and strong. This impression was confirmed when she took both my hands in hers. "It is good to finally meet you, J. I'm overwhelmed by your generosity."

I stood awkwardly, not knowing how to respond, still trying to reconcile expectation with reality. "Why don't I make us all a drink, then we can go out on the deck and get to know one another," I blurted. "What would you like?"

She raised her eyebrows. "Extra cold vodka up with a twist?"

I was going to like Mrs. Simpson.

Small talk over cocktails led to current events during dinner. Mrs. Simpson—*yes, she wanted me to call her Mrs. Simpson*—had received a bit of a shock when she saw remnants of police crime-scene tape around Charlotte's house. Apparently, Charlotte had failed to mention the bomb, saying that she was staying at my house while she underwent a kitchen renovation. The bombing introduced the topic of Zach, Charlotte's former employee. Despite her concern, Mrs. Simpson couldn't quit laughing as I described the angry naked man coming out of Charlotte's bedroom when I went in search of her mother's bracelet. But as we talked about possible suspects, the discussion turned more serious.

"Do the police think Zach planted the dynamite?"

Charlotte stood and began her interminable pacing. "Initially I think they did. But then I told the cops about Stephanie, Corey, and Cody. Now, Zach just happens to be the only local on the list of people who would be happy to see me dead."

Mrs. Simpson shook her head. "I know the twins are upset about the estate. Hell, before I left this morning I had to make sure the security service at the house was 24-7, and all the guards understood your brothers are not allowed in the main house under any circumstances. But I just can't imagine Corey or Cody actually wanting you dead. You're still their sister."

Charlotte stopped pacing long enough to make a face, her incredulity obvious. But Mrs. Simpson remained undaunted. "Well, then, look at it this way. Cody is too narcissistic to risk prison, and Corey is too disorganized to plan . . ."

Charlotte's cell rang. "Speak of the devil. It's Corey."

As she answered, Mrs. Simpson gestured vigorously by pointing to herself and shaking her head, so Charlotte would understand she was not here.

Charlotte nodded while she listened to her brother. "No, Mrs. Simpson is not with me," she said flatly.

"Is Mrs. Simpson coming to see me?" Mrs. Simpson shook her head.

"I can't imagine why. I don't think Mrs. Simpson even likes the mountains. What's this all about, Corey?" Charlotte's eyes widened as she listened. Mrs. Simpson shook her head, looking both embarrassed and angry.

"If I talk to her, I'll tell her you need her, Corey. But I wouldn't hold my breath. If you're in so much trouble, you better handle it yourself."

Once the phone call ended, Charlotte turned to Mrs. Simpson. "Corey's in love with you? When did you start going out with him? Hell, *why* would you go out with him?"

Mrs. Simpson straightened her shoulders and lengthened her spine. "I've never gone out with your brother, and never will." Her shoulders slumped and she added wearily, "Corey has been following me around for months, telling me we were meant to be. At first I thought it was humorous and he would lose interest, like he does with everything that isn't medicine. But he only seems to grow more insistent."

Almost more to herself than to us, Charlotte said, "Maybe that's why Stephanie said you were sleeping with one or both of my brothers."

Mrs. Simpson stood up. "She said what?" Indignation shaded her voice.

Charlotte flicked her hand. "Oh, you know Stephanie. She's always trashing other people. But this is interesting. Did Cody ever ask you out?"

Mrs. Simpson's eyes narrowed, but Charlotte was too caught up in the possibilities to notice.

"Charlotte, perhaps . . ." I started, but Mrs. Simpson finished my sentence.

"Perhaps . . . you should mind your own business."

Mrs. Simpson's tone drew Charlotte's attention. When she saw her face, Charlotte look mortified. "I'm sorry. I didn't mean anything. It's just that I never thought of you as a woman. No. That's not what I mean . . . it's just, well, you know . . . you're . . . you're Mrs. Simpson. You're part of the family."

Mrs. Simpson's face softened. She put a hand on her friend's shoulder to quiet her, but Charlotte continued. ". . . I mean. I just never thought the boys would . . ."

"Charlotte, instead of babbling on, would you please get us all another glass of wine," Mrs. Simpson suggested, visibly relaxing. I rose, but she looked at me and said, "Charlotte can do it." I sat back down, comprehending that while Mrs. Simpson might have been the youngest in the household, she ran a tight ship.

As Charlotte poured, she begged, "Please. I'm dying to know. Did Cody ever ask you out?"

After a couple of sips of wine Mrs. Simpson chuckled. "Cody never actually asked me out. He was a bit more direct than that."

"What do you mean, more direct?" I asked.

She rolled her eyes. "About five years ago, he was home on a Saturday night, which as Charlotte knows, is quite rare for him. He knocked on my cottage door and said, "Since neither of us have anything to do tonight, do you want to smoke a joint and fuck?""

Stunned silence was quickly obliterated by peals of giggles. "What did you say to him?"

"I didn't. I just calmly shut the door and double-locked it. The subject never came up again."

Charlotte broke the mood, asking gently, "May I ask one more question?"

"Sure. What is it?"

"Was Dad really going to marry Stephanie?"

Mrs. Simpson studied her hands as she replied. "Until I overheard your Dad ask his attorney about prenuptial agreements, I would've said no. Your father and Stephanie seemed to be spending less and less time together. I think you know she had her own room in the house, and most nights she stayed in it rather than with your father. They seemed to have lost some connection. I still don't understand."

"Don't understand . . .?"

Turning to me, she answered. "After Charlotte's mother died, I kept a close eye on Charles. They'd been so much in love I feared the loss would kill him. Each night before I left the house I made sure to say goodnight, so I could check on him once more before going to my cottage. If he looked particularly down, I would sit with him and we would chat." She sighed. "I loved those evenings."

As Mrs. Simpson took a sip of her wine, I could see she was back at the house talking to Charlotte's father. "I tried to continue this ritual even after Stephanie moved in, which of course, annoyed her no end. When Charles was out of earshot, she would tell me to leave them alone. But after a few months of cohabitation they were more often apart in the evening than together, so Charles and I resumed our routine."

There was an odd hollowness in her words. I ventured softly, "Mrs. Simpson?"

She continued to look at her hands, which were clutched tightly in her lap.

"Mrs. Simpson?"

When she still didn't respond, Charlotte went to her.

Charlotte whispered, "Marge?"

Mrs. Simpson looked up. There were tears in her eyes.

"You were in love with him?"

She nodded.

Chapter 34

"It's all my fault," cried Charlotte. "If I hadn't told Dad to get a personal shopper . . ."

Mrs. Simpson took her hand. "It's not your fault, Charlotte. You didn't make your father fall in love with Stephanie. He just did. Besides, I read more into our relationship than was there. I guess Charles didn't see me as a woman, he saw me like everyone else did—he saw Mrs. Simpson."

"But you would have been perfect together . . ."

Mrs. Simpson momentarily brightened. "Do you think? You know, there was a time I thought he felt the same way I did," she mused. "Our nightly conversations were magic. Sometimes we would just start talking—about politics, sports, a movie, it really didn't matter—and when we decided to call it a night, we'd both be surprised to see the sun was coming up." Mrs. Simpson looked at Charlotte with such sadness it made my heart break.

I felt like a reluctant voyeur so I left to busy myself in the kitchen. Neither woman noticed. They were holding onto one another and quietly crying. When I returned an hour later they had retired downstairs.

The next morning, I found a note from Charlotte taped to the coffee maker. She and Mrs. Simpson had gone for hike in the

Lakes Basin and would return late morning. She suggested we go out for a late lunch at Burgers. I was pleased. A morning in the mountains would be good for both of them. I was a firm believer in nature as a salve for emotional hurts. It certainly had worked for me over the last few years. And I smiled at Charlotte's choice of restaurants. While it might always have been Ross's and my café for important discussions, it also had the best burgers in town.

Besides, my work had fallen behind since Charlotte's arrival. A free morning meant it was time to be productive. I picked up my phone and listened to the messages I'd been ignoring. Linda Taylor and Kate wanted me to call as soon as possible.

The last message was from Ms. Germaine. "Good morning, J. No need to call me back, just wanted you to know all the staff who left have returned—minus Kyle, of course—and all but one of our clients have reengaged, as well. Thank you. One of the most important lessons I learned during this debacle is to ask for help when I need it. But I guess you probably figured that one out. Listen, if there's ever anything I can ever do for you, please let me know." Ms. Germaine and I had come a long way.

I returned Linda's call. "Hi J. When I didn't hear right back from you I went ahead and scheduled a meeting of the Labor Day weekend Gala committee tomorrow afternoon at three. Please tell me you can make it, because everyone else can."

I could hear the exasperation in her voice. It was usually harder to schedule a meeting than lead it. "No problem, Linda. I'll be there."

"Thank you," she said with a loud exhale, and then commenced to give me a review of the committee's progress. "Helen, Berta, and Bill have really come through for us. They've accomplished in days what it would take most people months to achieve. Even your friend Olli has been doing some quite exceptional work. I just wish she wasn't so . . . so . . . so attractive."

Linda's comment was a painful reminder that I was going on two days without seeing Ross. Attempting mild curiosity, I asked, "Olli's looks are getting in the way of writing press releases and marketing materials?"

"Olli isn't the problem, John is. Wherever she is, he's not far away, unless he's schmoozing with the greens crew at Snow Star. I'd hoped he could do a lot of the leg work, but unless Olli's involved, he just doesn't seem to get around to it." She sighed. "If he'd come to us through anyone other than our second biggest donor, I'd have a serious talk with him." She sighed again. "I guess I'll just have to live with it."

"Do you want me to see if I can talk to Olli about discouraging John?" The words were out of my mouth before I could stop them. If I could have sucked them back in I would have.

"Would you?" Linda asked. "Please."

I felt queasy. What was wrong with me? Why did I make such an outrageous offer? The last thing I wanted to do was talk to Olli.

More than a few seconds must have passed because Linda said, "J, are you still there? If you're having second thoughts, I understand. It's not a comfortable conversation."

Now in addition to feeling sick, I was mortified. I tried to sound light. "Sorry, Linda, nothing's wrong. I just became momentarily distracted. Don't give it a second thought. I'll speak to Olli this week."

"Thanks, J. I really do appreciate it. I better say goodbye, lots to do."

I sat for a moment stunned by my stupidity. If I hadn't had houseguests perhaps I could've invited Olli and Ross for dinner and casually raised the issue of John over a glass of wine. But even that would be awkward. As I searched for a simple strategy, my cell vibrated in my hand.

"Hello," I answered distractedly.

"Don't you ever return your phone messages?" Kate demanded.

"Oh, hi, Kate."

"Oh, hi, Kate?" she mimicked. "What's wrong?"

So, I told her, starting with Mary and Bob following Olli two nights before at Couloir, Ross's decision to watch out for Olli, and ending with my idiotic offer to talk to Olli about John.

I could hear the smile in Kate's voice. "You just can't help yourself, can you? You have to help fix things, even when they don't concern you."

The truthfulness in her words got under my skin. "I'm not that bad. I only help out when asked."

"Ahem." Kate was laughing now. "Correct me if I'm mistaken, but wasn't it you who planned out Michele's next five years within twenty-four hours of meeting her?"

My pique evaporated. "Rest your case, Kate. You win." With a bit more energy I asked, "So what can I do for *you* today."

"Actually, it's what can you do for Nathan. First, he wanted me to thank you for sending Charlotte to him. New clients are always welcome. And he wanted to ask if you could ask *her* to return *his* calls." She paused, seemingly for dramatic effect, "Ironic, isn't it?"

I ignored her jab. "No problem. Tell him not to take it personally. If Nathan has been calling her in the last forty-eight hours, it's been pretty emotional around here." I filled her in on Charlotte's depression, the decision to invite Mrs. Simpson to Mammoth, and last night's revelations.

"Sounds like you've your hands full. Call me if I can help or you need a sounding board."

"Wait, why are you calling and not Nathan?"

"The official reason is that Nathan is in court this morning, the real one is that your life is always so much more interesting than mine. Don't get me wrong, I wouldn't trade places with you. I love Nathan, our home, even learning to golf. But you have such a knack for finding drama. Bye, love."

I looked at the phone in my hand and snarled.

Chapter 35

I was loading packages into my car when Charlotte and Mrs. Simpson returned. Both women looked like they'd spent as much time crying as hiking. But even grief couldn't quell Charlotte's curiosity.

Pointing to the mound of parcels in the back of my car, she asked, "What are all those?"

I smiled." Presents for my last houseguests."

"They must be pretty special. What's the occasion?"

"No occasion," I said cryptically. "I just miss them." Assessing the stack, I added, "I might have gone a bit overboard."

Mrs. Simpson walked to the back of the car, her interest piqued.

Charlotte raised her eyebrows, "Does this mean I can expect occasional prizes when I move out? Or do I live too close to be missed?"

Mrs. Simpson smiled. "Perhaps you should tell us what makes these particular guests so special, so Charlotte and I know how to compete."

"They're for one-year-old twin girls and their mother."

Charlotte groaned. "Way too domestic for me." Turning to Mrs. Simpson she said, "We better get showered so we can go to lunch. I'm hungry."

"I'm off to the post office and a few other errands," I said. "See you at Burgers at one o'clock."

When I reached the post office the service line was out the door. In a town without mail delivery, I spent a lot of time waiting in lines to pick up and send packages. I made a quick U-turn in the parking lot and went to Mammoth Business Essentials, a business started several years ago by Marsha and Craig Hansen. For the self-employed and small businesses in town, the term "essential" could not have been more appropriate. It took me three trips to get all my presents inside, but in relatively short order they were on their way to Michele, Meg, and Max.

It was after one when the last parcel was processed. The rest of my chores would have to wait until after lunch. I was both gratified and horrified as I drove past the post office to see the line had made little progress. When I pulled into Burgers' parking lot, Charlotte and Mrs. Simpson were standing next to their car waiting for me. Charlotte seemed distressed as she approached my car.

"Something wrong?"

"Uh . . . no . . . not really . . . there's just too long a wait, and I'm hungry. Let's go to the Rock & Bowl. They have great food and Mrs. Simpson hasn't been there."

With that, she headed back to her car and the two women took off. I sat there for a moment, stymied. There just weren't that many cars in the parking lot. To my knowledge, Mrs.

Simpson had never been to Burgers, either. And more importantly, Charlotte hadn't chided me for being late. I didn't get it. When she passed me, I backed up my car to follow her out of the lot. As I waited to make a left turn onto the busy street I saw the problem in my rearview mirror. My heart fell. Olli and Ross were walking out of Burgers deep in conversation—so engaged they didn't see me.

Anxious to escape unnoticed, I almost ran down two cyclists and nearly T-boned a Ford pickup leaving the parking lot. I could see angry gestures in my side mirror as I sped away, but the loud buzzing in my head blocked out their words. I wanted to head home instead of to lunch with friends to be silently pitied. Over the course of the last few weeks I'd told Charlotte all about Olli, and I was sure by the time they reached the restaurant, Mrs. Simpson would know all the details.

Taking a few calming breaths to regain some sense of composure at a red light, I was alarmed to hear the front and back passenger doors open. Mary climbed into the seat beside me. I didn't have to look to know Bob was now sitting in the backseat. Even more surprising was that Mary shook her head then rolled her eyes at me as if I were a child throwing a tantrum. Before I had time to interpret her response or react, impatient drivers with loud horns announced the light had turned green.

I accelerated and asked indignantly, "What am I not getting?" and turned for Mary's response to find an empty seat. Pondering whether it had been a visit or a hallucination, I reached Rock & Bowl where Charlotte and Mrs. Simpson waited next to the only empty parking place.

I was going to pretend I bought Charlotte's story of a full restaurant when she said, "You saw them." It was a statement not a question.

I felt the pinpricks of tears building, so the response was nonverbal, a nod and a shrug.

Charlotte and Mrs. Simpson approached me. Fearing they would turn my shame into an opportunity to hug, I took a step backward.

Without hesitation, they each took one of my arms, and guided me indoors. "This is why martinis were invented."

Our timing was perfect. A party of four was just vacating one of the tables on the coveted downstairs back deck—far enough away from the bowlers to be quite tranquil. We took in the craggy, reddish rock of the Sherwin Range, as our table was cleared and set. I could just make out Couloir, certain that if I had not known its location, I would have just seen the slope-side. As always, the mountains brought back my sense of calm and equilibrium. I could see the Eastern Sierra had done the same for my companions.

As I explained that the Sherwins were named for Jim Sherwin, a prospector who operated the first toll road across the Sierra, ending in Mammoth, a waitress arrived and took our drink order.

Charlotte tentatively asked, "Did you see them or did you just guess?"

My heart gave a little stutter. "I saw them as they were leaving."

"Did they see you?"

I opened my mouth to say I didn't think so when my phone buzzed. I glanced at the display. It was Ross. Holding it up so Charlotte and Mrs. Simpson could see who was calling, I pressed "decline" and it immediately vibrated again. It said "Olli." I threw the phone in my purse. "I guess so."

My bag continued to vibrate while our drinks were served.

I reached to turn my phone off, when I remembered. "Charlotte, you need to return Nathan's calls."

"I forgot," she said sheepishly, and grabbed her own cell.

While Charlotte punched in the number, I explained to Mrs. Simpson who Nathan was, and my relationship to Kate, his wife.

Charlotte's side of the conversation was unusually monosyllabic.

"Nathan?"

"Sorry."

"Yeah."

"Stephanie."

"Gates, Stephanie Gates."

"Yeah?"

"Oh!"

"I'll call you back in thirty minutes." She glanced around the table. "Better make that an hour."

"Thanks."

She stuffed the phone back into a pocket of her cargo pants, took a big swallow of her martini, glanced at the menu, and said, "Order me an Angus Burger. Get something for yourselves. Make our orders to go, and meet me back at the house as soon as you can." She drained what was left of her drink and left without further explanation.

Having no clue as to what just happened, Mrs. Simpson and I did as instructed. When we got home we found Charlotte uncommunicative and vigorously rooting around in boxes she had stored in my garage. So, we set the table on the upstairs front deck and waited for her to join us and explain what the hell was going on.

Moments later she appeared, clutching a bottle of Dom Perignon. This was getting crazier by the minute!

She set the bottle on the deck and pulled out a small silver ring box out of a pocket, placing it reverently on the table. Then she called Nathan.

"I'm putting you on speaker, Nathan." She placed her cell on the table. "Can you hear me?"

Nathan said, "Sure can."

"Good." She looked at us as she spoke. "When I was going through Dad's things, I found this in a locked drawer in his office."

Mrs. Simpson and I looked at the box. Mrs. Simpson visibly deflated.

"I knew I shouldn't take it, but I was going to be damned if I was going to let the bitch have it."

Tears spilled from Mrs. Simpson's eyes.

I started to stand in protest; this was too cruel. Charlotte commanded me to sit with her eyes.

She opened the box. Inside was a rounded square sapphire surrounded by delicate pavé diamonds. It was exquisite.

Mrs. Simpson wept openly.

"Nathan, can you repeat what you told me earlier?"

Nathan must have sensed the moment, because his voice was low and respectful. "Charlotte had all her father's files sent to me from his former attorney. A few days ago, I sorted through them. One of the documents I found was a draft of a prenuptial agreement. I was confused when I read it, so I phoned Charlotte. I know that Stephanie Gates is pursuing actions against Mr. Caron's estate based on their engagement." Nathan paused as if he didn't know how to proceed.

Charlotte said, "Why don't you tell them exactly what question you asked me?"

We turned toward the phone as if Nathan were sitting there.

"Who is Margaret Bouvier?"

Mrs. Simpson's hand flew to her mouth, as if trying to stop the "Charles" that escaped it.

Charlotte asked Nathan to send her a copy of the document, and disconnected. She turned to Mrs. Simpson and handed her the silver box. "I believe this is yours."

Chapter 36

Mrs. Simpson clasped the box to her chest and then doubled over—hands hugging her body, head in lap, trembling. Charlotte and I looked at one another in alarm.

After a few agonizing minutes, Charlotte stood and placed her hand gently on Mrs. Simpson's back. "Mrs. Simpson?"

No response.

Her shaking became more violent.

"Marge?"

No response.

Charlotte looked at me and whispered, "Perhaps we should . . ."

Mrs. Simpson raised her head. She was laughing and crying. "He loved me," she breathed. "He really loved me."

We exchanged anxious glances. Charlotte finally said, "I'm so sorry. I can't imagine how hard this must be to learn now that Dad is gone."

"Oh, dear. You don't understand." Mrs. Simpson appeared downright jubilant. "Today I'm going to revel in the knowledge Charles loved me. Tomorrow I will mourn." She paused, peering at Charlotte. "I hope that's okay with you?"

Charlotte's response was to pop the cork on the Dom Perignon.

It wasn't quite dawn and someone was pounding on the front door. Poking my head out from underneath the pillow, I opened my left eye first—no daylight. I held my breath and waited for them to go away but the noise just got louder. Finally, I threw on a robe and stumbled downstairs, ready to give whomever was on the porch a piece of my mind. I could hear Charlotte's curses from the guest room as I flung open the door. Linda Taylor flew past me and up the stairs carrying two cups of coffee. My irritation turned to bewilderment. I meekly followed.

She sat down at the dining room table, pointed to all of Charlotte's coffee makers on one of the kitchen counters and said, "If I'd known you were so well equipped I wouldn't have stopped at the Looney Bean." She shoved a cup in my face. "Cappuccino with two sugars, the way *I* like it."

I opened my mouth to speak, but couldn't think of anything to say. I took a sip of the coffee and stared at her.

She took a couple of big gulps from her cup and asked, "Don't you EVER answer your messages? God knows we all sent you enough of them over the last eighteen hours."

A picture flashed of tossing my cell into my purse yesterday at the Rock & Bowl and never retrieving it. I opened my mouth again with the same lack of results.

Linda shook her head as if she'd never seen anyone so pathetic. "Well sit down, J. I have something unbelievable to show you."

While I fumbled into a chair, Linda pulled out the California section of the L.A. Times. This came out yesterday early afternoon online, and this morning in print."

On the front page in large bold letters was: CALIFORNIA MOUNTAIN TOWN TAKES FUNDRAISING FOR CHILDREN TO NEW HEIGHTS.

I was wide-awake now. I stood, grabbed the newspaper from Linda, and skimmed the article.

". . . fundraising event of a lifetime being held in Mammoth Lakes, a renowned Eastern Sierra resort town in Mono County . . ."

". . . collaboration between the California nonprofit Hope for Our Children and Mono County Health & Human Services . . ."

". . . multi-service program aimed at assisting working poor families . . ."

". . . $1,000,000 goal . . ."

". . . fully underwritten so all monies go directly to program . . ."

". . . Labor Day weekend . . . two-day event . . ."

". . . auctioning meals with a former US President, a former Speaker of the House, a current Prince; a round of golf with a Masters winner . . ."

". . . NFL and NBA players have volunteered to serve as waiters during the event . . ."

Startled, I looked at Linda. "I was going to announce it at the meeting this afternoon," she said. "We've been getting nonstop calls from sports, entertainment, and political celebrities volunteering their time. Basically, offering to do anything so they'll be included."

I went back to scanning the end of the article.

". . . fully subscribed . . ."

". . . international model for fundraising . . ."

". . . rumored to have already passed their million-dollar goal . . ."

Falling back into my chair, I took another sip of coffee. "*Wow.* This all happened since yesterday morning? That was when we spoke, right?"

Linda nodded. "I thought you better know before people start calling, and they will find you one way or another. After all, you're the one who put the fundraising dream team together . . . they'll want to speak with you and Roberta Hart."

I started when I heard a "whoo hoo" and applause coming from the staircase. Charlotte and Mrs. Simpson appeared. From the smiles on their faces they had heard most of Linda's and my conversation.

As I made introductions I was pleased to see the sapphire ring on Mrs. Simpson's left hand. When my houseguests went into the kitchen to make coffee, Linda took her leave.

As I followed her downstairs to the front door, Linda admonished, "Don't give any statements to press or volunteers until we have an agreed-upon game plan." I promised I wouldn't. Before she reached her car, she yelled, "And answer your goddamn phone."

Charlotte, Mrs. Simpson, and I drank cappuccinos while I told them about the event. Mrs. Simpson read the article, Charlotte checked out the social media coverage, and I listened to my thirteen voice messages. The last twelve corresponded in order to twelve texts waiting to be reviewed. The first message, the only one not followed by a text, was from Jeff Boucher, the prominent local who was going to be a host for our Gala visitors. He said he'd drop by his idea list for entertaining our guests, and asked that I review it before tomorrow's—now today's—meeting. He also said it would be early, so he would just leave the envelope on my front bench.

I hesitated when I reached Ross's message, but only for a moment. He said "Hey, J, congratulations. Was having lunch with Olli when we saw the LA Times article. You're unbelievable. Talk to you soon. Love you."

It was followed by Olli's call. "This article is fabulous. I've never seen anything like it. Congratulations. See you at tomorrow's meeting."

I realized how badly I'd overreacted to seeing them at Burgers on Monday. Hell, they were roommates, what was the big deal about eating lunch together? My self-recrimination was interrupted by a loud knock on the front door.

Expecting another member of the committee, I opened the door without concern about my early morning attire. A strange but slightly familiar man stood on the porch. I was about to ask if he'd come because of the article when he asked, "Is this where Charlotte Caron is staying?"

"Excuse me for a moment," I said, closed and locked the door, and went upstairs.

Charlotte barked, "Who in the hell was that? It's just dawn."

I hesitated for a moment, my fingertips to my lips. "I believe it's one of your brothers."

Chapter 37

Silent pandemonium broke out.

Charlotte jumped up, spilling her coffee, and whispered, "How do you know? Which one is it? What did you say to him? Where is he now? Why the fuck is he here?"

Mrs. Simpson leapt up and was looking for a place to hide. She asked, "J, can I wait in your room? I can't go downstairs or he'll see me through the beveled window in the door."

I took charge. Pointing to Mrs. Simpson, I said, "Of course you can stay in my room. Why don't you freshen up your cup of coffee, and get a scone from the pantry if you're hungry? There's a nice sitting area in the bedroom."

"Charlotte, he's been standing outside for almost five minutes. Go down and invite him in. We might as well find out what he wants. I'll stay unless *you* ask me to go. You don't have to do anything but listen." Then I grabbed some paper towels to clean the coffee off the floor.

Charlotte didn't look happy as she turned to go. "And, please, try not to lose your temper," I reminded her.

She scowled.

She came back upstairs with Cody, and introduced me through clenched teeth. I offered him coffee, and he asked for a

218

nonfat latte with two shots and extra foam. On my way to the kitchen, I asked, "Do you mind if I record you?"

He sneered. "I don't care what *you* do."

I turned on my Mr. Coffee, and brewed him a cup of decaf.

When I handed him the cup he studied me, then looked around the room. I suspected he was looking for a recording device, which he didn't find, so he accepted the coffee.

His eyes narrowed as he took a sip, and I asked in my cheeriest voice, "What brings you to our part of the world at this hour of the morning?"

The edges of Charlotte's mouth twitched, though I didn't know if was my words or Cody's reaction to the coffee that gave her pleasure. She relaxed a little, which was good for all of us.

He set the hot mug purposefully on the only antique table in the room. "I suppose it is early, but I'm on my way to Tahoe with a friend to consummate a business proposition." He drew out con-sum-mate, articulating each syllable.

Everything he said sounded crude, but I supposed that was what he intended.

He turned to Charlotte as I took his coffee to the kitchen and returned to wipe the table. "I really didn't come to argue, Char. I have a simple request."

Charlotte cocked her head as if an idea had just struck. "How did you know where to find me?"

"Mrs. Simpson told me." With a hint of a smile he added, "I see you're finally renovating the old vacation house. It's about time. Though I still don't understand why anyone would want to live here."

He paused for effect? "But back to business. If all goes as planned, I'll be moving off the estate next week. That means someone needs to look after Corey. I am no longer willing to accept the responsibility; it costs too much. Mrs. Simpson is on some sort of holiday, and Corey has barely left his hovel since Father died."

"He's a grown man. He should be able to take care of himself," Charlotte snapped.

"Indeed." He gave me a brief nod and headed for the stairs. Before he descended, he said, "I suspect this is the last time we'll speak directly. With the upcoming litigation, it would hardly be appropriate. If there is need of communication, we can do it through our attorneys."

I followed Cody downstairs at a distance. As he strode resolutely down the driveway, he passed Jeff Boucher on his way up, clutching a manila envelope. Jeff did a double take and yelled after Cody, "Hey, it *is* you. Remember me from the bar at Nevados a few weeks ago? We talked about mutual friends from my ski patrol days? Avalanche control? I can't remember your name, but it'll come to me. I'm Jeff. Jeff Boucher. Remember?"

Jeff was still shouting by the time Cody reached his is car, which was parked halfway down the street. Without a glance backward, he drove off.

Then Jeff saw me. "Can you remember his name? It began with a C or a K. Damn. I just can't…"

"Cody?"

"That's it. Cody. I wonder why he's in such a hurry?"

I almost smiled. Jeff wouldn't think someone was being rude, just that they were preoccupied.

"You know Cody?"

"Well, I can't say I *know* know him. I was having a drink at Nevados and he and this gorgeous chick he was with sat next to me. Friendly guy. Her, not so much. He and I struck up a conversation about the old days on the mountain. She sat there looking bored." Then Jeff gave me a very strange look. "It's none of my business why this dude is leaving your house at dawn, J, but this *is* a small town, and Ross *is* a nice guy."

I didn't know whether to laugh, blush, or explain. But I was interrupted by Charlotte calling from the upstairs deck, "What the hell are you doing down there? We need to talk."

Jeff looked embarrassed. He shoved the manila envelope in my hand. "Sorry, J. But you can't blame me. It was odd."

I smiled. "No worries. Do you think I could talk to you about Cody after this afternoon's meeting?"

"Sure. Though I've already told you almost everything I remember." He turned to go.

"Hey, Jeff?"

"Yeah?"

"What was the girlfriend's name?"

"Don't know. We were never introduced." He cocked his head, in thinking mode again. "I know he referred to her by name a few times. I just didn't pay attention. But I do know it's the same chick who was waiting for him in his car just now." He pointed to where Cody had been parked.

I looked up quickly, but Cody was already turning the corner at the end of the cul de sac.

"Last question. Do you remember what day it was when you met Cody?"

He paused, giving it some serious thought. He pulled out his cell and scrolled through his calendar. "Yeah. A week ago, last Friday. The fifteenth. Denise had a late showing for a house she listed, so I was on my own for the evening. I remember because she was late . . ." He grinned. ". . . And she sold it!"

"Thanks."

I ran back into the house.

Mrs. Simpson was livid. "I did *not* tell anyone where I was going, especially not one of the twins."

Charlotte was pacing. "How can I call that prick my brother? And what in the hell were you doing outside for so long, J?"

I held up my hands for quiet and pulled out my cell from behind a plant on the antique side table. "Cody was in town the night before your garage blew up," I said as I punched the number of the police chief.

I explained to Ian what I had just learned from Jeff Boucher as Charlotte and Mrs. Simpson listened open-mouthed.

"Yes. Jeff remembers precisely what day it was because Denise sold a house that evening."

"Well, if you can't arrest him, can't you stop him for questioning? Jeff said he was with the same woman he brought to the bar."

"He said he was going to Tahoe."

"I don't have to write down what Cody said. I recorded it."

"Calm down. I got his permission. It's on the recording."

"Sure, I'll bring the recording by the station. Now, go get him before he leaves town."

"Okay, I get it. You don't want to spook him. But you'll talk to the LA police?"

"No, we won't say anything."

"Thank you. And if I haven't heard from you by tomorrow morning, I'll call you."

As I hit end on the cell, I turned to Charlotte and Mrs. Simpson. "Well, you've heard everything I know. Not a word about what just happened until we've had some food. I'm famished. Let's make breakfast."

Chapter 38

Mrs. Simpson scrambled eggs, I toasted muffins, and Charlotte sliced melon.

I was uneasy about Charlotte using a knife right now. As I kept an eye on her I mused that when you knew someone from afar—like the neighbor down the street—your impressions are superficial. I had always thought of Charlotte as successful, optimistic, cheery, and high energy. Since she'd become a houseguest I saw less optimism and more mood swings, and her constant movement as fear of ambiguity—though I had to take into account the family and personal drama she'd experienced these past weeks. I was praying Mrs. Simpson could help get Charlotte's anger under control. I was glad she was here.

Charlotte blurted angrily, "My brother tried to blow me up!"

"We now know he had the opportunity but we can't jump to conclusions. Besides, we aren't discussing this until after we've had some food and can do so in an organized, non-emotional fashion."

Charlotte said defiantly, "I can't believe you recorded the conversation. You even asked the bastard if he minded, and he agreed."

I smiled. "I guess the flannel pajamas and robe made him think it was just a bluff."

Charlotte giggled.

"I also couldn't believe he asked you for a cappuccino with two shots and extra foam. Who does that in someone's house?" Charlotte scrunched up her face. "What did you give him? It looked nasty."

"A decaffeinated cup of coffee compliments of Mr. Coffee."

She giggled again. Mrs. Simpson was unusually quiet, even for her.

"What's wrong, Mrs. Simpson?"

"I guess I better go back and take care of Corey."

The knife Charlotte had been using fell to the floor, barely missing her right foot. "*No*, you will not. He's forty years old. He's a surgeon, for God's sake." Her face softened, her voice pleading. "Besides you need to stay here and take care of me. I have big plans for us."

Despite herself, Mrs. Simpson looked curious.

When she didn't say anything, I asked, "What kind of big plans? Or is it none of my business?"

Charlotte picked up the knife and placed it in the sink. "Actually, you're a little involved in the first part of the plan, J." She directed all her attention to Mrs. Simpson. "I was thinking since my house is already half gone, we could demolish the whole thing and start over. It's a perfect location, and there's enough space to build a duplex. That way we would both have our own home, but still be close to one another."

I'd never seen Charlotte this vulnerable. She took Mrs. Simpson's hands and said, "We're family. Hell, if Dad were alive you'd be my step-mom. Eventually, we're going to have to sell the estate, so why not stay here. When it's time to dismantle everything, we can do it together. There's really nothing left for either of us in Cheviot Hills. And you already said you loved being in Mammoth; just wait until winter. It'll blow you away. What do you think?"

Mrs. Simpson stared down at their clasped hands, looking up after a few seconds. "But I do need my own space. Sometimes, Charlotte, you can be a bit overwhelming."

Charlotte hooted. Mrs. Simpson wiped the tears from her eyes.

I was surprised to feel tears in my eyes as I asked, "How am I involved?"

Waggling her eyebrows up and down, Charlotte said, "Well, I thought we could stay here until the house is built, if that's okay with you."

I shook my head in humorous resignation. "Of course, it is. How could it not be? Before I get too emotional, let's eat. I'm starving."

Once food was on the table, no one spoke. We just ate. When our hunger pangs were sated, we got down to business.

"Agenda," I announced. "First, I'd like to look at what we learned from Jeff, and from Cody."

"Agreed," Charlotte said.

"And we need to discuss options for Corey," Mrs. Simpson said. "I'm concerned about him." She raised one eyebrow at Charlotte's grunt. "He's still family."

"All right," Charlotte conceded. "And I want to talk about architects so we can get going on the house."

Mrs. Simpson rolled her eyes. "If there's time."

Ever the consultant, I fetched a legal pad and pen. At the top of the first page I wrote: "what we know, assumptions, questions."

Know: Cody and a woman were in Mammoth the day before the bomb. Same woman was in Mammoth with him today.

Questions: Who was the woman? How long were they in Mammoth? Whom did they interact with? What did they do?

Charlotte chimed in. "It was probably Stephanie. She's such a slut."

"We can't make any assumptions. Do you have a picture of her? I could show it to Jeff this afternoon."

Charlotte shook her head. "Why would I keep a picture of that bitch?"

"I do," Mrs. Simpson said.

We looked at her. "You do?"

Her cheeks grew scarlet. "It's a wonderful picture of Charles. I was going to Photoshop her out . . ."

"And replace her with you. I love it," Charlotte hooted.

Mrs. Simpson looked sharply at her, and she quieted.

"Would you text me the picture so I can show it to Jeff at our three o'clock meeting today?"

Mrs. Simpson picked up her cell.

"Now, let's add what, if anything, we learned from Cody's visit."

We played the recording since Mrs. Simpson had only been able to hear bits and pieces from the bedroom.

"He's so arrogant," she said.

Question: How did Cody know you were staying here?

Question: What is his new business proposition, and with whom is he consummating it?

Charlotte snorted.

Assumption: He's on his way to Tahoe.

Mrs. Simpson cocked her head. "Don't we know that?"

"No," I responded. "Just because he told us he was didn't mean he was telling the truth."

Charlotte snorted again.

Mrs. Simpson gave Charlotte a raised eyebrow. "Okay, I get it. Then another assumption is that Cody cares about Corey."

"Yes, and we're assuming that he's entering into litigation against the estate—though I think that's a pretty good assumption," I responded.

"Basically, the only thing we know for sure is that Cody was here with someone the night before my house blew up, and we know he was here this morning. Where the hell is that going to get us?" Charlotte looked frustrated.

"Well, I think it's a start," said Mrs. Simpson.

"So, did he come here this morning because he's concerned about Corey, or to intimidate Charlotte?" I asked.

I answered my own question. "Both, I think. There was one thing that bothered me about what Cody said that I just can't get a handle on. What did he mean by saying taking care of Corey costs too much?"

We sat in silence. No one had an answer.

"If there's nothing else we can do about Cody, could we please talk about Corey?" Mrs. Simpson asked. "It sounds like he's in trouble, and no one is going to help him. He *is* your brother, Charlotte. And we both know how emotionally unequipped he is to handle family stress."

Charlotte broke in. "I've been giving that some thought. His old medical school roommate became a psychiatrist. They were close at one time, and his practice is in Thousand Oaks. Perhaps I could call him and see if he can drop in on Corey and do an evaluation at the same time. I know it's unusual, but if I explain the circumstances, I'll bet Kevin would see him. He has firsthand knowledge of just how fragile Corey can be."

"I think that's a good idea," said Mrs. Simpson in her command voice. "Why don't you go downstairs right now and call him?"

I was flabbergasted when Charlotte stood up without comment or complaint and headed downstairs to make the call.

I turned to Mrs. Simpson. "Can you teach me how to do that?"

She smiled wistfully. "It's a skill that takes years to learn."

Chapter 39

Mrs. Simpson and I were cleaning up the breakfast dishes when Charlotte returned.

"At first Kevin told me Corey needed to phone him directly, and all kinds of crap about confidentiality. He was nice but uncompromising. So, I told him about Dad's suspicious death, his estate provisions regarding the twins, my house blowing up, and Cody's visit. Kevin said he would go out and visit Corey this afternoon. He said while he would not breach Corey's confidentiality, he would make some general recommendations to both him and me."

"Charlotte, it was a brilliant idea to get a professional to check in on him. Let's just hope Corey will see him." Mrs. Simpson still looked concerned.

"One way or another, the visit should give us more information." I checked my watch. "I need to shower and prepare for my committee meeting. What are you two going to do today?"

"We have a three o'clock with an architect," Charlotte said.

"We do? That's a surprise," Mrs. Simpson said. "When did you make that appointment?"

"I called her before I called Kevin. We need to get started, winter's coming."

My phone chirped an incoming text as I pulled into the Snow Star parking lot. It was Ross. "This is crazy not spending time together. How about a dinner on the Sherwin side of the golf course? I could pick up a picnic dinner at Bleu and meet you with a golf cart after your committee meeting. What do you say?"

My heart grew lighter. "Definitely," I said, and headed to my meeting.

I was greeted at the conference room door by David in his Green Bay Packers jersey and Jeff Boucher in his Minnesota Vikings jersey. Each had a plate of cookies decorated like footballs and cheerleaders. I noticed they were only handing out the football cookies.

The mood in the room was high and I knew from experience it was going to be difficult to bring focus to the tasks at hand. But precisely at three o'clock, Linda called the meeting to order. "It's apparent everyone has read the LA Times article. I thought we would start this afternoon by separating fact from fiction, then we can address the more mundane chore of pulling the gala off."

She had everyone's attention.

"Fact: We've had several NFL players offer to serve as waiters for the Awards dinner." She turned to Brian. "How many of those offers did we accept?"

"Twenty. Some will work in the bar, others in the dining room."

"And how many have we turned down?"

"Another twenty, and offers are still coming in."

"Any Packers?" David asked from the rear of the room. "Any Vikings?" he added as he looked at Jeff.

Brian smiled. "One of each."

Jeff and David growled at one another.

"Fiction: Cheerleaders will perform during the gala. There were some offers but we declined. They would compete with, not add to the scheduled activities."

An "Awww" rose from the back of the room.

"Fact: We are fully subscribed. We cannot accept any more golfers, or for that matter, house any more visitors. For those of you who had the forethought to purchase your foursome when they first came available, I applaud you. Not everyone did."

Tony stood. For once he wasn't dressed in bike clothes. "I think the Mayor and the Town Manager should participate. After all, this is one of the biggest events we've ever had in Mammoth." He turned to me and said, "J, why don't they ride in your foursome?"

"Sorry, Tony, my foursome is full."

"Whoever is in your foursome, they can't be as important as our town officials."

"Actually . . ."

Fortunately, Linda interrupted me. "I'll look around for you, Tony, but I wouldn't make any promises you can't keep. Perhaps they should have purchased tickets before the newspaper article came out."

Linda continued. "Fact: Brunch with a member of royalty will be auctioned off, though that person's name will not be made public until the auction."

There was some light applause.

"Fact: We've received offers from other dignitaries to be auctioned, but we decided not to accept. Berta, Kate, and I believe that less is definitely more. And we do not want to trivialize the commitments of those we asked and who accepted."

Most everyone at the table was nodding in agreement.

"Fact: In addition to having sold out all our foursomes, we've received some generous financial donations that have placed us over our million-dollar goal." This time there were cheers and applause from everyone in the room. "All of which will be acknowledged in our program and press statements. This does not mean; however, we can slack off. We need to ensure our auction brings in big bucks. It's for our Mono County families. Besides, if this is going to be, and I quote, an international model for fundraising, let's knock it out of the park."

More hoots and hollers.

"Now let's get down to the business of putting this event on."

Each committee member made a report. I noticed Olli was seated between Berta and Helen. John sat four seats way from the trio, staring at Olli. When it was Tony's turn, he boasted that since the LA Times article had come out many business owners who'd turned him down for contributing items to the gift baskets had called with a change of heart. "But my best news," he said with obvious pride, "Is that our local brewing company is going to come out with a limited edition nonalcoholic brew they are calling "Labor Day Hope."

After the applause died down, he added, "Labor Day Hope will not only be available for the event, but they'll sell it at local establishments, with a portion of the profits going to the charity."

Another round of applause.

Jeff Boucher made the final presentation, listing a number of activities planned beginning Friday of Labor Day weekend, ending Tuesday. He said a number of local celebrities, including one of the town's Olympians, had volunteered to help, assuring that each event had its own leader. The events program would be included in the registration mailing to all participants.

Then David brought in the drink cart and everyone started talking.

Chapter 40

I found Jeff and David in the back of the room, munching on the last of the cheerleaders. "Do you mind stepping outside for a moment?" I asked Jeff. Over my shoulder I saw Tony making a beeline toward me. "I'd like to talk to you in private. It'll only take a minute."

Following my gaze, Jeff said. "I'll be right there." I turned to leave, but Jeff remained in place.

As Tony approached, he yelled, "J, I need to talk to you."

Jeff timed his move to follow perfectly, blocking Tony's exit to pursue me. "Sorry, Tony, J and I are about to have a meeting. Maybe you can catch her later."

Tony looked up at Jeff who stood six plus inches taller, and gritted his teeth. "When you're through, tell her I'm waiting and that it's important."

I was fumbling with my cell phone, trying to find the picture of Stephanie, when Jeff reached me. "Thanks, Jeff, that was brilliant." I found what I was looking for and held the phone up. "Is this the woman you saw with Cody at the bar and again in his car?"

Jeff barely looked at the photo before saying, "That's her. Who's the old dude with her?"

"Cody's father." Realizing I probably just revealed more than I should have, I added. "Not to freak you out, but the police chief will probably contact you about seeing Cody and his girlfriend. So best not to say anything to anyone since it's part of an active investigation."

Jeff laughed—the kind of genuine laugh that makes people happy. "You sound like someone off a cop show, J. But don't worry. I won't say anything. And tell Ian if he wants to talk to me, it's his turn to buy."

"Thanks, Jeff. Are you going back in?"

"Yeah. David and I are going to the Chip Shot for a beer after everyone leaves. You?"

"Nope. As soon as I share your photo confirmation with Ian, I have a date."

"Lucky you. Say hi to Ross for me."

I responded with a wink.

Ian came on the line just as I reached Ross in a golf cart next to my car. I covered the phone and whispered "Ian Williams." Ross gestured to take my time; we were not in a hurry.

"I just spoke with Jeff Boucher and he confirmed that it was Stephanie Gates who was with Cody in Nevados the night before the bomb went off, and again today she was waiting in Cody's car."

"What do you mean 'that's nice but it doesn't matter'?"

"LAPD already has a suspect? For both the suspicious death and the bombing? Who?" I knew my voice was rising, but I couldn't help it.

"The *maid?* They didn't have a maid."

"Margaret Bouvier was *not* the *maid.*" I was beginning to sound like Charlotte. "And she did *not* abscond with valuables and leave the country. She's staying with me. And if the LAPD wants to know where she is they should speak with the security firm that's taking care of the estate, *not* one of the suspects and a person who has been banned from going onto the estate."

"I will *not* calm down. How can you guys mess this up so badly?"

"*No.* Not tonight. Mrs. Simpson . . ."

"Mrs. Simpson is Margaret Bouvier."

"*No.* It's not an alias. It's a nickname."

"Why don't you—just you—come out to the house tomorrow morning and Mrs. Simpson, Charlotte, and I will explain what's happening. Then you can explain it to the LAPD."

"How about ten?"

"Do you really want to see Charlotte before she's had coffee?"

"Yes, we'll serve you breakfast."

I was saddened when I looked up to see a very confused Ross. In pre-Olli times Ross would have known everything I knew. But that had changed, at least for the time being.

I opened my mouth to explain, but I didn't know where to begin.

He put his arm around me and drew me to him. "We have all night." He guided me to the passenger side of the golf cart.

Just as he got in his side, Tony came around the corner and said, "J, I've been looking all over for you. We have to talk."

Ross shook his head. "Not tonight, Tony. Tonight, she's mine." We sped off toward the fourth fairway.

We decided that all "business" would be discussed on the ride out, and once we arrived the evening would be about us. So, I quickly filled him in on Charlotte, Mrs. Simpson, and the drama surrounding them. Ross laughed when he heard how Mrs. Simpson got her name; and worried when he learned it might have been Charlotte's brother who planted the bomb. He told me not much had changed with Olli. By day she was involved in work and relatively happy, by night still paranoid and withdrawn. We finished just as we arrived at our destination.

The fourth hole of the Snow Star's Sherwin course is bordered on one side by a spectacular meadow just beneath the Sherwin Range. Some of the most breathtaking sunsets are where the Sherwin Range and Mammoth Mountain meet. We reached our spot along the meadow just in time to spread a blanket, set out the picnic, and pour the wine before the sun began its elegant journey to the other side of the world. When the last of the rays were vanishing, we said goodnight to the sun, and turned to be with one another. Ross had even remembered electric candles, so as the twilight inevitably dimmed, we could still see one another perfectly. I felt the happiest I had in a very long time.

Chapter 41

I was up with the dawn birds. The house was quiet. After making a cappuccino, I left a note on the coffeemaker telling Charlotte and Mrs. Simpson about our ten o'clock breakfast meeting. Then I stole away to my bedroom to make notes for our meeting with Ian. It seemed important for some reason to get the chronology right. List making once again.

Fifteen years ago, Charlotte's mother hires an assistant (show photo) they call Mrs. Simpson. Mother is diagnosed with cancer and Mrs. Simpson stays with her through illness. When the mother dies, Mrs. Simpson takes over running of household. Lives in one of three cottages on property. (Brothers live in other two).

Charlotte's father drowns. Police later decide to investigate as a suspicious death.

Charlotte returns home. Learns father left live-in (Stephanie Gates) only fifty thousand dollars of a 471-million-dollar estate. Live-in claims they were engaged and will contest the estate. Father also left instructions that twin sons must move out within a month and support themselves for two years or they will be disinherited. If Charlotte agrees, this final amendment to trust could be nullified; she refuses. If sons are disinherited, Charlotte and a designated charity will split estate.

While Charlotte is in Southern California her employee moves into her house with his girlfriend and trashes it.

Discovered only because I needed to pick up an item for Charlotte and overnight it to her. Employee was arrested and fired.

The same day Charlotte returns home, her garage and half her house blow up. Only reason she isn't killed is because she's taking me home.

Father's attorney wants to settle with live-in because there is "plenty of money to go around." Charlotte fires attorney. Hires new attorney.

Live-in calls Charlotte to vent anger that Mrs. Simpson— whom live-in refers to as the maid—received a larger bequest than she. (Do not know whether live-in knew this for a fact.)

Live-in and twins threaten to take legal action against estate, but to date no actual documents have been filed.

New attorney reviews father's files and finds draft of a pre-nuptial agreement naming Margaret Bouvier, aka Mrs. Simpson, as his intended.

This past Tuesday Charlotte's brother Cody shows up on my doorstep at dawn. (Meeting recorded).

Jeff Boucher comes to deliver an envelope to me. Cody passes him on way out the house. Jeff recognizes Cody who he claims he drank with at Nevados on July 15—the night before Charlotte's garage/house explosion. Jeff states Cody was with a woman at the bar, the same woman he just passed waiting in Cody's car.

Later Tuesday I show Jeff a picture of Stephanie Gates, and he confirms it is the same woman who was with Cody on July 15, and again yesterday.

I was rereading the timeline when there was a sharp knock on my door and Charlotte burst in. "What's this meeting with the Chief about?"

If Charlotte heard the truth—law enforcement's assumption 'the maid did it'—she would go ballistic. "I want to review the sequence of events from the time your father died through yesterday. It would probably also be beneficial for Ian to meet Mrs. Simpson." I handed her my iPad. "Why don't you read this chronology while I get breakfast started."

She looked suspicious as she took the tablet. "Mrs. Simpson has breakfast under control. And it's a good thing. It's almost ten."

I'd lost track of the time. "Let me put something on and I'll be right out."

Before either of us could utter another word, there was a loud knock on the front door.

It was obvious Charlotte thought something wasn't right about this meeting as she returned the iPad and ran downstairs to answer the door.

I stepped into my sweats before Charlotte reached the mudroom and rushed down behind her. I wanted to control the conversation we were about to have. We greeted Ian together. His response surprised both of us. Pointing to Charlotte's car in the driveway, he asked. "Who owns the silver Toyota?"

"I do. Why?" Charlotte snapped, alarmed.

"Someone doesn't like you. Or did you already know about the graffiti on your car?"

We ran out to see what Ian was talking about. Crudely spray-painted in red on the driver's side of the car was the word, "KABOOM."

"*Shit.*" Charlotte screamed so loudly Mrs. Simpson came out to the upstairs front deck to see what was happening. "*Shit, shit, shit.*"

I glared at Ian who was making little attempt to hide his amusement, and tried to get Charlotte to calm down. Mrs. Simpson took control of the situation. "Charlotte, stop it and come inside now," she commanded from the deck.

Unbelievably, Charlotte obeyed. Leaving Ian and me in the driveway. I was stupefied.

When we reached the dining room, Mrs. Simpson was talking in calm, hushed tones. As she turned to fetch something from the kitchen, she saw us. She held out her hand to Ian. "I'm Marge Bouvier, but you may call me Mrs. Simpson—everyone does."

She asked us to be seated, so I went to get the chronology.

I returned with the iPad just in time to hear Charlotte say, "You're a goddamn cop. What're you going to do about my car?"

"Charlotte . . ." Mrs. Simpson warned sternly.

"Well, yesterday morning my brother surprises us with pre-dawn visit, then last night we see Zach partying at Nevados like there's no tomorrow," she whined. "So, w-h-a-t are you going to do?"

Ian was unperturbed. "After breakfast you can come down to the station and file a report."

Charlotte stormed, "You don't think it's significant the vandalism in question is KABOOM written on the side of my car? A car, which, by the way, should be residing in my garage, but that garage was blown up? Or that two of the prime suspects in the destruction of my house were nearby when the vandalism occurred? Or, for that matter, that my brother seems to have been in Mammoth on only two occasions in years: the day before my house was bombed, and the day my car was vandalized? We damn well better talk about it before you leave."

Mrs. Simpson came between the pair, and led each by the arm towards the dining table. "The food is hot *now*. It won't be in few minutes."

The room was quiet while I served fresh-squeezed grapefruit juice, and Mrs. Simpson passed around melon, berries, toast, eggs, pancakes, and bacon.

Surreptitiously Mrs. Simpson and I looked at one another. It was becoming clear the pressure of her father's death, her brothers' dysfunction, and the destruction of her house were getting to Charlotte more than she had been letting on.

Chapter 42

"So why do people call you Mrs. Simpson? Is it your married name or are you divorced?" Ian asked while piling food onto his plate and ignoring Charlotte's death stare.

Ian might as well have told Mrs. Simpson she was under arrest.

Charlotte leaped up, looking outraged. "What's this about? *Now* you're accusing Mrs. Simpson of something? I think you better leave."

"Charlotte, please sit down. It's obvious Chief Williams came here to question me," she said. Isn't that right, Chief?"

Ian colored. "Actually, it is."

Mrs. Simpson placed a hand on Charlotte's shoulder and gently pushed her back into her chair. "Charlotte, I *am* going to answer Chief Williams's questions, and you *are* going to remain silent." She turned to me, "I guess the picture is the easiest way to explain the pseudonym. It's downstairs in the box. Do you mind getting it, J?"

Charlotte began to rise and Mrs. Simpson placed a firm hand on her arm. "Not you, Charlotte." A little more gently she added, "I want you close."

It took me a moment to find the picture, which somehow had managed to work itself to the bottom of the box. As I headed back upstairs I heard Charlotte yell. "What are you saying? You think Mrs. Simpson stole her own engagement ring? Did you learn how to be a cop by watching late-century crime shows?"

The scene couldn't have been much worse. Charlotte was in Ian's face. He looked ready to pull his gun, and Mrs. Simpson was in tears.

"Stop," I intervened. "Charlotte, please be quiet! Ian, I said we could meet over breakfast because I believed we could share everything we've learned, in hopes it would provide you with additional information. If this is an interrogation, I'll ask Mrs. Simpson to remain silent while I call an attorney."

Ian said, "I just said that the ring Ms. Bouvier . . . er, Mrs. Simpson has on matches the description of an item purchased by the deceased for his fiancé, which Ms. Gates claims to be."

Charlotte turned beet red and opened her mouth to object. "Charlotte, would you please get Mrs. Simpson some Kleenex and keep your mouth shut," I begged in desperation.

"It would be helpful if you would explain what you know, Ian. When you're through, we'll walk you through Ms. Bouvier's nickname, why she's in possession of her ring, and the chronology of events that should help you direct your attention—as well as the LAPD's—in a more fruitful direction."

Ian sighed. Loudly. "With the explosion coming so quickly after Mr. Caron's death, the LAPD and I have been working together on the premise the two events are connected."

Charlotte exhaled loudly.

"Because Mr. Caron's death was suspicious, the team wanted to know what he'd been doing in the days leading up to his demise. This included looking for any unusual financial activity." Ian poured an obscene amount of syrup on his pancakes. Turning to Charlotte, who was trying to stare him down, he continued. "For an extremely well-to-do man, your father was quite frugal. So, when we learned that he had purchased a thirty-seven-thousand-dollar ring . . ."

Mrs. Simpson, Charlotte, and I gasped in unison.

". . . we became interested. Especially since we'd asked Ms. Gates in multiple interviews if she had proof of her engagement to Mr. Caron. We were looking for something like a ring, a prenuptial agreement, even communications referring to the engagement or wedding plans. She gave us nothing. So, an officer was sent to the jewelry store to interview the person who sold Mr. Caron the ring. The store owner remembered the sale quite well." He picked up a slice of bacon and took a bite. "I mean who wouldn't? You don't make a thirty-seven-thousand-dollar sale every day."

I cleared my throat, and gestured, hoping to get back on track.

"Anyway, the owner said that no one was with Mr. Caron, but he, quote: 'wanted the most beautiful sapphire for the most beautiful woman in the world'."

Mrs. Simpson sucked in her breath. Fresh tears came to her eyes but she made no move to brush them away.

Ian took a notebook out of his back pants pocket. He rifled through it until he found what he was looking for. "Mr. Lucia also quoted Caron as saying: 'How can a guy get so lucky twice in one lifetime'?"

To his chagrin he looked up and saw all three women crying. Ian took a large bite of his pancakes and waited for the box of tissues to make its way around the table.

He had finished his plate and was helping himself to seconds, or was it thirds, by the time we had composed ourselves.

"Since Ms. Gates was living with Mr. Caron, we assumed the ring had been purchased for her. I was just a little surprised to see it on Ms. Bouvier's finger."

I picked up the fifteen-year-old picture and handed it to Ian. "Thanks for explaining, Ian. Now it's time to put everything in order. First, this picture was taken when Marge first went to work for the Caron's. It should explain her nickname."

Ian quickly swallowed his food, and then let out a loud guffaw. "Mrs. Simpson! I get it! The TV show. The Simpsons! The mom with blue hair!"

Charlotte rolled her eyes.

I went through the chronology I'd drafted.

Ian's eyes widened when he heard the value of the estate was 471 million.

Charlotte rolled her eyes and shook her head.

He scribbled furiously as I explained the trust amendment the twins were so upset about.

He straightened upon hearing about the name on the prenuptial agreement, and whispered, "I'm sorry" to Mrs. Simpson. He asked for an electronic copy of the prenuptial and Nathan's information so he could send it to the LAPD.

Although he'd heard it before, Ian listened to the tape of Cody's visit, and continued to write in his notebook.

When I finished, he asked me to email him a copy of the chronology. "I should have come and talked to you sooner, ladies. This was extremely helpful." To Charlotte, he added, "It also puts the vandalism of your car in a new light. I'm sorry for not treating the incident with the seriousness it deserves when I first arrived. I really do, however, need to have you file a report. Would it be possible for you to follow me down to the station now? I would like to include it in the package I send the LAPD so they also can see the broader picture."

Charlotte made a show of looking at her watch. "Then we better make it now, because Mrs. Simpson and I have a one o'clock meeting with the architect."

Ian shoveled a few more bites of pancake into his mouth. "Well then, I guess we better go," he said, his mouth very full. He gave an awkwardly gracious smile to Mrs. Simpson, and swallowed. "Thanks for the best breakfast I've had in years." Glancing at Charlotte, he amended. "The best breakfast *food* I've had in years. And, Mrs. Simpson, I'm uh, sorry for, uh, your loss."

"Not so quick. Mrs. Simpson is coming with me," Charlotte said, heading downstairs.

"I need to clean up the dishes," Mrs. Simpson protested.

"No need," I said, glancing at the table. Ian's plate was the only one scraped clean. The other three had barely been touched.

As we all walked downstairs onto the porch I was alarmed to see Mary and Bob standing next to Charlotte's car. Their arms were outstretched as if to bar our passage. They adamantly shook their heads 'no'.

"Stop," I yelled. "Don't go near Charlotte's car."

My three companions looked at me as if I were mad. Only Mrs. Simpson hesitated. Charlotte and Ian kept going.

"I . . . I think the car is booby-trapped. It could be a bomb." I hoped I wasn't misreading Mary and Bob's message.

Charlotte and Ian froze in their tracks. "Why would you say that?"

"Please. It's just a feeling I have. If I'm wrong, I'm sorry. But please don't go near that car until someone examines it. Please."

Despite his clear skepticism, Ian called for his bomb expert.

Chapter 43

We went back upstairs and the wait commenced. Ian stood on the back deck making calls. Mrs. Simpson cleared the dishes from the table. I put them in the dishwasher. Charlotte paced. Every so often Ian stuck his head through the French doors and said to me, "I hope this feeling of yours pans out." Charlotte would glare at Ian until he retreated outside.

What seemed like hours later—in truth, it was a matter of minutes—Ian announced his guy had arrived, and we were to stay in the back of the house and away from any windows until he returned. I could tell Charlotte was about to make a smart-ass comment when she was distracted by the chirping of her phone. She answered it as she moved toward the back deck. Mrs. Simpson and I busied ourselves brewing cappuccinos.

When our coffees were finished, our conversation petered out, and no one had returned, we turned our attention to our smart phones. Mrs. Simpson played a game that made her phone ding periodically, while I reviewed my emails. Or to be more precise, the one email that awaited me.

It was from Linda. *I'm at my wit's end. John doesn't do anything except interfere and follow Olli around. Have you spoken with her yet? If you have, whatever you suggested didn't work. Help!*

I was ashamed of myself. Since I had no desire to talk with Olli and discover yet another of her remarkable talents, I'd simply ignored my promise to Linda. Considering options, I decided to start with an email to Olli. An email could be carefully worded. An email could provide Olli with time to think through how she wanted to handle John without being placed on the spot. Most importantly, an email could still fulfill my commitment without having to meet face to face with her.

In the middle of formulating the message, Charlotte burst back into the house, looking alarmed. "You're never going to believe this."

At the same time Ian walked up the stairs. "You all need to leave. In fact, I have officers evacuating the neighborhood. Looks like your intuition is working, J. We found a bomb."

Ian's announcement had the impact of a fire alarm. For a moment, I froze, and then flew into action, grabbing my iPad, phone, and purse. Mrs. Simpson said there was something in her room she had to get and rushed off. Charlotte had turned chalk-white.

Ian gently guided her downstairs. I brought up the rear. When Mrs. Simpson returned, Ian handed us off to one of the growing number of police officers who had appeared on the street. "Take them wherever they want to go." He whispered to me, "Text me where you land. I'll come pick the three of you up as soon as this is resolved—one way or another. Don't talk to anyone, not even another police officer, until we've spoken." He started to turn away, and then grabbed me by the arm. "No one. Talk to no one."

Ian's vehemence frightened me, but another problem loomed: Where were we going to go? What was left of Charlotte's house was being demolished—an action required by fire officials. Olli was living with Ross. If I went to a friend's house they would want to know why. Finally, I made a decision. On the way to the officer's car down the street, I called the Westin, checked that they had a room that could be immediately occupied, reserved it, told the reservations clerk what I wanted in the room, then texted Ian our destination. By the time the cop asked where we were going, I could tell him.

Mrs. Simpson and Charlotte were still in a mild state of shock as we entered room 217. Both followed me without comment or question. Mrs. Simpson was the first to speak. "What's all this?" she asked, sweeping her arm. I wasn't sure if she was referring to the suite or to the room service table, which held a six-pack of Pellegrino, sliced lemons, two bottles of Rombauer chardonnay, and a large cheese and fruit tray.

I explained the dilemma of finding a place to retreat. She looked confused until I added Ian's warning against speaking with anyone.

"And the food?" she asked.

"Well, judging from the amount of food I tossed out when we were cleaning up from breakfast, I suspect none of us has eaten since last night. And it's now midafternoon."

Charlotte came out of her stupor when I mentioned the time of day. "We missed our meeting with the architect."

Mrs. Simpson put an arm around her shoulders. "I think the architect will understand once we can explain." She turned to Charlotte and looked directly into her eyes. "Are you okay? You looked upset even before Ian told us about the bomb."

Charlotte fell into a large, gray upholstered side chair. "That was Kevin who called. He said Corey was depressed and uncommunicative." She put her head in her hands. "It seems he tried for more than an hour to engage him, but Corey just stared at him while he clutched his cell phone between his palms. Or at least that was what Kevin thought he was holding. I'm not clear how he figured it out, but at some point, Corey's grip must have slipped because it was a Beretta, not a phone."

"A gun?" Mrs. Simpson cried. "What was he doing with a gun?"

"That was Kevin's first concern. As he put it, he casually asked Corey if he could see his gun. And Corey handed it to him. It wasn't loaded. Kevin asked why he had the gun. Corey finally looked at Kevin and said he would only tell Mrs. Simpson."

Mrs. Simpson inhaled sharply.

"I had to explain to Kevin who Mrs. Simpson was. Kevin said he didn't want to leave Corey by himself, so with no other alternatives, he asked him to come home with him. He convinced Corey with the promise he would find Mrs. Simpson. Apparently, that's all it took. Kevin packed some of Corey's clothes, and drove him back to his place."

She turned a sad face to Mrs. Simpson. "I promised you and I would fly down and see them tomorrow. I hope that's all right with you?"

"Of course, it is."

We sat stunned. Charlotte broke the silence. "I think I'd like a glass of that wine, if you don't mind, J. It's not every day you find out your brother is possibly suicidal, *and* someone puts a bomb in your car.

Chapter 44

For a few minutes, we sat, still a little stunned, sipping on the wine. Partly to break the silence, and partly because I was curious, I asked Mrs. Simpson, "It's none of my business, but may I ask, what did you rush downstairs to get before we were evacuated?"

Her cheeks turned pink.

"I'm sorry. I didn't mean be intrusive."

Charlotte's interest was piqued. "Come on, Mrs. Simpson, tell us. What couldn't you leave behind?"

"Charlotte," I frowned at her.

Mrs. Simpson shook her head. "You know Charlotte. She doesn't let things go." She went to her large purse and pulled out a well-worn, blue and green tartan flannel shirt.

Her blush was in full bloom. "One night when your father and I were talking I got chilled. He went to his closet and draped this shirt around my shoulders." She took a long slow breath. "And I never returned it."

There was a long silence. I think we all got lost in the romantic image until I was startled out of it by a loud rap on the door.

A little put out by his timing, I yelled, "Come on in, Ian. The door is unlocked."

He walked in, looked around the room, and made a beeline for the cheese and fruit tray. "You're one lucky little lady, Charlotte. All you had to do was put the car in reverse and BOOM."

Charlotte looked sick.

"That was sensitively phrased," I said.

Ian looked chagrined. "Sorry."

"Does this mean we can go home now?" Charlotte asked.

"Afraid not. It's going to be a few more hours."

"J, you didn't talk to anyone about what happened, did you?"

"No." I was getting a little annoyed. "But I don't understand why we had to keep quiet. By now most of the town knows about the bomb."

"Yeah, but they don't know that the reason we looked for a bomb was because *you* had a *feeling* something was wrong. Not even my officers know that."

"J had a feeling. What's the big deal? It saved my life, after all," Charlotte said.

Ian sat down on the couch with his plate of cheese and crackers and a glass of wine. "I've gotten to know J over the last year, so I'm used to her prescience. Hell, I kind of expect it from her now. But the rest of the force might find it a little suspicious."

"Ian, what do you mean?" I asked, alarmed.

He gestured for me to calm down. "Less than two weeks ago you just happened to need a ride home from the grocery store when you saw Charlotte. She gave you a ride, and when she reached her house, she automatically hit the garage door opener. But she didn't turn in because she had to drop you off at the top of the street. That saved her life. Today, you look at a car and say, I have a feeling it's booby-trapped? Then we find a bomb magnetically attached to the bottom of the car just under the driver's seat. There's no way you could've seen it. But you stopped Charlotte anyway, and once again inadvertently saved her life."

Charlotte was out of her chair and in Ian's face. "Are you accusing J of having something to do with the bombs?"

"No, but someone who doesn't know J might."

Mrs. Simpson took Charlotte by the hand and led her back to her chair. "I see what you're saying, Chief. But we can't change the facts." She studied him closely. "Can we?"

Ian smiled. "That's why I didn't want you to say anything until we spoke. When our bomb expert asked how we knew there might be a bomb, I told them I had a feeling. I said it was cop instinct."

"You mean you wanted to look like the hero," Charlotte snapped.

"No, Charlotte," I said, comprehension dawning. "Ian was stopping me from becoming the red herring in the investigation, and from wasting a lot of my time being questioned."

Ian nodded, smiled, and ate a hunk of Camembert on a wheat cracker.

As he was leaving, he said he'd call or text when the coast was clear for us to go home. He asked that each of us schedule an interview the next day at the station. Charlotte said she and Mrs. Simpson could be there first thing in the morning, because they would be on the early afternoon flight to LA for a family emergency.

Ian looked alarmed. "When will you be back?"

"Friday. Saturday at the latest."

"Okay, we'll interview you at eight tomorrow morning, but I want you check in with me when you return."

We finally received the all clear around seven. Since we had no vehicle, and it was only five blocks home, we walked. The fresh mountain air was a welcome relief after our confinement. As we strolled up our street I noticed Ross's car stood where Charlotte's had been. And Ross was on the upstairs deck, pacing while he talked on his cell.

We were in the driveway when he saw us. "J, I've been calling and texting. Where have you been? I came by to see you more than two hours ago and the street was full of cops. They said there was a car bomb. Did someone try to blow you up? I've been out of my mind with worry."

"Sorry. I turned off my phone when it all started and forgot to turn it back on. It's been a long day. I'll be up and explain everything." I turned to Charlotte and Mrs. Simpson. "Neither of you touched the food. Want me to make you something? You must be famished. I know I am."

They both looked spent. Charlotte held up the second bottle of wine, which had not been opened. "I think I'll just come up and get a couple of glasses, and Mrs. Simpson and I will have this for dinner."

Mrs. Simpson's whose arms were crossed, gently caressing the sleeves of the flannel shirt she was wearing, nodded in agreement.

When we were alone, Ross took me in his arms, and held me tight. "This isn't working, J. I can't stand not knowing where you are or what you're doing. When Olli and Charlotte have returned to their own lives, we need to talk."

I was no longer hungry. We called it an early night.

Chapter 45

Friday afternoon found me impatiently standing in a long post office line to pick up a package. I spent the time brooding that I still hadn't called, texted, or emailed Olli to discuss John—as I'd promised Linda. My guilt trip was interrupted when a postal employee from the back office came out and collected the yellow cards that indicated a package was waiting for its holder. At least ten of us rushed forward to thrust our cards in the worker's hands. Olli was one of them.

"J, it's so good to see you. It's been a while."

"Actually, Olli," I said sheepishly, "I was just thinking about you. I wanted to talk to you about . . ." Looking around, I saw several people who seemed interested in why I wanted to talk to Olli. "Can we talk outside as soon as we get our packages?"

Moments later, parcels in hand, we headed toward a bench under the trees. Olli was talking about something that had happened in one of her yoga classes, but I wasn't listening. I was too busy trying to come up with the right words so I wouldn't sound snarky when I asked about John. I must have really been lost in thought, because Olli gently shook my arm.

"J, your phone is ringing."

Embarrassed, I looked at caller ID. It was Charlotte. "Sorry, Olli, I have to take this."

Olli flicked her hand. "Don't worry. I can wait."

"Charlotte, is everything okay?" I answered.

"No, I'm at the post office. Why?"

I briefly glanced at Olli. "I'm just going to meet with a friend."

"If it's that important, I guess so."

"Give me ten minutes."

I held my hands up in a shrug. "Go," Olli said. "That sounds important."

I felt a mixture of relief and frustration. I had a legitimate reason to postpone our conversation. On the other hand, we'd have to go through all this again.

"Instead, have a drink with me this evening, J. We can talk then. Let's say Le Coquetier at six?"

Before I could come up with an excuse, Olli was gone.

On my way home Kate phoned.

"Hi, Kate. Don't have time to talk. Can I call back later?"

"It's okay, J. If you have time this weekend, call and we can catch up. Just wanted you to know that Nathan and I can't make your big golf tournament next week. He's got a new client, and just can't get away. Sorry."

"I'm the one who's sorry." And I was more than sorry, I was disappointed. I missed Kate and Nathan. "You should tell

Nathan you're going to miss meeting lots of celebrities, politicos, and possibly some royalty."

"Really?" Kate asked. Then laughing, added, "If I didn't suck at golf so badly, I'd come by myself."

"Kate, it's not about playing golf. It's about charitizing."

"Charitizing?"

"Participating in activities to raise funds for important causes."

"Hmmm. If you're sure no one will care about how I golf, I'm in. Fortunately, I called you before I cancelled our room reservation."

"It's a full house, but you could stay here."

"No way. I was lucky enough to score one of the rooms at Couloir. You may want to stay with me."

"It's a pretty spectacular place. I just might take you up on it."

My phone started to vibrate as I entered the house. "Uh oh. There's the call I've been waiting for. Talk to you later."

"How's your brother, Charlotte?" I asked as I walked upstairs. "For that matter, how are you and Mrs. Simpson?"

Charlotte let out a long breath. "So much has happened, I don't know where to begin."

I didn't need to state the obvious. She continued. "When we arrived in LA we drove straight to Kevin's house. He seemed pretty relieved to see us. He told us Corey was waiting, and took us to him.

"As Kevin led us through the house, I noticed four people sitting in a den. They weren't talking, just sitting there. They seemed out of place. I asked Kevin who they were and he told us they were waiting to talk to Corey. Before I could pose any more questions, Kevin said he would explain *after* we saw my brother.

"When we reached a closed door at the back of the house, Kevin told us to go in, and he would wait for us in the hall. Neither Mrs. Simpson nor I knew what to expect, but we did as we were instructed.

"We found Corey pacing in Kevin's study." Charlotte snickered. "Before you ask, it's a family trait."

Her voice quickly returned to its somber note. "I don't think Corey even saw me. As soon as we entered he rushed up to Mrs. Simpson, and told her he'd been looking all over for her. J, Mrs. Simpson was so calm. She led Corey to a chair, pulled one up across from him, so close their knees almost touched. She asked: 'What do you want to talk to me about, Corey.' And then he told her how he killed Dad."

"It was so crazy. I'm still not sure how it happened. I don't know if I told you but I'm taking a class to get my scuba diving certification. I heard you tell someone you wanted to learn, and thought maybe I could teach you. Anyway, that Thursday I went down to the pool with my tank and weight belt to get more comfortable with the equipment. I was in a really good mood because I finally made a decision about you." He paused and reached for Mrs. Simpson's hands. She kept them clasped in her lap; he went on.

"Dad was just getting out of the pool. When he saw me, he said, 'You look unusually happy, Corey. What's up?' So, I told him I was going to ask you to marry me." He glanced longingly at Mrs. Simpson, who did not react. She just seemed attentive, waiting to hear what Corey had to say.

Corey scowled. *"Instead of telling me how happy he was for me, Dad laughed."* Corey started to stand, but Mrs. Simpson gently pulled him back into the chair and asked him to continue.

"He . . . he said: 'So am I.'" Corey's voice was rising. Mrs. Simpson's expression never changed.

"I told him he was going to marry Stephanie, and I was going to marry you. Dad said 'no,' Stephanie was just living at the house long enough to rent her own place, then she was moving out. So . . . so, I told him he couldn't have you just because Stephanie was moving out. It wasn't fair. YOU WERE MINE.

"The last thing I remember is Dad smiling and shaking his head as if I were a little kid." Corey's hands went to his face, and he began to weep.

I stood in the corner watching; Mrs. Simpson never moved. Eventually, Corey cried, *"I didn't mean to do it. I mean one minute he's treating me like a child and telling me he's going to marry you, and the next he's floating in the water with blood all over the side of his head. And . . . and . . . blood all over the side of my scuba tank."*

Mrs. Simpson and I watched while Corey cried like a four-year-old, then composed himself back into his full forty years. Finally, he looked deeply into her eyes. *"I felt so guilty. I* thought if I could find you and explain, you would know how to make it better. When I gave up searching for you, I thought I might kill myself. I mean I killed my Dad." For the first time, he looked at me. "Our Dad," he whispered.

He stared at his knees for an eternity. "But," he said, gazing at Mrs. Simpson, "I would never want you to think of me as a coward. So, I asked Kevin to get me an attorney, and I'm turning myself in."

Finally, Mrs. Simpson spoke. "Are those the people waiting to speak with you?"

"Yeah. I'll talk to the attorney, and then we'll meet with some law enforcement people. I just wanted to see you first. I wanted you to know the truth. So, you'd know I didn't mean to kill Dad. And . . . and to ask you a question."

"What question, Corey?"

His voice broke. "Will, uh, will there ever . . . ever be a chance you would marry me?"

Tears moistened Mrs. Simpson's eyes, but none fell. She took his hand in hers. "Corey, I'm . . . I'm more like your mother or sister than I am a girlfriend."

Corey sounded earnest, and a little hopeful. "I don't care, really I don't. There are only two times when I'm happy and really know what to do—when I'm in surgery and when I'm with you."

She couldn't hold the tears back any longer. "But I do care, Corey."

I was speechless.

"Are you still there, J?" Charlotte asked. "Corey killed Dad. Can you believe it?"

"From everything you and Mrs. Simpson have told me about Corey, no, I don't believe it." Thoughts raced through my head. "Certainly he didn't plant the bombs. He doesn't sound stable enough to pull that off."

"Kevin agrees with you. For that matter, so do Mrs. Simpson and I."

My energy vanished. I sighed. "So, we're back to square one."

"Not exactly. . ."

Chapter 46

"What do you mean, not exactly?" I pleaded, beyond exasperation. *I felt like Charlotte was spoon-feeding me the information.*

"Bear with me. I want to walk you through our discoveries as they occurred."

Now *I* was pacing. "Fine. Just, please, don't drag it out."

"The first thing Mrs. Simpson and I noticed when we pulled into Dad's garage was that one of the cars was missing—a 1991 500E Mercedes sedan. When we talked to the security guard on duty, he said Stephanie came by and told him she'd left some of her belongings on the estate and needed to pick them up. So, the guard went up to her bedroom, found the box, and brought it down to her . . ."

"What does a box of old clothes have to do with anything?"

"Be patient, J." I thought I heard Charlotte giggle. Before I could call her on it, she continued. "Stephanie produced the pink slip to the missing car, and said it had been a gift from Charles, and she was taking it, too. The guard said the pink slip had all the necessary signatures, so he couldn't stop her."

"Your father gave her the car?" I was lost.

"No, he didn't. When I was here for the memorial, I went through all Dad's personal papers, and found the pink slips to his four cars, including the 500E. Besides, J, he bought that car for Mother. He would never have given it away. It held so many memories. Hell, he wouldn't let anyone even drive it, except the mechanic who kept it tuned."

"Did you call the police?"

"I was about to, when Mrs. Simpson had the foresight to ask if anyone else had been in the house while she was gone."

"And?"

"Just Cody, who needed to get his passport from the safe."

"I thought your brothers were barred from going into the house?"

"So did I," Charlotte said hotly. "Apparently five-hundred dollars buys temporary amnesia. That particular member of our security team is no longer employed."

"I'm getting really confused. Do you think Cody forged the pink slip? Why would he do that? Even if he and Stephanie are sleeping together, that's a felony. He's got to know he'll get caught sooner or later. Come to think of it, did Cody even know the combination to the safe?"

"I was sure Dad, Mrs. Simpson, and I were the only ones who knew the safe passcode. But anything is possible. We decided before we called the police, or even you, we'd better go through the safe and take inventory."

"And?" I was getting frustrated. Charlotte could be so damn dramatic.

"And, five-hundred-thousand dollars in cash that Dad kept in case of an economic emergency, and an undetermined number of gold coins were missing. But we did find an envelope addressed to me."

"Wait," Charlotte had the audacity to say. "I need to take a break. I'll call you back in five minutes."

I was beside myself. She hung up on me. I was about to let out a stream of expletives when I heard a pounding on the front door. Then I heard it open. I knew it was Ian even before he called out as he ascended the stairs, "Have you talked to Charlotte yet?"

"For the last half-hour, but then she said she'd call me back in five and disconnected."

"Good," Ian grunted. He reached the refrigerator just as the phone buzzed.

I shouted into the phone, "What the hell?"

"Put her on speaker," Ian instructed.

I reluctantly complied.

"He hasn't told you, has he?" Charlotte asked excitedly.

"No, I haven't," yelled Ian. "Where are you in the story?"

"We just found the envelope . . ."

"Great. I arrived in time for the good part."

I couldn't take it any longer. "Charlotte, what was in the fucking envelope?"

"A note from Cody, and a thumb drive with a recording on it." It was obvious she was enjoying the suspense.

"Start with the note, and quit messing with me," I said.

"Okay, okay . . . I'll read it to you."

Ian handed me a glass of chardonnay. "This might help you calm down."

I glared at him, but accepted the wine.

Charlotte began.

Charlotte, Sorry I tried to kill you, but you really gave me no choice. The day after Dad died, Stephanie came to me and showed me iPhone pictures she took of Corey whacking Dad with his scuba tank. Not sure what they were fighting about, but I couldn't have my twin go to jail. Of course, the bitch demanded money to keep quiet. If you'd agreed to void the fucking amendment, I could've paid her off. But you were so fucking self-righteous, you basically signed your own death warrant. You must lead a charmed life, though. I still can't believe neither bomb did the job. Can't hang around to try again, I've pushed my luck as it is. Took some of the money Dad owed me. It's your turn to watch out for Corey. The enclosed drive will take care of Stephanie . . . plus, technically she's driving around in a stolen car. Guess this is adios. Cody

By the time Charlotte finished, there was no wine left in my glass. "So, let me get this straight, Charlotte. One of your brothers killed your father, and the other tried to kill you?"

Ian jumped in. "Yep. I've heard of some screwed up families, but Charlotte's brothers win hands down."

I ignored Ian. "And what was on the thumb drive?"

Ian was eating; Charlotte responded. "There are two separate conversations. The first was Stephanie describing Corey hitting his father, and then blackmailing Cody. I couldn't believe it, there were a few times when Cody asked her to repeat what she just said, and she did." I could hear Charlotte smirk.

"And the second . . .?"

"Stephanie suggesting the best ways to blow me up."

"Cody left you a tape of the two of them planning the bombings?"

"No, just the blackmail demand. It appears Cody was carefully edited out of the bomb discussion. It may not be of any use in court, but it should be helpful when Stephanie is interrogated."

Ian took over. "We should have Ms. Gates in custody within twenty-four hours. It may take longer to find Cody, but we will." Then he started explaining various search strategies that would be employed.

As he droned on, I thought about Charlotte. In less than a month she'd lost her entire family, in one way or another. That was more than most people could handle, even with a Mrs. Simpson. I signaled for Ian to be quiet. He ignored me, so I took the phone off speaker mode.

"Charlotte?"

There was no response.

"Charlotte, are you still there?"

Still no response.

I didn't think she'd disconnected. I could hear muffled background sounds.

"Charlotte?"

Mrs. Simpson answered softly. "She handed me the phone and went to her room. I think it's finally all beginning to hit her, J. Not sure when we will be back. We'll probably spend the weekend here, back Monday or Tuesday."

"If I can . . ."

"Don't worry, J. I'll take care of her. With Charles gone, that's my job now."

Chapter 47

I t took a while to get rid of Ian, who crowed like he'd singlehandedly solved the mysteries of Mr. Caron's death and the bombings—instead of acknowledging Charlotte's brothers' voluntary confessions. A sense of peace entered the house as he left it. I was looking forward to the evening of drama-less solitude that lay before me. Then my cell played "Does Anyone Really Know What Time It Is," alerting me to my appointment, and all tranquility vanished. I exchanged my shorts and tee for a summer dress, ran a brush through my hair, and headed off to meet Olli.

The bar at Le Coquetier was packed. Finding a place to stand, much less sit and talk, was going to be a real challenge. When Ryan and Sue, the owners of the establishment, spotted me, they signaled me to follow them. We entered the restaurant, and the noise level decreased significantly.

We hugged as if we hadn't just seen each other last week. After pleasantries, I said, "Unfortunately, I have to go back into the crowd. I'm meeting a friend."

Sue smiled. "We know. When Olli saw how busy it was, she asked if you two could have a table in the dining room." She pointed to a table in the back corner for four where Olli was sipping on a glass of white wine—while Mary and Bob drank red.

I was so startled by the tableau I almost missed Ryan saying, "Anything for you, Olli, or Ross. You're family."

Fortunately, both Sue and Ryan returned to their tasks before I could react to their words. They didn't see my jaws clench, and my determination kick in. I couldn't help it. It felt like Olli wasn't satisfied with taking Ross away. Now she had *my* friends calling her family, and Mary and Bob were spending more time with her than with me. I couldn't take it anymore. The pressures of the last few weeks had pushed me to my limit. It was time to set things straight.

Olli gave me one of her dazzling smiles when I sat down across from her, and I lost my resolve. While I stumbled through an awkward greeting, Sue placed a drink in front of me.

"Olli said you'd like an extra cold Absolut up with two olives." Sue gave Olli an inquisitive look; Olli gave her the thumbs up, then Sue left to tend to other patrons.

Staring dumbly at the cocktail, I screamed in my head. *Dammit; don't be so damn nice; it will only make our conversation harder.*

My face must have reflected my mood. Olli said, "I'm sorry. I shouldn't have ordered for you. It's just that Ross said it was your favorite, and I thought . . ."

"No, it's not that. I just have a lot on my mind right now. Sorry for looking ungrateful. This is just what I would have ordered."

Her smile returned. "I was glad to hear you wanted to talk to me, because there's something I need to talk to you about. But you first." She looked at me expectantly.

While my head and heart fought for dominance, words would not come. I took a big swallow of my martini, trying to decide whether I should be passive, aggressive or both.

"Okay," Olli said. "I guess I'll go first. Maybe it's best to get it out of the way." She took a sip of her wine, and calmly asked. "Why don't you like me? I've tried everything I know, but nothing works. I thought if I could work with you, albeit at a distance, we would have a chance. Now, when I walk into a room, you walk in the opposite direction. If it's something I did, please tell me. I promise I won't do it again. I thought . . . I'd hoped we could be friends."

I looked at the cocktail napkin for the right words. My inner-self screamed: *Because, bitch, you're beautiful, accomplished, athletic, and everyone—and I mean everyone, including Ross and maybe even my twin—seem to love you . . . more than they love me.* I knew I was being juvenile and irrational, but I couldn't help it. When I looked up, Mary, Bob, and Olli were waiting for my response.

I took a deep breath—too many words and I would screw it up, so I simply said, "Look at you. You're everything I ever wanted to be, but didn't know how inadequate I was until I met you. I'm ashamed to say I'm jealous." I turned to see if Bob was smirking, but he and Mary were gone.

A series of emotions crossed Olli's face: surprise, outrage, finally disappointment. "So, you want to be an abused lesbian?" She spat out the words. Her hands frantically flew to her mouth as if trying to push her words back in—which only succeeded in sending both our drinks sprawling.

Cleaning up and replacing our cocktails gave us both time to calm down and process what had just happened. We were two different people by the time we were alone again.

"I didn't mean to say that. Please don't tell anyone, J. No one knows, at least not here in Mammoth."

"I won't. I promise. But are you saying Ross doesn't know?"

"No one. I came to Mammoth to hide, regroup, come up with a plan. Ross was the only person I trusted who lived in a remote location, and who I knew would ask no questions. Just be a friend."

"Weren't you two dating in high school—I mean really dating." Hearing the words come out of my mouth, I was mortified. "I'm sorry. It's really none of my business."

Olli's smile was wistful. "Oh, we were a couple all right—through our junior and senior years of high school. It wasn't until college when I realized I'd been playing the role I thought I was supposed to play instead of being me. It's hard to explain, but I went from acting to living."

I leaned forward, trying to comprehend how difficult her self-discovery must have been. "If what you're saying is true, it must be hell. I mean, every man you meet falls for you. The night we had dinner at Couloir I thought Brian and John might fight over you." Deciding to keep the conversation honest, I added. "Actually, I wouldn't have been surprised if Ross joined in the competition."

Olli gave a spontaneous, full-throated laugh. "Even if I weren't a lesbian, I'd be no competition. Ross spends most of his time either talking about you or worrying about you. By the way, did someone really try to blow you up again?"

"Not me." I told Olli about Charlotte, her father, the two bomb-related incidents, and what we'd learned that afternoon about Charlotte's father's death, and the bombs.

We talked through a second drink and dinner as if we'd known one another all our lives. I realized both of us were avoiding anything related to our love lives, which was fine with me. We were exploring friendship, and that meant building trust over time.

Over cappuccinos Olli asked, "When I saw you at the post office you said you wanted to talk to me. What about?"

Theatrically, slapping my hand to my forehead, I responded. "I completely forgot. As we know, among your many admirers is John Collins. Instead of working on the gala, he seems to be following you around. We were hoping you could find some way of redirecting his attention."

Olli shook her head. "I'm sorry, J. I've done everything I can think of, and nothing works. Every time I turn around, there he is. Sometimes I even duck into the ladies' room and surf the net, hoping when I leave he'll be gone. But no matter how long I stay in there, he's waiting nearby."

Olli pondered for a moment. "I thought this guy was supposed to have headed up an executive search firm. Either he had a big staff helping him from the beginning, or he wasn't that successful. He's an electronic-idiot. I don't even think I've ever seen him use his smartphone for anything but making calls. And, he won't go near a computer."

"That's odd. Though I know he said it was social networking rather than building talent banks one professional at a time that made him want to sell his business."

Sue came over. "Sorry to interrupt, but we're getting ready to close."

Olli and I looked around. There was no one left in the restaurant, and we could hear the last of the drinkers leaving the bar. It was past midnight. We paid our tabs with profuse apologies and big tips.

In the almost empty parking lot impulsively I asked, "Olli, are you playing in the gala golf tournament?"

She shrugged, self-deprecatingly. "When there were openings I didn't really know anyone to play with."

"I spoke with Kate earlier today . . . Yesterday. You remember Kate . . ."

Olli giggled. "Ah, oui."

I shook my head. "I still can't believe everyone speaks French but me. Anyway, Kate is coming, but Nathan had to cancel. Would you like to join our foursome? It would be Kate, Ross, you, and me."

She seemed genuinely taken aback. "Really? No, don't answer that. Absolutely. I'd love to golf with you."

"Just one condition," I said, trying to look serious.

"You don't want me to ride with Ross?" she tried to squelch a snicker.

I arched an eyebrow. "No. You can't speak French."

We hugged, and went to our cars on opposite sides of the lot. A great weight had been replaced by the possibility of a new friend. I turned to wave, and saw with dread that Mary and Bob were getting into Olli's backseat.

Halfway through the evening I'd decided Mary and Bob were letting me see them follow Olli to show how wrong I was about her. After all, they had left once Olli and I started being honest with one another. But now I knew Olli really was in danger.

Chapter 48

The next morning, I phoned Ms. Germaine.

"J, this is an unexpected pleasure. Are you checking up on us?"

Since she usually answered her own questions, I jumped in. "Lynette, I'm calling to ask a favor."

I could almost hear her click into business mode. "Certainly. I'll do whatever I can to help you. What kind of trouble are you in?"

I laughed. "Not that kind of favor, but thank you. There's a man working with the Hope for Our Children Gala committee, and something just doesn't feel right about him. Do you think you could do a thorough background check on him? I'm assuming the firm has that capacity."

"Of course, we do and I will. One question, though. Why didn't you ask Bill, I think I'm correct in believing he's on the committee?"

I'd expected the question. "Lynette, if this feeling is wrong I don't want to prejudice Bill. Does that make sense?"

"Perfect sense. I admire your forethought. Now, please tell me everything you know about this individual."

"Let's see. His name is John James Collins. He owned an executive search firm in Boston, which he started twenty years ago, and sold within the last year. He's fortyish, blond, blue-gray . . ."

Ms. Germaine interrupted. "I don't need to know what he looks like. He should be pretty easy to find. Do you have any other *relevant* facts?"

I managed to stifle a laugh. The woman would never change. "Hmm. He told me he's related to one Susanna Angelina Montoya, who owns a marketing firm in Santa Barbara. Ah . . . and, his father passed away within the last two months. His funeral was held in Cambridge, Massachusetts." I studied my memory for a moment. "I think that's it."

"That should be enough. Now let's discuss timing. Mags and I are at a spa in Ojai this weekend, returning Tuesday. This appears to be a simple search. May I get the results to you Wednesday or Thursday, or is this a rush?"

"No rush. We're going to be busy since the gala is only a week away. And even if the report comes back negative, there's really nothing much we can do about it. Mr. Collins was loaned to us by a major donor, whom we don't want to offend. As I said, this is more about a funny feeling than anything else."

"Great. I'll start working on it as soon as we return."

"Thanks, Lynette." Smiling at the thought of Mags taking time away from work, I asked. "How did you get Mags to go to a spa?"

Ms. Germaine chuckled. "Now that her brother is out of the picture, I thought it would be easy. But it wasn't. So, I promised to help her study for the Bar Exam if we could do some of the prep work here in Ojai. Worked like a charm."

With one week until the Gala, everything began to blur into fast-forward mode. Disasters followed victories, followed disasters. Somehow the committee managed to stay focused, fix the problems, and not go bonkers.

Among the almost-disasters:

The Grammy winner who was set to perform at the Friday night Rock & Bowl opening event cancelled because of illness. Fortunately, Brian was able to get one of last year's nominees for Academy of Country Music Awards Entertainer of the Year.

The company that printed the labels for the limited edition non-alcoholic beer *Labor Day Hope* misprinted all of the labels to read *Labor Day Hype*. We found a new printer and gave them a rush job.

Tony was able to collect some fantastic gifts for the gift baskets each golfer would receive, but somehow forgot the baskets needed to be assembled. Linda called the school's summer athletic director and kids from the soccer and swim programs arrived to assemble the goodies. Their only compensation request was a constant stream of pizza and soda.

The supplier called and said the fresh lobsters, crab, and scallops ordered for the awards dinner would be delayed because of a major storm moving onto the East Coast. We found our seafood on the West Coast.

Among the victories:

Four of the NFL players who had volunteered to be wait-staff for the Awards dinner, agreed to challenge guests in bowling contests at Friday night's Rock & Bowl event—as long as the guests made a donation.

Three of the more famous golfers from the Arnold Palmer era said they would play with guests—again for a sizable donation—at the establishment's golf simulators on Friday night.

When asked, a local Marathon Olympian agreed to lead a morning run each day of the event for the more athletically inclined.

But by far the biggest victory was when the auction's Royal called Roberta to say he and his wife would be in California over the Labor Day weekend. They were adamantly committed to enriching the lives of disadvantaged, abused, and neglected children. And, if invited, would like to attend the awards dinner and perhaps say a few words about the cause.

Among the smiles:

I found a sky-blue polo shirt on my front porch with "team hope" imprinted on it. There was a note from Olli. "One for you, will give one to Ross, sent one to your friend Kate. Now we are a team. Thank you."

Chapter 49

A nd suddenly it was Thursday. Preparations were being finalized. Guests would start arriving in town. In five exhausting weeks, the committee had pulled off what took most event planners a year or more.

I mentally reviewed the day ahead of me as I made a cappuccino. I needed to clean the house in the morning—a chore long neglected—since Charlotte and Mrs. Simpson would return in the afternoon. Also, requiring attention was the laundry. Every respectable piece of clothing I owned was dirty. At two o'clock the committee was to meet to go over last-minute details, and at six I was picking up Kate at the airport. I downed my coffee and got to work.

Midmorning, Ross phoned from work. After Mary and Bob got into the car with Olli the previous week, I called Ross and said we needed to be hyper-vigilant. We agreed I would call Olli once a day to check in, Ross would try to spend as much time with her as he could, and he would call each morning and let me know how the previous evening went. Fortunately, he kept reporting that Olli seemed happy and less paranoid. We kept our fingers crossed.

The last housekeeping chore of the day was to tackle my bedroom. After changing the linens, I started straightening the small desk in the corner of my room. It had become the temporary repository for all my work and gala-related documents. Underneath a schedule of gala events I found the three business cards I'd been given at Helen's when I first met

Roberta Hart and Susanna Montoya. John James Collins's card was on top. It dawned on me that I hadn't heard back from Ms. Germaine, which was quite unlike her. I thought of calling or texting, but realized by Sunday John would no longer be in Mammoth. Tossing the cards back onto the desk, I returned to my chores.

I could feel the energy even before I walked into the Snow Star conference room. It was like walking into electricity; even the air seemed charged. For the first time since the group formed, no one was paying attention to Linda, who was trying to call the meeting to order. I asked David to help her out, and went to take my seat. David let out the loudest, shrillest whistle I've ever heard.

Before all were seated, Tony asked, "Is it true we've already raised a million-two and change?"

Linda speared him with a look. "It is, but we'll have to return the money if we fail to put on the gala." Point made, she got down to business. "We have, indeed, taken in a shade more than one-million-two-hundred-thousand dollars. About a third of those dollars were donations resulting from the recent press coverage. We expect to increase this amount significantly with the proceeds from Friday's competitions, and Saturday's auction."

David started to take out a couple of bottles of champagne, but Linda told him not until after the meeting. "Brian, will you please make the first report?"

"Couloir is fully booked, with a waiting list. I brought in staff from two of my other hotels. They've already started training new staff, and will ensure our guests are taken care of. When reservations were made, we explained their accommodations would be comped, through the gala weekend. Interestingly, more than half of our guests chose to extend their stays in Mammoth through next week!"

Brian turned to Roberta. "I know you said you'd pick up the lodging, but for those guests staying with us, I'll cover it."

Roberta started to protest, but Brian cut her off. "Berta, I couldn't buy this kind of advertising. It's a gift for a new property—especially a boutique hotel."

Turning crimson, Helen stood. "I've been working with Andrea Revy, the owner of Rock & Bowl, and they're ready. We have three professional golfers who will challenge guests to a game of golf on the upstairs simulators. Each pro has chosen a California course to play . . ." Helen fumbled through a notebook. "Er . . . ah . . . the names of the courses are Spyglass Hill, Cyprus Point, and Pebble Beach." She shrugged. "Anybody ever heard of them? I'm not much of a golfer, but Andrea seems excited."

The golfers in the room laughed at Helen's expense. She blushed and continued. "In addition, the restaurant upstairs will be open. We decided since this is a casual affair, there will be a tapas buffet with wine pairings. Guests can either eat in the restaurant or on the upper deck at their leisure."

Helen took a deep breath and let it out slowly. "There's more. Downstairs, four of the twelve bowling lanes will be occupied by NFL players, challenging guests for a game and a donation. The other eight lanes will be available for anyone who wants to play. The downstairs restaurant and bar will be open. Since we have," she blushed even deeper, "a singer who

I consider the country music entertainer of *all time* performing on the downstairs deck, we decided to go with barbecue and beers. And, of course, there will be wait staff taking all drink orders wherever you are."

Helen sat down looking pleased, but a little wrung out from her report.

Linda stood up. "Not much new to report on the actual golf tournament. It's fully subscribed with a long waiting list."

Tony raised his hand.

"Yes, Tony," she said, "the Mayor and Town Manager are on the top of that list." Looking more seriously at him, she said, "Why don't you tell everyone what's in the goody baskets the golfers will receive."

"Thank you, Linda," Tony said as if he were accepting an award. "I approached this assignment . . ."

Tony didn't see Linda shake her head. "Not the process of procuring the gifts, Tony. Just the contents."

"Oh . . . well, sure. Instead of a lot of stuff, I went for a few very nice items. They include a Nike golf jacket for each player, inscribed with his or her name and 'Hope for Our Children, Snow Star Golf Club, Mammoth Lakes, California." The most special gift is a certificate for a signed Stephen Ingram fourteen-by-twenty-inch framed Eastern Sierra landscape photograph. Each participant will get to choose the photograph. And, of course, a couple of bottles of Labor Day Hope beer, and a bag of Mimi's cookies. Instead of baskets, these items have been placed in small, soft coolers, again with the name of the tournament embroidered on the side."

Tony received a round of applause—even I joined in. Nice touch with the Stephen Ingram photographs. I wondered how he pulled that one off.

Bill, David, and Jeff Boucher made brief reports. But the audience was getting restless. I could feel the meeting winding down. As Jeff finished, David walked over to open champagne. But, again Linda held up her hand.

"One last order of business. There'll be many wealthy and well-known people attending this weekend. I've emailed you the roster of participants, and would like you to look it over carefully. We need to make them feel welcome, appreciated, and secure. Also, we need to handle their donations responsibly. Both Friday and Saturday nights' guests will make donations, either to play golf, bowl, or participate in the auction. I've asked Ian to arrange for and supervise all security matters for Friday night, Saturday at the golf tournament, and Saturday night. He has enlisted the services of retired and off-duty police officers for the events. If you see something or someone out of place, regardless of where you are, text or call me and I will make sure security responds. They, too, are donating their services, so thank the officers when you see them."

"Does that mean Ian won't be playing golf, and there's a tournament opening?" Tony asked.

Instead of looking annoyed, Linda just laughed. "There's no way Ian's not golfing. He'd quit the MLPD before he'd miss that opportunity. He's paired up with the one of the golf pros who is challenging guests to a round on Friday night."

Finally, Linda nodded at David, and the champagne corks flew.

Chapter 50

As soon as the meeting ended, I rummaged around in my purse for my cell, which had been vibrating through most of the meeting. I had two voicemails and three texts from Kate. I took the glass of champagne David offered me, and went to the corner of the room to call.

"Kate, please don't tell me you're cancelling."

"No, I'm not cancelling, exactly. But I can't fly to Mammoth tonight."

Trying to mask my disappointment, I asked casually. "Why? What's up?"

"I've let you down, J. I'm sorry. There's this Bar Association dinner tonight . . . and Nathan is receiving this award . . . and I messed up and put it on the calendar for next week . . . and Nathan said it wasn't a big deal, but it is . . . and I'm either going to let you down or Nathan . . . and . . ." Kate's voice cracked.

"It's okay, Kate. It's just a golf tournament. I'm probably going to be running around like a crazy person, anyway."

"I can still come to the golf part. I just won't arrive until tomorrow evening. Is that all right?"

"You're still coming?"

"Of course, I'm just going to miss Friday's activities."

I let out a long breath. "Most of the action will be on Saturday, anyway. What time will you arrive tomorrow? I can pick you up."

"Don't worry. It'll probably be while you're at the opening dinner. Couloir has a shuttle."

"You'll text me when you arrive so I know you landed safely?"

"Absolutely."

"Oh good." Curiosity piqued, I asked. "Kate. What award is Nathan getting?"

"Barrister of the year."

"Wow. Congratulate him for me. Clearly I'm pretty good at picking attorneys."

Kate giggled. "Technically Mary picked Nathan as her attorney. You inherited him. On the other hand, I married him."

"Details, details." As I dropped the phone back into my purse, I saw Tony standing just a few feet away, looking hopeful. "Did I hear you say someone cancelled?"

Eavesdropping was over the top even for Tony. "No luck, Tony. She'll be here for the golf tournament."

An hour later I discovered a red Tesla Model S sitting in my driveway. I parked next to it and went inside. Charlotte yelled from upstairs, "Great timing, J. The hors d'oeuvres will be out of the oven in 5,4,3,2 . . ." the timer binged. "Now."

Mrs. Simpson handed me a chilled martini when I reached the top of the stairs. "We weren't sure when you'd be home, so I made one and put it in the freezer."

I followed her into the kitchen where Charlotte was placing beef and chicken satays on a platter. Mrs. Simpson set two small bowls of dipping sauce in the center of the platter. "Shall we have these out on the deck? It's so good to be back in Mammoth."

"Wow," I gasped. "Last week you were reeling from Corey and Cody's confessions, now you're on top of the world. The mood change is beyond dramatic. What's up? And whose Tesla is that in the driveway?" I asked as I sipped my drink.

Charlotte and Mrs. Simpson looked at one another and chuckled.

"The Tesla belongs . . . ah, belonged to Charles. Technically I believe it's Charlotte's. We decided we wanted to drive back to Mammoth instead of fly. Besides, the police still have her car, so Charlotte needed something to drive. Then when her car is returned, I'll have something to drive."

Charlotte interrupted. "I hope you don't mind but I have an electrician coming tomorrow to install a high volt charging outlet just inside the garage. I'm paying, of course. Maybe you'll want to buy a Tesla, yourself, in the future."

And there was a time I thought Charlotte might not feel comfortable while staying with me?

Mrs. Simpson continued as if Charlotte hadn't said a word. She sounded like a kid bursting to tell her secrets. "But, J, we have so much to tell you it's hard to know where to start."

Charlotte chimed in. "Okay, the police caught Stephanie. She was driving back from Tahoe in Mother's car when they found her. It helped that Dad had put a tracking device on it after the rash of car thefts in Southern California a few years ago."

"She must have been pretty pissed."

"According to the LAPD detective in charge of Dad's investigation, the CHP officer eventually had to restrain her. When he told her she was driving a stolen car, Stephanie pulled out the pink slip Cody had given her. The Officer said he was sorry but the car had been reported missing, and she would have to come with him. Then, she tried to seduce him." Turning to Mrs. Simpson, she said, "That was what the officer said, or did I make that up because it would be so like her?"

Mrs. Simpson smiled. "No, I believe that's what the detective told us."

"When did he restrain her?"

"Right after he turned her down. Fortunately, he had one of those cameras on his uniform and recorded everything Stephanie said, and it wasn't very lady-like."

Mrs. Simpson added with an uncharacteristic smirk, "According to the LA detective, the arrest by the CHP was the best part of Stephanie's day."

"You won't believe this, J." Charlotte's eyes gleamed. "But the bitch actually phoned *me* to ask if I would get her an attorney and pay her bail."

"Wow. I wouldn't have seen that coming." I could see how Stephanie's arrest might make these two women happy, but this happy? "Stephanie's arrest is what put you two in such a good mood?"

"No," said Mrs. Simpson, her expression sober. "We found out Charles kept a diary." She slipped a small leather-bound book out of the pocket of her jumper and held it up. "And for both of us, it's like having a little piece of him."

"Read J *the* passage . . . please, Marge." I don't think I ever heard Charlotte call Mrs. Simpson by her real name when she wasn't panicked or upset.

Chapter 51

June 3 What an old fool I've been. When I returned home this afternoon from my board meeting, I saw Margaret staring out the window that overlooks the pool. At first I was captivated by the way the sunlight revealed little streaks of red highlights in her hair. I almost got lost in it. But she let out a long, unhappy sigh and turned away from the window. So, I quietly backed out of the room, I didn't want her to know I'd been watching her. She left without seeing me. I went to the window to see what had disturbed her, and there was Stephanie, wearing only the thong bottom of her bathing suit, stretched out on a chaise between Corey and Cody. Corey was oblivious, but she had Cody and she knew it. It's time for me to act my age.

"That's not the passage I meant. But finish this string, and then read J one of my favorite parts."

I could tell by Mrs. Simpson's lovesick smile she knew all along what section Charlotte wanted her to read. She thumbed forward a few pages in the journal.

June 15 Last night Margaret and I spoke in my study until the sun came up. I know that since Celia died, she's been checking on me most evenings to make sure I'm okay before she goes back to her cottage, though I have never let on that I know. I have come to cherish those conversations. We talk about everything: economics, politics, global warming . . . I just can't get enough of her.

"Enough. Now read one about me," Charlotte said petulantly.

Mrs. Simpson flipped a few pages backward. "I think J should hear the part about your brothers first."

Charlotte grudgingly agreed.

June 4 Steph was livid when I told her it was over, and somehow that invigorated me. I realized I didn't just make a chump of myself; I've also failed Celia and the children, especially the twins. I thought we gave the boys everything, now I think perhaps we gave them too much. I should have been more of a father and less of a financial sponsor after Celia died. Corey has always needed structure, and Celia provided it for him. When she died, it went away. I've wondered whether he's an idiot savant. I'm told that he's an exceptional surgeon, yet he approaches the rest of his life like a spoiled teenager. Cody lost some of his humanity when Celia died. It's a feeling I can't explain. Perhaps if I'd been there for them, they both would be living productive, normal lives on their own instead of continuing this symbiotic dance we've created . . .

Charlotte broke in. "Here's the good part."

Mrs. Simpson shook her head affectionately, and continued.

. . . And then there's Charlotte. What a perfect human being she turned out to be. She's smart, accomplished, caring, honest, loyal, full of integrity, and one of my anchors. She's never come to me for financial assistance, only advice—and rarely for that. I've often thought she would be offended if I offered either. She's independent and headstrong—in the very

best way. When Celia died, she was there, doing whatever she could for me. I wish Celia could see her now. She would be so proud. I know I couldn't be prouder.

Tears rolled down Charlotte's cheeks. "What a gift he left us. I can feel him in the words."

Mrs. Simpson also appeared to be a bit teary as she closed the diary. "Perhaps we should prepare dinner."

"I'll put the halibut on the barbecue." Charlotte offered.

Mrs. Simpson stood. "I'll finish the salad and slice the bread."

I was the last to get up, still a bit overwhelmed by what I'd just heard. "I guess I'll set the table and open some wine."

"Who gets custody of the diary?" I asked when we were seated at the dining table.

They smiled at one another like sisters.

"We both do," Charlotte said. "Sort of a joint custody arrangement. Since we'll be living next door to one another, it shouldn't be a problem."

I took a bite of the fish, and almost swooned. *Why doesn't my fish ever taste like this?*

"What's happening with Corey?"

"That's a bit complicated. Initially, he was arrested for manslaughter, leaving the door open for more charges as information came in. When the District Attorney heard Stephanie's blackmail recording, and then interviewed her, they quit fighting bail. Corey is out on bail under Kevin's supervision in a small clinic he runs. Mrs. Simpson and I spent time with both Kevin and his attorney. Dad's observation about Corey turns out to be on target. He thrives in a structured environment; he's unable to cope without it."

"What does the attorney think will happen?"

"If they go to trial, he thinks he'll plead diminished capacity. But for now, he's working with the DA to see if they can agree to a plea bargain. He and Kevin think Corey needs to be institutionalized and work on his capacity for self-care."

"What does Corey think?"

"He wants to be taken care of. Corey trusts Kevin and believes he will help him."

"How good are his chances of getting a desirable plea bargain?"

"Pretty good. With Stephanie's recording and the subsequent information she's provided, the fact that he's never been in trouble, and has multiple endorsements from the reputable medical organizations he's worked with, I think they might just pull it off."

I sat back and saw I'd scraped my plate clean—a habit I'd previously only ascribed to Ian. Perhaps I'd been spending too much time with him. "You two have been busy."

"Ah," said Charlotte. "We saved the best for last."

I waited.

"This morning we approved architectural plans for our duplex, and officially engaged the contractor."

"How in the world did you manage that so quickly? It takes months, sometimes years to get a custom home built in Mammoth. There are waiting lists."

Charlotte's smile was larcenous. "And one of those contractors called me Monday because his system crashed and he's screwed if he loses all his files. I'm back in business."

Chapter 52

To avoid illegal parking and encourage carpooling, the committee decided on valet service Friday night. Still, I left early for the event, hoping to avoid the crush. Or so I thought. The line of cars inching down Old Mammoth Road toward Rock & Bowl was evidence that many had the same idea. After several minutes, it occurred to me that the number of vehicles did not justify the lengthy wait.

When at last I reached the valet, he wouldn't let me out of the car until he confirmed I was on the guest list and I'd shown him a valid photo ID. Then I joined the line to get into the Rock & Bowl, which moved just as slowly as the one I'd just left. Finally, at the entrance I went through a metal detector and received a name badge with an embedded microchip on it containing my personal information—only then was I permitted to enter the event.

Clearly, Ian had taken his job as head of security way too seriously, even for a police chief. I was furious. Looking around for him so I could call off this charade, I ran into an irritated Andrea.

"What's this all about, J?" Andrea asked, sweeping her arm toward the screening equipment. "Do you know I had security people here all day, checking every damn entrance and exit?"

Before I could respond, one of her managers signaled her, and she left, no happier than when she arrived.

Through the noise of the crowd I heard my name and saw Ross, Olli, Linda, Helen, Denis, and Berta at a table in the back. Ross was holding up a martini. Immediately, Ian faded from my mind.

As I took a sip, I looked around. The place was alive and packed. Every table, chair, barstool, and inch of space was occupied by revelers. Bowlers filled all twelve lanes. Every so often players cheered or groaned. It was obvious which lanes the NFL players were using, not only from their jerseys, but also because the large-screen TV at the end of the alley was screening one of the team's games from last season, while the TVs showed scenes of the Eastern Sierra.

"You must've arrived really early to score this table, though I was hoping to sit out on the deck. Were all those tables taken?" I yelled above the din.

Ross pointed to the "reserved" sign in the middle of the table. He shouted in my ear, "We were supposed to be outside, but Berta said there was a change of plans." He shrugged.

I noticed a table identical to ours, standing empty.

"Whose table is that?"

Ross shrugged again. "All I know is that when anyone goes near, they get shooed away by that guy." He pointed to a very large man standing in the corner.

"Perhaps Helen knows." Before I could ask her, Andrea came over to our table.

"We have a big problem. Two of my bartenders were in a mountain biking collision today. I just got word they're in the hospital."

Olli and Ross glanced at one another, nodding. "We'll fill in," Olli said as they both stood.

I looked at Olli in amazement. "You're also a bartender?"

She laughed. "One of the best."

As she and Ross left, I said to their backs, "I don't doubt it."

I moved toward Helen to ask her about the empty table, when the lights flashed on and off. Slowly, the room began to quiet. I could hear the upstairs crowd quieting too. Some started to come downstairs to see what was happening. Others came from the outside deck. I turned to see Berta, Helen, and Denis rise. Helen looked so excited I thought she might explode. What the hell was going on?

As all the TV monitors changed to Rock & Bowl's entrance, we watched the former President of the United States and First Lady walk into the building.

I turned my attention to Berta and Helen, and pantomimed, "What?"

Berta said quietly, "I've held a few fundraisers for him. I just asked if he would return the favor."

The strains of "Hail to the Chief" sounded throughout the establishment.

By nine o'clock I'd met the President and First Lady, watched the professional golfers beat the pants off the amateurs, listened to some fabulous country music, eaten the best barbecue I'd ever tasted, and learned we had raised in excess of another hundred thousand dollars for the cause. I returned to my table tired but proud of what the committee had accomplished.

Only Linda and Ian remained seated, deep in conversation. I checked my phone to see that Kate had texted her arrival. She was not going to be happy when she learned she'd missed meeting the President and his wife.

As I finished a coffee, I watched Olli and Ross who were at opposite ends of the bar, and mused that while Olli might not be competition, she had certainly set the bar high. My attention was diverted when there was a commotion at her end. With so many people it was difficult to see what was happening. It seemed a male patron was picking himself off the floor, swearing at an empty barstool. As the crowd shifted I saw the barstool wasn't empty. Mary was sitting on it, drinking a glass of red wine. Bob, of course, stood next to her. I watched as the man tried to sit down again, and Mary shoved him away. When the guest started yelling profanities at the "empty" stool, a security guard whispered something in his ear. By the man's reaction, he'd just been cut off.

On my way out I said goodnight to Ross and Olli. Both said they'd see me at the golf cart at eight a.m.

Driving home, my anxiety level ratcheted-up several levels. This much attention by Mary and Bob could only mean Olli really was in extraordinary danger.

Chapter 53

I was in a deep sleep when there was a roar and my bed shook. Earthquake! Disentangling myself from the bed sheets, I jumped out of bed and leapt smack into Charlotte.

"Don't you have a golf tournament at nine o'clock?"

I stared at her dumbly.

"Remember. Your G-A-L-A event?" She cocked her head and widened her eyes.

"Oh shit! The tournament. What time is it? Why didn't my alarm go off? What time is it? Why didn't you wake me? Dammit. What time is it?"

"I did wake you up, or you'd still be sleeping. It's five of eight. And, I have no idea why your alarm didn't go off. But I wouldn't worry about it now." She handed me a cappuccino and left.

Fifteen minutes later, clad in the "team hope" golf shirt Olli had designed, I was on my way to the golf course, all the while thanking God the actual tournament didn't begin for another forty-five minutes. When I pulled out my cell to let Ross know I was running a little late, three business cards fell into my lap. I reached for them up as my phone rang. Thinking Ross had beat me to the punch, I answered, "I'm here. I'm looking for a parking place."

Ms. Germaine answered, "That's nice, but I'm not expecting you."

"Oh, Lynette. Sorry. I thought you were . . . it doesn't matter."

"By the panic in your voice, I would guess you're late for something." There was a tinge of the old smugness in her tone. "So I won't keep you. I was about to send you an email and wanted to give you a heads-up."

I was half paying attention, while I eyed an empty spot in front of a trash dumpster.

"Uh huh."

Ignoring my lack of a real response, she went on. "The reason your background check was delayed is that there's no John James Collins who has owned a search firm in Boston, or in the United States for that matter, at least in the last thirty years. While there is a plethora of men named John James Collins in the country, none match the criteria you gave me."

The side of my car scraped the dumpster as I began to comprehend what Lynette was saying. "None? That can't be right." She had my full attention.

"It is. I double, then triple-checked. I am nothing, J, if not thorough."

I felt sick. "Thanks, Lynette. I need to run."

Now I knew how the business cards had found their way to my pocket from where I left them on my desk. *Thanks, Mary. Thanks, Bob. Sorry I didn't understand right away.* I got out of my car and ran to where I was to meet Ross, Kate, and Olli.

As soon as I saw our two carts, with Ross, Kate, and Olli's golf clubs, I relaxed. Olli was okay. Ross saw me and asked where my clubs were. I sheepishly gave him directions to where I parked the car and promised to explain later. He said Kate was in the golf shop, and Olli was making a call. Then he ran in the direction of the trash bin and my illegally parked car.

I glanced around and saw Tony talking to the Mayor and Town Manager—all three decked out in new golf attire. Despite all the drama, I couldn't help it. I stared. Tony saw me and strutted over to me.

Pointing to the town officials, I said. "Looks like you found them a foursome."

Tony frowned. In a low voice, he said, "No, I didn't. But we figured no one would know if they're here when everyone goes out to play, and when everyone returns." He glared as if the ruse was my fault.

Fortunately, Kate chose just that moment to run over and throw her arms around me. "I'm so excited. Do you know who I just talked to in the golf shop?"

I hugged her back and was about to ask who, when the sound system broadcast David asking for everyone to return to their carts because the tournament would begin soon.

Just as we reached our cart, Ross came running up with my golf bag. "What's in this thing? It weighs a ton."

I was trying to come up with a snappy retort, but Ross was sweating and didn't look like he wanted an answer. I vowed to clean out my bag soon.

Kate and I would ride together; Olli and Ross were partnered. An arrangement I wouldn't have considered a few days ago. Kate was texting Nathan when the fifteen-minute warning sounded, alerting players to be in or near their carts. Ross and I looked around for Olli.

"I thought you said Olli was making a call?"

"I think she was taking a call, but what's the difference?"

My heart started beating hard. "Everything."

Ross must have heard something in my voice. I saw him shift to high alert.

I took a deep breath. "I'm probably making something out of nothing. Which way did she go? I'll go get her."

"She headed toward the registration desk by the parking lot." Ross's voice was tight. "I can go."

"No," I interrupted him. "I'm sure everything is fine." I saw Tony talking to Kate. Kate did not look like she wanted to continue their conversation. "But you could rescue Kate."

"I'm on it," Ross said. He looked over and, despite himself, laughed, because every time Kate took a step backward, Tony advanced.

Helen, Linda, and Berta were manning the registration desk. As I approached I heard a woman ask for the local's discount in response to learning mulligans—purchased "do-over's" without penalty after making a poor shot—were a hundred dollars apiece. Then the man next to her handed her the two mulligans he'd just purchased, saying, "If I use one of these it'll probably ruin my reputation." As he walked away I realized he was one of the golf pros who had been challenging guests to play with him at the Rock & Bowl last night.

"Helen, Ross said Olli came this way. Did you see her?"

Helen shook her head. "I've been too busy to see anything."

"I saw her about fifteen minutes ago," Linda chimed in. "She was talking on her cell, heading for the parking lot. She looked a little upset."

The lot was full of cars, but no people.

"Was she with anyone? Did she get into a car?" My questions were coming too fast.

"Is everything all right, J?" I had Linda's attention.

"Probably." I tried to tamp down my anxiety. "The tournament is about to start and she's in my foursome."

Linda eyed me skeptically. "Olli seemed to be heading toward a dark blue Audi, but I couldn't be sure."

"Susanna drives a dark blue Audi," Helen said. "So, it could be Susanna or John. He's been using her car while he's in town."

My skin began to prickle. "So, it's John . . ." I said, "because Susanna isn't in town."

"Oh, no. John picked Susanna up at the airport last night. I ran into them when I went to fetch Denis. Denis was in LA. He had to go there to meet . . ." Helen was oblivious to the tension that oozed from my pores.

Rudely, I interrupted. "I thought Susanna wanted to remain anonymous?"

"She does." Helen didn't seem bothered by the interruption. "She's hoping to meet with the committee on Monday or Tuesday to hear how the gala went."

My voice was tight and getting louder. "Do you know where John is staying in Mammoth?"

Now all three women were staring at me.

Berta said, "Why yes. They're staying in my guesthouse. Is something wrong, J?"

Just then David announced the five-minute warning for the golfers. I glanced over to where our carts were parked. Kate was snapping pictures of various celebrities with her iPhone, Ross was looking as anxious as I felt, and there was still no Olli.

"Yes," I said softly, "I believe there is."

Chapter 54

I felt paralyzed by all the possibilities. What if I was wrong, and Olli had just gone home, or lost track of time. On the other hand . . .

"Linda, you need to get Ian."

Linda looked at me as if I was crazy. "J, do you know how upset he'll be? He said nothing short of a terrorist attack could stop him from playing. What do I tell him?"

I sighed because I knew how this would sound. "Tell him I have a feeling."

Before Helen could react, I spotted David and I said I'd be right back.

I ran over to him. "David, I don't care how you do it, but you need to delay this event for at least fifteen minutes."

To his credit, he pointed his index finger and thumb in a finger-shot at me and said, "Will do."

Tony was still lurking. "Tony, this is your lucky day. You can tell the Mayor and his sidekick you just found two open spots in the tournament. And tell them in no uncertain terms this is a charity fundraiser for Hope for Our Children, not the town."

As Ross approached, David's voice came over the loudspeaker system. "Well, folks, there's going to be a little delay." I heard groans. "It appears I don't have enough drink carts on the course, and that just won't do." There was some laughter. "To apologize for the late start, I've told all the servers the first drink is on the house." There was applause.

"Ross, I'm going to look for Olli. You ride with Kate and apologize for me. The Mayor and Town Manager will make up the foursome."

Ross's response was a mixture of tenderness and anger. "No fucking way. I'm with you."

Tears welled up in my eyes. I'd hoped that was what he'd say.

David rushed up. "I'm going to have to start this thing pretty soon."

"Are you playing?" He was put off by the non sequitur, but recovered quickly.

"I don't have that kind of money, J." With a wicked smile, he added, "Yet."

"Well, you're playing now. If you don't mind, you can use Ross's clubs. Now let me introduce you to your partner. Please take care of her; she's one of my closest friends. And don't let the boys from the town get out of hand."

David waggled his eyebrows. "I'll take great care of her! Don't worry about a thing."

Ross and I rushed back toward the parking lot to find one extremely pissed-off police chief.

"This better be good, J. I was teamed with my all-time favorite golf pro. And if this is just another one of your goddamn feelings . . ."

So, I explained how Olli came to town; her extreme paranoia; how John was volunteered to work with the committee; his obvious obsession with Olli; and, the subsequent investigation I'd asked an attorney to conduct for me. When I came to the part about John's credentials being false, Ross let out a long breath and explained how excited Olli had been to participate in the tournament, and that she wouldn't have missed it voluntarily. Then Linda told Ian the last sighting of Olli was her walking toward a dark blue Audi, which looked like the one John had been driving. My anxiety grew as he asked questions and waited for answers, but his inquiries were valid.

Finally, Ian picked up his cell and called for a team to pick him up.

"Ross and I will be right behind you."

Ian turned purple with indignation. "No, you will not. When will you learn you're not a cop, J. If you want to join the force, go get training. But I will not have civilians interfere."

He stomped off without another word to anyone.

Linda shook her head and headed in the opposite direction.

I knew Ross was feeling the same sense of impotence I was. We couldn't just stand there, but there was nothing we could think to do.

We walked back to the tournament staging area, which was occupied by a few course employees, and some volunteers cleaning up. I was just about to suggest we go home and wait to hear from Ian, when Bob Gibson, the greens superintendent for Snow Star, asked no one in particular where David was.

Despite my frustration, I smiled, as I always did when I saw Bob. He stood six-foot-two, and was lean with sharp, attractive features. He sported a mop of sandy hair and usually a goofy grin. He was adorable. I'd never seen him upset, but he was now.

"I made David take my place in the tournament. What's wrong?"

"It took us a month to schedule someone to repave the parking lot of the Creekside garage. Now there's a car parked in the lot, and we don't know where it came from. To make matters worse, it seems every cop in town is either working for this event or playing in it."

"There shouldn't be a car there," Ross said. "The garage is closed today." Ross's boss rolled his eyes.

"Okay. What kind of car? Maybe we know the owner," Ross said.

"Something expensive and dark blue."

Ross and I broke into a sprint. I could hear Bob yelling "Hey, what's up?" as we ran toward my car.

I tossed Ross the keys, and got into the passenger seat so I could call Ian. Ross threw litter from the driver's seat to my side of the car, and took off. I called Ian. My call went to voicemail. I left a message, but held little hope he would listen to it in the near future. I was a civilian, after all.

"Tell me about John Collins," Ross said.

"You've never met him, have you?" I said, incredulous.

"No. You and Olli have both mentioned him, but I don't even know what he looks like."

Absentmindedly, I picked the trash up off the floor—it was the business cards I discovered in my pocket earlier. "He's fortyish, tall like you, blond hair, fair . . . uh . . . sort of looks like a polo-playing type of guy."

I stared at the cards, while Ross asked, "You don't mean JJ, do you?"

Most of my attention was focused on the cards I held. "Hmm. I think he once told me people call him JJ. Why?"

"He's been hanging out at the course a lot lately. He seemed like a nice guy. Now you tell me he's probably kidnapped Olli?"

I didn't respond. I was having an epiphany of my own.

"J." Ross was getting irritated. "Do you think John Collins and JJ are the same person? And, that he has Olli?"

"No," I whispered. "He doesn't have Olli, Sam does."

Chapter 55

Ross jerked the car over to the side of the road so fast I slammed against the door.

"Sam? How in the hell did Sam get involved in this? I don't think Sam even knows where Olli is."

How could I have been so stupid? "Actually, she's known for weeks where Olli is."

"She? What the hell are you talking about? J, look at me. Talk to me. What are you saying?"

I handed one of the business cards to Ross. The name imprinted on it was Susanna Angelina Montoya. I said quietly, "Last week when Olli and I met for dinner she told me she was a lesbian. It was a discovery she made in college. She asked that I not tell anyone."

All the breath escaped Ross as he slumped against his seat, stunned.

Calmly but firmly I said, "I know this is a lot to take in, but when Ian gets to Berta's guest house, he'll probably find John—alone with a plausible alibi. My money is that Sam has taken Olli to the garage, and is going to kill her. If Sam has kidnapped her, she can't afford for Olli to live. Are you with me?"

Ross pulled back onto the road. "Yes," he said deliberately. "Now let's talk about how we stop Sam."

As we drove past the garage, we saw a navy-blue Audi, a fairway mower, and a greens mower parked in front. "She's moved out some of the equipment," Ross said. "Makes sense. There's no room to move when all the machines are in the garage.

We left our car outside the athletic club a half-block away and headed back on foot after texting Ian an update.

Ross said the building was divided into three units. The two end units had both a regular entrance and a garage door; the middle unit only had a garage door. Inside the building the three units were accessible to each other by passages covered with long plastic strips instead of regular doors. The golf course's corner unit was on the north end.

My plan was to enter via the south-end unit, and cross the building through the inner passage, to see where things stood. If the situation had escalated, I would walk in and distract Sam, pulling her attention away from the doorway, so Ross could surprise and overpower her while Sam was focused on me. If it did not appear Olli was in immediate danger, we would exit as we came and wait for the police.

Ross's plan and mine were identical except in his, I would wait outside the entire time for the police.

I claimed that Mary and Bob had protected me from all kinds of danger, and I was counting on them not quitting on me now.

Ross was about to object, when we heard a muffled cry from within the garage. We both headed toward the south door.

"We forgot to change out of our golf shoes," Ross said as we reached the entrance. He was right. "Take off your shoes."

There was very little ambient light in the building and lots of equipment and boxes filled the space, so the going was slow. I almost tripped twice. Both times, Ross caught me. We knew surprise was all we had going for us. When we entered the middle unit, Ross looked around for something he could use as a weapon, and I inched toward the plastic flaps covering the entrance to the next unit, trying to silently step over the hoses and cords strewn haphazardly on the floor.

As I got closer I could hear Sam, but not Olli.

"How many times did I tell you? We pledged to love, honor, and obey. Somehow you forgot it all, especially the part about obeying. I could have had anyone I wanted, but I chose you. And *you* have the hubris to think you can just walk out with no word, no forwarding address . . ."

I had to get a peek at Olli to make sure she was okay. I peered through the slats. I saw Sam, knife in hand, pacing and ranting. But I couldn't see Olli. Quietly, I moved to the other side of the passage to see if I could spot her from that angle. And there she was, her ankles and wrists duct-taped to a chair. Her mouth was duct-taped too, but her eyes were wide-open and terrified. From where I stood I saw several knife cuts on her arms.

"Who did you leave me for? I know you never would've left me if there wasn't someone." She walked up to Olli and ripped the tape off her mouth, taking patches of skin with it. Olli shrieked, and I gasped out loud.

Sam looked at the doorway and smiled. "Come out, come out, whoever you are."

I couldn't move. Ian was right; I was no cop. What in the hell was I doing?

Sam walked up to Olli and held the knife to her cheek. "Come out or Beauty here isn't going to stay so pretty." Her voice was almost singsong.

I couldn't move. I stood like a statue. But Mary stood behind Olli and Sam. She pointed to the far corner of the room near the outside door, and mouthed "*now.*"

I could feel Ross rushing up behind me, but I pushed him back so Sam wouldn't see him and stormed into the room. I was no longer afraid.

I moved toward my mark, demanding, "This is the bitch you married, Olli? You could've done so much better."

"You!" she cried. "Little miss organizer. I thought you had a guy at home." She looked me over slowly. "Or was that just for show?"

We stared at one another. Sam walked toward me brandishing her knife. "Olli wouldn't have left me for you. Look at you. You're nothing."

I could see her processing it all, and it wasn't adding up. I also sensed movement at the passage; it took all my energy not to look. Sam heard it, too. As she was about to turn away I asked in the ugliest voice I could muster, "So is JJ your brother? Your fuck-buddy? Or both?"

Her look was filled with such naked hatred my first instinct was to run. But this skank wasn't going to win. I went on, hoping Ross, Mary, or Bob still had my back. "Do you have to pay people to be with you or do you just beat them into submission?"

With a scream, she lunged, knife extended. I saw Ross leap from the doorway to stop her, only to fall hard when his feet got tangled in gas hoses strewn across the floor. Then someone shoved me to the left, and a wrench was pressed into my hand. I smacked Sam on the head as she passed me.

I looked up to see Mary and Bob high-fiving one another as they vanished. As for the rest of us—Sam was knocked out by the blow to her head; Olli was tied up, crying and bleeding; blood poured from Ross's forehead as he furiously worked to extricate himself from the hoses tangled around his ankles; and, me, my heart beat so hard, I thought I might pass out.

Ian found us moments later.

Chapter 56

After one look at the chaos in the room, Ian took command. He called for an ambulance; instructed one of his officers to go pick up John Collins before he had a chance to leave town; asked another cop to help Ross; and went to Olli. Once he freed her from her bonds and assessed her condition, he looked at me as if I were an afterthought. He had Officer Jon Cole escort me to the backseat of his police car.

As soon as we were outside, Jon said, "Boy, J, I don't know what you did, but I've never seen the chief this angry with anyone before."

I shrugged, but Ian had every right to be mad at me. I was angry with myself. I'd been stupid enough to think nothing could go wrong just because I had right on my side when I provoked Sam to come after me. After all, our plan was to distract Sam, when Ross would run in and save the day. A bunch of garage hoses changed all that. Without Mary and Bob, we probably would've all been killed. And, I had no way of knowing whether they were even still around. I certainly couldn't see them. I curled up in a ball on the car seat and brooded about all the bad decisions I'd made.

What seemed like hours later, Ian got into the driver's seat without a word and started the engine.

"Where are we going?"

No response.

"Look, I'm sorry, Ian. You were right. I'm not a cop. I did try to call you, and I left a text once we figured out what was happening."

No response.

"Will you at least tell me how Olli and Ross are?"

A long sigh came from the front. "Olli is in shock and has lost a lot of blood. She has small cuts all over her arms and legs, but I suspect the greater injuries are emotional. Ross has a concussion. We're on our way to the hospital."

Fear, relief, anger, frustration, and shame filled me. I started to cry, and couldn't stop.

When we pulled into the hospital parking lot, Ian made no move to get out of the car. He handed me a packet of Kleenex and waited for me to compose myself. I wasn't sure whether he just didn't want to be seen escorting a hysterical woman, or if he was just very uncomfortable with such raw emotion coming from me.

As we entered, Ian spoke quietly with a woman at the admissions desk. Soon after, we were taken to an empty patient room.

"I need to speak with Olli and Ross, then I'll be back. In the meantime, I've asked that someone come in and check you out." As he was leaving, he added, "And do not leave this room for any reason."

I felt so numb I just nodded. I sat in a chair and played the garage scene over and over in my head.

A nurse came in. She asked me questions, gave me a brief examination, and announced I was fine—though a bit emotionally overwrought.

She returned with a bottle of water and plate of cookies. "In case you're hungry."

I tried to smile, but failed.

An officer I'd never met before came in. She introduced herself and recorded my statement. I walked her through the events of the day, beginning with Olli's absence after taking a call, ending with Ian's appearance in the garage. My only omission was Mary and Bob's intervention. Other than asking a few clarifying questions, she just listened. She left as efficiently as she arrived.

The sun was setting when Ian returned. He was all business. "Both Olli and Ross are spending the night here. Mostly as a precaution." He sat on the edge of the bed. "J, I don't want to argue with you. You look like you finally comprehend the gravity of your actions."

I nodded.

"I've listened to your statement, which is generally consistent with what little Ross and Olli were able to tell me. I'll interview each of them in more depth tomorrow, if they're up to it. I do have a question at the moment, however."

I looked at him, and waited.

"How did you get the wrench you hit Ms. Montoya with?"

I should have anticipated this would come up. I shook my head. "I really don't remember. It all happened so quickly . . . and I was so terrified."

Ian ran his hand over his jaw and studied me.

"Ross said he'd fallen by the time you hit Ms. Montoya and he only heard the blow. Olli told me a wrench flew through the air into your hand."

He looked at me expectantly.

I tried to slow my heart. "For all I know, Ian, maybe it did fly through the air. All I remember is that one minute I was going to die, and the next Sam was down on the ground.

Ian sighed loudly. "Something's going on with you. I wish I knew what. You attract danger like no one I've ever known; yet you remain unscathed. In the last several weeks you've miraculously avoided being blown up by two bombs, and, now a wrench mysteriously appears when you're being attacked by a psychopath."

He shook his head and stood. "I know you want to see Olli and Ross. An officer will escort you. We need to conduct full interviews before you can speak with them privately, which we plan on doing tomorrow morning when they're a little more coherent. I'm sure you understand." He narrowed his eyes as he appraised me. "I suggest you avail yourself of the facilities and clean up before you go see them. You look like hell."

As he left I realized Ian hadn't touched the plate of cookies. I walked to the bathroom to take his advice. When I returned a totally different Ian stood in the room. He looked anxious and embarrassed.

"I almost forgot. The timing is a bit awkward, but I'm not sure when we'll speak in private again. What are you doing next Saturday?"

The change in his demeanor was so dramatic I had no idea how to respond. "Uh . . . nothing, I guess."

He looked at the ceiling instead of me. "Linda and I are getting married."

I smiled. "I knew you were engaged, just didn't realize the ceremony was so soon. Congratulations."

"Uh, yeah." He was still staring at the ceiling. "You remember Fran, don't you? She's standing up for Linda."

I did remember Fran. What a lady. She was Linda's secretary at the elementary school. District regulations had forced her to retire after thirty-two years of service. The day after her retirement party, she shocked everyone by returning to her job as a volunteer.

I smiled. "Perfect. Who better?"

Ian was looking at everything in the room but me. "Um . . . I . . . er . . . I was wondering." He took a deep breath. "Would you stand up for me?"

"Me? Why in God's name would you want me?" The question was out of my mouth before I could stop it.

Now he was staring at the floor. "I don't really have any close friends outside the police force. And it wouldn't be appropriate to ask one of the guys. You know, favoritism and all." He finally looked at me. "Let's face it, J. I don't understand it, but you've got to be one of the luckiest people I know. Perhaps some of that luck will rub off on me. I mean, I'm marrying one of the most beautiful, smartest women in the world. And, look at me. I think I'm going to need some luck to keep her."

The self-deprecating Ian left, and the man I knew returned. "So," he demanded. "Will you?"

"Yes."

He grunted his satisfaction, grabbed a handful of cookies and left.

Chapter 57

My visits were brief and highly emotional. The head nurse, Nurse Fitzpatrick, insisted I see Olli first, since she refused to take a sleeping pill until we spoke.

"Ms. Parker is in a fragile state. Please be brief and don't upset her any more than she already is." Nurse Fitzpatrick glanced at my police escort. "Is it really necessary that you accompany Ms. Westmore into the room? Your very presence will probably upset Olivia."

The young man, who introduced himself as Officer Stark, turned bright red under the nurse's scrutiny. "Sorry, ma'am. I'll stay in the background, but those are my orders."

The nurse looked unimpressed. After a brief knock, she opened the door to Olli's room, saying, "Five minutes at most."

Our eyes locked as I entered.

"J. J, how did you find me in that garage? How could you be so brave? You called Sam out even when she was going after you with a knife. You . . . you saved my life," said the small, pale woman covered in bandages and bruises. She burst into tears.

Nurse Fitzpatrick gave me a venomous scowl for upsetting her patient, and then closed the door.

Moments later I entered room 217. As soon as I saw Ross, all my defenses fled and I broke into inconsolable sobs. My arrogance could have cost him his life. Thoughtfully, Officer Stark guided me to the bedside chair lest I destroy something in my path. Our visit was more about comforting and holding than speaking. We both knew words would come later.

I was completely spent by the time Officer Stark and I reached the lobby. He was offering to escort me to my car, which had been moved to the hospital parking lot, when a voice from the entrance announced, "I'll walk J to her car, Officer. I need to speak with her."

My heart sank when I saw the mayor.

"J, if this wasn't imperative, I would leave it to morning. But, I'm afraid I can't." He led me to a far corner of the empty lobby. I followed numbly.

He cleared his throat, and cleared it again. The third time, I finally looked at him. This wasn't a bureaucratic delay, he was nervous.

I tried to sound interested. "What can I do for you, Mayor?"

"I know we haven't met formally, but please call me Wally, J. It's alright if I call you J, isn't it?"

"That's fine, May . . . uh . . . Wally."

"First, let me tell you that your golf tournament, hell, the entire gala was a smashing success for the town, as well as Hope for Our Children. You should be congratulated."

Oh, shit. The Gala. I'd abandoned Kate with no explanation, and sent her out with three people she'd never met before. She must be worried sick.

Wally was still talking. "I'm sorry I missed that last part."

"I was explaining why I believed it would be best for all concerned that we keep the um . . . incident at the garage confidential—out of the press. We wouldn't want our guests to end such a spectacular weekend in Mammoth with, er . . . safety concerns, would we?"

News of the incident could destroy Olli, particularly in her current vulnerable state. Olli's abuse and sexual orientation were hers to share, not gossip to be spread.

"I couldn't agree more, Wally. You can be sure we'll keep it to ourselves. Can you do the same with the paramedics, hospital, and law enforcement staff?"

The mayor looked both relieved and a little surprised. "I certainly can, J." He stood. "I'm sure you want to go home and put this day behind you. And thank you for including the town manager and me in your foursome. You made a great civic contribution."

My cell was where I'd left it, on the front passenger seat of the car. I frantically punched in the number.

"Well, I hope your day was as exciting as mine." There was a party going on in the background.

"Oh, Kate. I'm so sorry." Both my brain and my mouth stopped working. I had no idea where to begin or what to say.

"Don't worry about me, I've been having a great time. I even got a prize at the awards dinner for the highest score. All of us who are staying at Couloir are having a nightcap at the bar."

A little less jovially, she asked, "Linda said you just had some unexpected issues related to the gala, and would explain later. You're okay, aren't you?"

Tears began to well; my voice got hoarse. "I've been better. Can I come spend the night with you?"

The approach to Kate's unit made me momentarily forget the angst of the past twelve hours. Subtly placed fairy lights made the mirrored-structures look mystical. Brian had reserved one of the suspended glass-cubes on the perimeter of the property for Kate and Nathan at my request. A romantic present for the newlyweds. Now I was grateful it was away from the partyers.

Candles and recessed lights lit Kate's suite, enhancing the view of the night sky above and the retiring town below. She waited for me with open arms.

Over a 2012 Silver Oak Cellars Cabernet Sauvignon and braised beef tacos—a Couloir specialty—I told Kate the entire story: from the evening I confessed my jealousy when Olli announced she was a lesbian, to leaving Olli and Ross in the hospital. Not having to exclude Mary and Bob's participation from the tale was a relief.

Kate listened without comment, question, or judgment. She moved only when I needed Kleenex or a hug.

I finished my saga. "What if Mary and Bob hadn't saved us? I don't know how long they're going to stick around. Maybe they're on some kind of time limit. I can't just count on them . . . you know . . . they probably have better . . . oh, you know what I'm trying . . ." I was babbling from exhaustion, frustration, and guilt.

Kate said, "You know, since I met Mary I've never believed in what ifs, only in what now." She gave me a beatific smile, looked to my right, and said, "But why don't you ask *them*?"

I followed Kate's gaze. Mary and Bob were sitting on the couch. Mary was shaking her head as if I was a child who just didn't get it, while Bob filled two glasses with the cabernet.

Chapter 58

The period from Labor Day to Thanksgiving is one of constant transformations in Mammoth Lakes. Changes in the night sky, leaf color, temperature, foliage, species of birds, wildlife migrations, and population density, to mention a few. Many of the locals also revere it as their favorite time of year. Whether it's because of the warm days and crisp nights, having hiking trails and lakes pretty much to themselves, or no more suffering in long lines at the one crowded grocery store in town. For me, it's usually the sense of quiet, as part-time residents and visitors go back to their real lives. This year, however, it was because everyone close to me seemed to be on the mend.

Olli was physically recovering at a rapid pace; it was the emotional damage that would take a while. After several interviews, she'd finally found a therapist she thought she could trust, and had begun treatment. She was still living with Ross, but now the two of them came to my house most nights for dinner. Fortunately, Mrs. Simpson did most of the cooking, except when she and Charlotte were on one of their many trips to Southern California to settle Charles Caron's estate.

Tonight, they were doing just that. From Charlotte's latest text I had the impression she was sick of arguing with attorneys and accountants. My money was on Charlotte.

I was preparing a late-summer Heirloom tomato soup when the cell chirped. Helen's name popped up on the phone screen.

"Hello, Helen. What's up?"

"J." I could hear the excitement in that one syllable.

"Sounds like something good."

"J, the final tally came in from the Gala. Are you sitting down?"

I wasn't but I said I was.

"We brought in . . ." She pounded her hands on a table to mimic a drum roll, I assumed. "One-million-eight-hundred fifty-five-thousand dollars. Can you believe it?"

I sat down. "Wow. That's mind-boggling. I can't believe we pulled it off in barely five weeks."

"I know," Helen crowed. "Word must be leaking out, because Berta has received calls from Time and Forbes to do interviews."

"Is she going to accept?"

"She told me she'll only agree if they include Jean McBride as the executive director of Hope for Our Children, and give her equal time. Berta wants Jean to talk about the various programs and services that will now be available in Mono County, and the need for developing the same capacity in other California counties."

"Good for her. Congratulations."

Helen dismissed the praise. "You put the team together, J." Her voice lost a little of its energy. "I'm just sorry about Susanna."

I stiffened at mention of Sam. To my knowledge no one other than those directly involved knew about her kidnapping Olli. "What do you mean?" I asked tentatively.

"Her check bounced," Helen declared indignantly.

I almost laughed out loud. Trying to sound serious, I responded. "It did?"

"Most certainly. When Berta tried to contact her, the number was no longer in service."

"Very strange." Trying a bit of redirection, "Don't let Sam's . . . uh . . . Susanna's rudeness distract from our success."

"I won't. Uh oh, better go. Denis is giving me that look. We're meeting some friends at Couloir. Night."

Ross and Olli arrived separately as usual, since they were both coming from work. Olli seemed a bit withdrawn, but I thought that was only to be expected. Being kidnaped, tortured, and almost murdered isn't necessarily something one gets over quickly. So, I nattered on through cocktails and dinner about the results of the gala and what it meant for Mono County children.

Halfway through dinner Ross asked, "Is something wrong, Olli? You seemed on top of the world this morning, almost like you won the lottery."

Olli used her spoon to make circle-eights in the soup. "This morning I decided I was going to stay in Mammoth and open my own consulting business, specializing in marketing, communications, and public relations." She put her spoon down. "This afternoon I found out that Sam cleaned out all my accounts, even ones I didn't think she knew about. I'm completely broke."

"If it's money you need, I'll give you what you . . ." I began.

"You don't need charity, Olli," Charlotte interrupted. "You need an investor, like me."

Olli was visibly startled, Ross dropped his bread, and I almost knocked over my wine. How could Charlotte and Mrs. Simpson—especially Charlotte—walk in and we not hear them? Besides, I wasn't expecting them back for another couple of days.

Mrs. Simpson started to apologize, but Charlotte spoke right over her. "I saw what you did for the Gala. And I've Googled your career, and read about your achievements on LinkedIn. I consider you a great investment."

Charlotte sat down at one of the empty dining room chairs next to Olli, and said, "I'm starving, J. I don't see any meat on the table, but the soup, vegetable salad, and bread will do. And, bring me a glass of wine, while you're up."

I looked at her with an arched eyebrow.

"Please," she conceded. "Olli and I have business to conduct."

Ross set two more places at the table while I poured the wine. Charlotte never quit talking.

From what I could discern, Olli didn't believe Charlotte but was playing along, until Mrs. Simpson whispered something in Olli's ear. I suspect it was Charlotte's net worth, or something of the sort, because Olli's eyes widened, and she started taking Charlotte very seriously.

They were still deep in conversation long after Ross left, Mrs. Simpson retreated to her room, and I went to bed.

Early the next morning while the house was blessedly quiet, I made myself a cappuccino and checked emails and texts.

The only email worth reading was from Linda. She and Ian were honeymooning on Maui.

J, Sorry, we didn't have a chance to talk before or after the ceremony. Everything seemed to be happening in triple time. I still can't believe you threw Ian a bachelor party the night before we got married. Ian was even more surprised. He said you made a toast then left. Ross must have told you the next morning leaving was a fortuitous decision. Oh, and I loved your tux. Wait until you see the pictures. We're having a fabulous time in Maui—snorkeling, golfing, eating and drinking too much. But I'm ready to return home. This is the first time in my career I wasn't present for the first day of school. Anyway, just wanted to say thank you, and let's have dinner when we get back. L

The wedding had been lovely. Around thirty people—most either of the law enforcement or elementary school persuasion—gathered in Linda's backyard for the ceremony and celebration. Linda wore a tea-length, off the shoulders white lace dress and silver sandals. It was both a casual and an elegant choice. Her blond hair, usually pulled back in a French braid, hung loosely at her shoulders. Ian's attire surprised me. Scruffy was his normal look. For the wedding, he sported a white long-sleeved shirt, rolled up mid-arm, dove-gray pants, and a buttoned dove-gray vest. His unruly curly black hair was combed. He looked surprisingly handsome and happy. The ceremony, conducted by the presiding Judge, was short but personal. The party after, raucous—without a hint of the elementary school principal or the chief of police personas.

The only text worth answering was from Ross, asking me to join him at Burgers for dinner that evening so we could talk. We had not dined there together since he announced Olli's impending arrival. I sent back, "See you at seven." This time curious, rather than worried, about the topic of our dinner conversation.

Chapter 59

Charlotte and Mrs. Simpson spent most of the day working with their contractor, making choices for the duplex. I, on the other hand, golfed. We arrived home at the same time. Even before Charlotte exited her vehicle, I knew she was not happy.

"December! He promised us we could move in before Thanksgiving. Now it's mid-December?"

Though I couldn't see her face, I knew Mrs. Simpson was rolling her eyes. "It is what it is, Charlotte. Let's just be grateful we'll be in by Christmas."

Charlotte rattled up a bag of Mimi's cookies in my face. "Do you have a wine that will go with snickerdoodles?"

I poured some prosecco while Charlotte placed the treats on a plate.

"Was your trip down south fruitful?"

Mrs. Simpson looked at me like "please don't get her started." So, I quickly added, "Did you see Corey?"

Mrs. Simpson's shoulders relaxed as Charlotte answered, "He's doing really well. His attorney and the DA worked out a plea arrangement. Corey will remain under Kevin's care. And after visiting him, I don't think Corey will ever be out on his own again. He doesn't just need; he craves the structure provided in Kevin's clinic."

"I realize you have the money, but that could get pretty pricey."

"Actually, Kevin has been delegating some of the minor medical responsibilities to Corey, and Corey loves it. Corey told us that his sense of helplessness and depression go away when he's working. Kevin plans on capitalizing on that."

Mrs. Simpson added, "And he appears to be over his infatuation with me."

"That must be a relief. Heard anything about Cody?"

Charlotte shook her head. "He appears to be in the wind. We'll see how long that lasts. Sooner or later he's going to need a capital infusion, I would think."

I went to grab another cookie and discovered an empty plate. The three of us had polished off a dozen snickerdoodles and a bottle of prosecco. It was time for me to get ready for dinner.

Ed Hurley was taking a phone reservation when I walked into Burgers. He smiled and pointed to the corner table. There was a large vase of red-tinged yellow roses on the table. My stomach did a flip. Ross was looking at his phone, but as I neared he set it aside, stood, and kissed me. A public display of affection? My stomach did another flip.

I looked at the flowers. "Pour moi?" I had begun to take French lessons on the Internet in preparation for our holiday trip to Paris.

His face altered. I didn't like that I couldn't tell what he was thinking. Ignoring the roses, I asked cheerfully, "What are we talking about tonight."

Ross looked uneasy. "I have some bad news, and an apology. Which would you like first?"

I sighed. "A beer."

As he poured me a glass from the pitcher on the table, he said. "Let's just get the bad news out of the way. Do you mind?"

I took a swallow too fast, and coughed. "No, I agree," I sputtered.

"I talked to Bobby and the rookies won't be coming onto Patrol until after Christmas. I'm sorry, J, but there's no way I can go to Paris with you and Kate and Nathan."

I wasn't surprised. We both knew Paris was a long shot. Mammoth was packed from Christmas through New Year's, and if there were snow, everyone would be skiing. Nonetheless, I felt like crying. I waited for the lump in my throat to go away before I said, "It's sort of what we expected, but it was nice to pretend for a while it would work out."

Needing to change the subject so I didn't let Ross see how truly disappointed I was, I asked, "You brought me roses as a consolation prize?"

Ross smiled. "No, the flowers are part of my apology."

"Apology for what?"

"Being so lame I thought it would be no big deal for my old girlfriend to live with me."

"It wasn't a big deal," I lied.

Ross gave me the "don't lie to me" look. "Now that Sam is incarcerated and no longer an immediate threat, Olli is finally starting to open up . . ."

"Just because Sam is in jail?" I asked skeptically.

Ross looked uncomfortable. "Well, that and the fact I finally know she's a lesbian."

I opened my mouth to ask how he felt about that, but realized this was his party, and how he felt about it was none of my business. I closed my mouth.

"Anyway, she told me about your conversation the night you two met at Le Coquetier."

My face turned hot. I spoke so quietly Ross asked me to repeat what I'd mumbled. "You mean the night I told her how jealous I was of her."

"Yes." He pushed the vase of flowers across the table toward me. "J, I know I don't give you many compliments, or tell you how much in love I am with you, but don't you know?"

"Know?" I whispered. My urge to hear him say it was greater than my desire not to torture him.

He took my hand. "I choose you, J. I choose you over every other woman in the world. That's not going to change."

For once I kept my mouth shut.

Epilogue

As I dressed for Christmas Eve dinner, I marveled at how fast the first two weeks of our Paris adventure had passed. It was everything Kate had promised and more. Steve's trial ended two days before we were to leave, giving us just enough time to celebrate his conviction and finish packing. Just before we left I surprised Kate and Nathan with early Christmas gifts—full-length down coats to keep out the damp Paris December. Both claimed they had plenty of warm clothes packed, but as soon as we left Charles de Gaulle airport, the coats came on.

L'Hotel was as advertised. Exquisite. Kate had booked a newly built top-floor, two-bedroom, two-bath suite with a large living room and a terrace overlooking the city's rooftops. Rain or shine—though there was little of the latter—we explored museums, galleries, and monuments. We bought gifts for everyone we knew, and many for ourselves. We walked almost everywhere, which was fortunate, since almost every journey ended in a restaurant.

I put on a forest-green sheath, and black strappy heels, walked into the living room, and admired the ten-foot Christmas tree, decorated with red, silver, and gold ornaments as I waited for my friends. Bells rang somewhere in the city, and I turned to the terrace. A light snow dusted the railings. I knew it would soon turn to rain, but it was still magical. The entire scene made me yearn for Ross. I whined in my head.

My pout was interrupted when the Hadleys emerged from their bedroom. Kate giggled as Nathan twirled her to show off her clingy cobalt-blue dress. She sparkled in the light of the Christmas tree.

"Shall we go downstairs for Christmas Eve dinner?" Nathan asked, as he offered me his other arm.

We walked into the elegant Le Restaurant, and were escorted to our table with its plush upholstered seating and unobstructed view of the terrace fountain and living wall. A few snowflakes danced in the outside lights, which perfectly complemented the subtle holiday décor. As we were seated, a waiter poured champagne into crystal flutes.

It was perfect except for . . . No, I decided. I would not ruin such a magical evening by wishing Ross were here. I offered a Christmas Eve toast to my dearest friends.

As we sipped our wine, we discussed our day. Most of it we'd spent walking the city, looking at the decorations, and popping in and out of boutiques. I got a vicarious thrill watching Nathan watch Kate shop. Every time she found something that delighted her, he beamed.

The maître d'hôtel approached, and I assumed he was going to tell us about the evening's fare. This was always a bit of an ordeal, because all would be explained to us in French, then Kate or Nathan would translate for me with the waiter looking anxiously on. Clasping a cell phone, the maître d'hôtel spoke much more rapidly than usual. At one point, I thought I heard my name, but wasn't sure. Then he thrust the phone at Kate with a slight bow.

Kate said to him, "Cela doit être plus insolite. Merci d'apporter le téléphone pour nous."

All three looked at me with interest. Kate smiled, "It appears a text was sent to the hotel for you." She handed me the phone.

I took the phone reluctantly. If I couldn't speak French, I certainly couldn't read it.

But there was a text from Charlotte.

"We had one hell of a time finding the right Christmas gift for you. But the porter should be bringing it to you momentarily. Mrs. Simpson and I hope you like it. It's an original."

The waiter seemed distracted by a disturbance at the restaurant entrance, because he turned away as I tried to hand the phone back to him. I thought I saw a blur of red, but my view was blocked by a green marble pillar and the waiter.

Then the phone vibrated again. I automatically looked to see the message.

"Sorry, J. I forgot to give him a change of clothes when I grabbed him from the mountain, or any luggage, for that matter."

I heard Kate's sharp intake of breath and looked up. There stood Ross in his ski patrol uniform, looking at me like I was the only person in the room.

He bent down, I thought to kiss me. I was wrong. He whispered in my ear, "I'll give you one choice."

I looked at him confused.

"Do you want us to live in your house or mine?"

About the Author

A southern California native, Terry Gooch Ross moved to the Eastern Sierra with her husband in 1993. She earned her living as an independent consultant specializing in leadership and organization development.

Terry lost her twin Mary suddenly in 2001. In an effort to get her grief under control, Terry began writing a mystery series set in the High Sierra—*A Twin Falls*, *A Twin Pursuit,* and now *A Twin Pique*— in which Mary and her husband Bob make regular appearances.

Terry divides her time among family, friends, work, and spending time in the mountains she loves.

CPSIA information can be obtained
at www.ICGtesting.com
Printed in the USA
FSOW03n0423160117
29581FS